Knight in Shining Amour

Amy Renee Sawyer

Published by Vantage Point Publishing
Indianapolis, IN 46218

ISBN 978-0-9883939-5-0

The publisher would appreciate notification where errors occur so that they may be corrected in subsequent printing and/or editions. Please send comments to the publisher by emailing to biz@amorousink.com

Printed in the United States of America

Acknowledgment

Thank you to Dawn Rivers my editor and publisher, the first person to read one of my projects, for encouraging me to continue and thank you to Vantage Point Media Company. To my family, friends and loved ones who have excitedly stood on the sidelines cheering me on to the finish line, your support has been invaluable. Finally, thank you to one person in particular who inspired in me all the necessary emotion to create this story.

Dedication

To the ever expanding, morphing, cradling, bending, illuminating universe in which we dwell, and the infinity of love that holds us all together. And to one star that burns brightest of all and eternally in my heart, my Chlore.

1.

Decaying maple leaves filled the air with the smell of a changing season and reflected beautiful orange light into the glistening mid-morning. I was visiting the campus of my alma mater with my best friend in southern Indiana, and we, with thousands of others, marched upon the football stadium grounds for a late November game. All around us friends greeted one another, and tents and grills were raised as we made our way to our tailgate site as the perfect day pushed us ever twisting through the crowd. Ava and I had been friends for over a decade. She had witnessed my trials and errors and was my biggest cheerleader. Regardless of the difficult situation, she was always there with a chant, a bottle of Gatorade, and a towel to wipe away the stains of failure and regret.

After several minutes of battling the chaos around us, we spotted our friend Henry's green SUV which had been turned into food pantry and jukebox in one for the festivities. The smell of brats and burgers hit our stomachs like a defensive end upon a quarterback. Henry, a big Dutch teddy bear, had been one of my closest friends in school, and many a night Ava and I had sandwiched him in his king sized bed after he safely got us home from the bars. It was customary for him to take us back to his apartment, fix us a snack and tuck us into bed. He was always very protective of us, always ready to help whatever the situation and he never seemed to tire of it.

After reuniting hugs and kisses, Ava and I visited with other friends that had arrived at the site and introduced ourselves to new faces. The morning sun crept higher and games were organized as we set alcohol the task of slowly warming our bodies against the crisp air. Ava and I had become perfect partners in numerous drinking games and I noted that our favorite was being played at a table a few yards away. Beer pong was a game of two teams throwing ping pong balls into cups set up on the opposite side of the table. I spied a sign-up sheet as I walked over the table and jotted our names down. I remained by the competition, leaning against Henry's car enjoying the sun and the happy soundtrack that only drunken college tailgaters can orchestrate.

Due to the nature of the game and southern Indiana's hilly terrain, every time the ping pong ball bounced haphazardly off the table it would roll toward me. I made it my responsibility to retrieve the white, hollow ball from under the car, catch it midair or dig it out of the muddy earth, and toss it back to the players. In the current competition were friends from school, Claude and Troy, playing against two men I had never seen before. Ava wandered over and as the game progressed the four of us old friends caught up, laughed and carried on with competitive banter all in the name of good school age fun.

The game came to a close. Claude and Troy reigned victorious and boastfully taunted their opponents after which one of the unknown players walked over and stood next to me. I cupped my beer bottle with mitted hands and looked up at him. He was tall. Very tall. Blonde hair stuck out just below his crimson baseball cap and a long sleeved tee shirt with my school's name stretched across his broad chest. I felt dwarfed, which rarely happened as a woman of five feet seven inches.

"Thank you for your help with the balls." He said. "I'm Cain."

"Anytime." The smell of cheap beer and fall air rolled off of him and I smiled self-consciously from behind my eye glasses. The night before had been a blur of drinking, bars and dancing which left my head a little less than clear. It had taken a lot for me to get out of bed that morning and I had very little energy left to make myself look presentable. My cinnamon brown locs were up in a ponytail, I had no makeup on and I was wearing a baggy thrift shop university sweatshirt complete with frayed sleeves. Ava and I had a habit of getting together in the little college town and letting loose in ways that often left us regretful the next day. This was a prime example.

Cain looked at my hands and frowned, "Your beer is gone. Would you like some more?" He gently relieved my grip of the empty bottle before I could answer and walked with long strides over to the cooler.

"So… how's it going?" I jumped at the slightly shushed voice of Ava who was standing behind me, holding two red plastic cups, her sky blue eyes shining. She looked at me intently as she took a gulp from the cup on the left, made a face that looked like she was in pain and then quickly took a long drain of the cup on the right.

"Straight vodka?" I asked with a shudder.

"Yup! You want some?" I shook my head violently and tried to push back the wave of nausea that rose up with the thought of ingesting cheap vodka followed by lemon-lime soda. Cain came back with two beers and opened them both in front of me, then handed me one.

"Hi! I'm Ava!" She said with a sly grin.

"Hello, I'm Cain." He answered back. "May I ask you a question?" Ava's face lit up.

"Sure!" she squealed. Ava thought he was cute. Whenever Ava thought a man was cute her voice raised at least two octaves.

"What is your friend's name?" he gestured at me. I, who had started to quietly sip my beer, removed the cold glass from my mouth.

"Oh. I'm sorry. I didn't tell you, did I? But did you ask? No. I don't think you did. I definitely would have told you if you would have asked." I stopped talking and looked at him innocently, confusing myself slightly. *Wait… what was the question?* It was at that point I began to notice the tingling feeling that was enveloping my limbs and head and also, how very cute Cain was as he inspected me.

"Her name is Myra. Myra Knight." Ava jumped in after giving me a look of disbelief. "And she is not being difficult on purpose, I swear." Cain's head was tilted to the side and he had a silly smile on his face. I could feel him examining my lips and I licked them, feeling exposed, then giggled.

"Why are you smiling at me like that?" I asked. The smile melted from his mouth.

"I don't know." He said thoughtfully. I believed him. The odd exchange was broken up by Claude, who called for me and Ava to come over and play him and Henry in beer pong.

"Would you like to come and hangout while we play?" I asked Cain politely.

"Absolutely."

During school, Claude and Henry had been roommates and created a monthly beer pong tournament at their apartment. Tons of people would crowd in their tiny garage and driveway for a Saturday afternoon of games and fun. Ava and I had attended most of them as partners and, at the end of many an evening, it was Claude and Henry versus Ava and me in the championship game. We were very evenly matched and playing again was nostalgic, and brought a sense of comfort as well as intense competition.

The four of us chatted happily over the next twenty minutes. Henry was finishing up grad school there on campus and planned to move to Chicago in the fall to work in a mid-level marketing position. During undergraduate his interests had bounced around and he and I had spent a lot of time talking about what he wanted to do with his life and why, but finally he felt that he had found something that could sustain him and that he was interested in.

Claude had moved to Kansas City and worked as a physical therapist. He was an almost overly confident guy, short with dark hair and olive skin. He knew that he was attractive. In my opinion, he thought he was more attractive than he actually was. Cain stood next to me, helping me wrangle ping pong balls. The first time his large fingers handed me a ball and our skin touched I felt a hot sting. The sensation was alarming and I stopped and looked at his fingers for a moment and then up at his face. He looked back at me, inquisitively, mouth slightly agape. *Well, that was weird.*

I turned back to the table, rinsed off the plastic ball and handed it to my partner. She sunk the ball deep into a cup on the opposing side.

"Nailed it!" She shouted out. I gave her an enthusiastic high-five and took my turn. I stepped up, glanced over at Cain who was smiling at me, aimed and fired the ball which landed with a plunk into another red cup.

"Nice!" Cain said, holding his hand in the air for me to hit with my own. I hesitated then met his hand. His long fingers folded around mine just for an instant. Apparently, he was not expecting his laudation to end so personally and turned slightly red then stepped back to lean against the car. *That was weird, too.*

The game persisted and for the duration Cain cheered us on, although he did not attempt to touch me again, I noted with annoyance. After several more minutes all but two of the cups had been cleared away by Ava's and my near perfect aim. It was her turn, and she gave a whoop, aimed and threw the ball into one of the cups. She and I did a loud and slightly vulgar dance involving her wildly swinging her arms in the air behind me as if she were slapping my behind. I laughed and then remembered that we, I in particular, had an audience that I was interested in impressing. I slapped at Ava teasingly and stepped up to the table. I looked over to see that the space where Cain had been standing was no longer occupied.

My eyes found him, pumping a beer at the keg, in conversation with a brunette girl in black leggings and a stocking cap. Trying not to feel too dejected, I lined up to the table, aimed and sunk the ball into the final cup. Ava and I shrieked and cheered loudly while dancing around again, then shook our opponent's hands. Per beer pong tournament rules, the table was ours to defend until we lost a game, but Ava and I decided to abdicate and allow others to play instead. She came up beside me as I walked away from the table.

"It should be illegal how good we are at beer pong. But I guess we have been playing forever." She lovingly wrapped her arm around me. "What happened to Cain?"

I surveyed the area and didn't see him, then pretended to be looking for the bathroom as I said, "I'm not sure. Hey, do you want to go to the restroom with me?" The lines were seemingly miles long and full of rowdy college kids. Facing them with a friend would make them seem less tedious.

"Sure!" She said happily.

When we got back, the scene had changed quite a bit. Different drinking games had begun and Henry was donning his chef's hat, standing by a smoking grill placing pink patties onto sizzling iron. I stopped at the cooler to grab two light beers and then continued towards him.

"Here, Henry." I said warmly, opening a can and handing it to him.

"Awesome, Myra. Thanks." He drank deeply, deep brown eyes on me the whole time.

"Do you need some help cooking?" The grill, specifically designed for tailgating, extended from the hatch of the SUV. Next to it was a table covered with every condiment known to man and a platter of marinated chicken, beef and pork.

"No. I think I have it under control for now." He surveyed his workspace proudly. "But how about you keep me company for a while?" I nodded enthusiastically and took a seat in a gray folding chair next to him. There was something about Henry that made me appreciate his attention. He was tough and masculine, but extremely thoughtful and kind. I felt special when he wanted to spend time with me.

The fact that he was pleasant to look at didn't hurt either. His tall, broad frame was covered with dark features and hair. Henry and I had engaged in mild to moderate flirtation for four years yet had never been on a date. Neither of us could seem to muster the courage to make a first move, so we stayed where it was comfortable. As friends.

"So how has campus life been treating you, honey?" I took a sip of my beer and glanced around at the rows upon rows of cars and the people milling around in between them.

"Not too bad." He answered with a sigh. "I am ready to get done and get out into the real world. I'm tired of not making any money."

"Don't get too excited, it's not all it's cracked up to be, sometimes." I responded bitterly, thinking about my own job. He laughed at this.

"Having problems in the workplace? How is the promotion?" We spoke for a few minutes about my job and some of the issues I was facing with new projects and he smiled and listened, giving me some suggestions and general support. It was comfortable to talk to him and I loved how genuinely interested he seemed.

Out of the corner of my eye I saw Cain wander back to the tailgate area with one of his friends. My heart began to race with adrenaline. I hoped that he would come over and join our conversation. Dejection struck as I watched him hover over to another group sitting on the back of a bright yellow Jeep Wrangler. Henry continued talking, but I found myself tuning in and out of the conversation, picking up on only bits and pieces which left me utterly confused. I subtly shifted in my seat several times to keep Cain in my peripheral vision while posturing myself, chest out and a curve in my spine, attempting to look shapely and attractive in case he happened to look over. It didn't occur to me that all I was managing to do was look uncomfortable.

"Are you OK, Myra? You going to be sick?" Henry had noticed my odd mating ritual and it had caused him alarm. *That is certainly not the look I'm going for.* I sat up quickly and tried to hide the embarrassment I felt while assuring Henry that I was fine. It was unfortunate that every time I returned to my alma mater I regressed four years back to being a college student. I binge drank, wore ridiculous college gear (at that moment I scratched my head through a cream beanie with our school's mascot on it) and composed

myself like a silly, boy crazy cheerleader. Mentally shaking myself and
snatching the hideous hat off of my head, I tuned back into Henry

"So, may I try?" I asked Henry, referring to the flipping of the burgers in
which he displayed such finesse. He sighed loudly like a child asked to
share his toys.

"Get on over here then, girl." He faked annoyance. I stepped in front of
him and he handed me the utensil by reaching his thick arm around my
body.

"Flip that one right there." He pointed. I delicately slipped the end of
the metal tool under the meat, raised it up slowly and squealed as half of the
patty fell apart, off of the spatula and through the grates of the grill into the
fire.

"Well, that one's yours!" Henry let out a howl and gave me a hug. "That
was truly pathetic." He said softly, looking down at me just inches from my
face. His plush lashes batted a few times as his eyes bounced back and forth
between mine. An awkward feeling rose in my throat as his gloved hand
rubbed my arm. *Is he going to kiss me?* "Now, move out of the way! This
is clearly man's work!" He quickly pulled me into a hug then playfully
shoved me in the direction of the chair I had come from. *Nope! I guess not.*
I swatted back at him playfully and then plopped down on the chair next to
the grill. I looked at Henry and felt warm. *Maybe it isn't too late to start
something romantic with him.*

Just as I was beginning to imagine what it might be like to hold his hand,
I heard someone approaching from behind.

"Hey Henry, how's it going man?" I turned around to see Cain with a red
cup in his hand, reflective aviator style sunglasses hiding his eyes. I smiled
softly at him and twisted back around towards Henry trying to conceal my
excitement at his reappearance.

"Oh, you know. Just trying to keep the women from burning down the
tailgating fields." Henry replied and shot me a wink. I stuck out my tongue
at him and grinned.

"So how long have you gentlemen known each other?" I addressed the
men who were now standing side by side. Cain had made his way over to
the grill and both men were now staring down at the meat like it held the
answers of the universe.

"Oh, about five years," Henry guessed. I smiled pleasantly and
pretended to be preoccupied with my phone while the two chatted about the
current news in their lives which proved to be very informative. I learned

that Cain worked in the same city as I did for a major corporation and lived downtown. He had graduated from one of the best business in the region. More importantly, I learned that Cain was single and had been for three months. As he spoke I looked up at him and caught him stealing a glance at me, and I turned away pretending to look for Ava.

The smell of the grill began attracting attention, and people started making their way over for their midday meal. I stood up from the chair and walked over to a girlfriend whom I hadn't seen in a couple of years and we began to chat and catch up like old times. I learned, as she brandished her new shiny ring, that she was to be married in the fall to a psychiatrist. After which, they would move to Manhattan where he would work in his family's practice. They had already purchased an apartment in Chelsea. I listened politely, trying not to scowl with envy. *Where does one find a rich psychiatrist anyway*? I wondered if her fiancée had any friends, or if she would at least give me a few tips on how she bagged him.

I was just opening my mouth to rather uncouthly ask her, when I noticed her gaze directed past my left shoulder. I looked behind me and faced Cain.

"Excuse me." He extended a plate with a hamburger and chips towards me. "I convinced Henry to let you eat this, even though you threw yours into the flames." My friend was summoned by some people by the stereo and she excused herself and walked away.

"I didn't throw it into the flames." I turned and faced Cain squarely. "It committed suicide and that is nothing to tease about." I took the plate dramatically and smiled widely at him. Cain flashed a cat like grin and invited me to sit with him while we ate.

During the next four hours Cain and I were never very far away from each other. We talked about our lives, and laughed about funny TV shows and movies, and joined conversations with other people, then found our way back to standing face to face becoming deep in conversation. I liked him. He kept a drink in my and his own hands at all times and was becoming increasingly intoxicated and, subsequently, increasingly hilarious.

The sun started to set as we leaned against an unknown car in very close proximity to each other, discussing football, a true passion of mine. After emphatically describing my opinion of the Wildcat offense, with the help of the liquid courage flowing through my veins, I finally touched him. My hand was placed delicately on his broad chest. Our conversation twisted and turned to two of his passions: skiing and snowboarding.

"I can't believe you have never been to Colorado. It is the most beautiful place. I want to retire there for a couple of years." His eyes, now unsheltered by his sunglasses which hung on the front of his sweater, were warm and glowing in the purple dusk.

"Maybe you just need a good teacher to go with you, show you the slopes." I decided not to tell him that due to a knee injury the chances of me going skiing or snowboarding were slim to none. Plus, I hated cold weather. His palm grazed the side of my face and I looked down.

"May I kiss you?" He asked, speech slightly slurred. *"What? No! Absolutely not!"* Is what I would have said if I hadn't been drunk. Instead, I smiled and nodded enthusiastically. He tilted my chin up with his hand, slowly moving his mouth towards mine. My heart was racing and every neuron in my body was shooting with anticipation. *Oh my God! I cannot believe this is happening. I barely know this person!* I wanted to look around to make sure no one was watching but I was unable to pry my attention away from him. Cain took a step towards me and just as I closed my eyes a loud squishing sound ripped through the dusk. The soft muddy earth gave way and Cain slipped back, legs straight into the air, and landed with a thud on the ground.

"Are you OK?" I screamed. Cain didn't answer and was attempting to get up out of the muck at my feet. He was obtaining no traction and was slipping and sliding around. I started to laugh as I watched, feeling positively mortified for him. Others from our site began to notice started laughing.

"Hey, you OK, stud?" Shouted Cain's previous beer pong partner. After a few moments my giggles turned into full on hysteria. He tried for several more moments, much longer than I would have, then resigned to the fact that he was going to need help. He looked up at me like a sad puppy and held his hand out for mine.

"OK," I said. "But if you pull me down into that mud, I will make you pay… and not in a good way." He smiled at this and I gave him my hand.

"You are the best," he said once he had returned to his feet, his arms held wide, ready for a hug. I screamed at his filthy hands and turned to run away but he caught me and pulled me close to him, muddying my sweatshirt. I didn't care in the slightest. It was the perfect moment for a kiss and I looked up at him expectantly.

"Hey Romeo!" Claude shouted from over at the keg. "Time to pack it up. Let's go!"

"Shit." Cain muttered. "Are you going out tonight?" He asked eagerly. I had heard earlier that the group was going to meet up later at some of our favorite bars in town.

"Probably. I will check in with Claude and try to catch up with you later maybe?"

"Yes, please do." He said with a large smile. As he walked away I leaned against the car and put my hand in my sweatshirt pocket, fingering the business card he had given me earlier with his cell phone number on it. Ava walked over to me.

"Hi, stranger. I haven't seen very much of you today." I smiled to myself then looked at her and grinned. "Things progressed nicely there, huh?" Her excitement etched in every syllable, she didn't wait for me to respond. "Come on, let's get home and get cleaned up so we can meet them out later." She took my hand and we skipped cheerfully cross the lot to find our car.

2.

When I realized that I only had five minutes until I was officially late, I also realized I was still ten minutes away from my destination. I navigated the one-way streets with notable difficulty considering I had lived in the city for fifteen years. I squinted to see the letters of the green street signs as they swung wildly in the early December wind and cursed myself for not bringing my eyeglasses. *Shit, I should have turned left there.* I could have worn them in the car but then I would have had unsightly compression marks on the bridge of my nose. Definitely embarrassing. I inched closer to the windshield and I made the next left turn and then another left turn and pulled into a parking spot. I applied a new layer of gloss to my full lips and straighten my eyeliner with the insides of my pinky fingers which shook with adrenaline. I was undeniably on edge. I took a deep breath and relaxed my shoulders. *This happens every first date. Every time.* No matter what I told myself to quell the annoying and pathetic beast, something deep inside me yearned for this date to be the beginning of an exquisite love story, for this first date to be my last first date. Ever. A pretty lofty goal for a single, twenty-three year old African -American woman or at least that is what statistics say. As a Business major, I know statistics.

I checked my still perfectly polished nails done at an over-priced salon that afternoon, opened the door to my beige sedan, placed the four-inch heel of my black leather boot onto the pavement and smiled. *Even if this ends badly, at least I look amazing.* My grandmother, Roslyn, had strongly advocated looking the best absolutely everywhere you went. Whether to the dollar store or to church, she believed that a woman and man should look like they were important people with important things to do. I had adopted the philosophy, as well as her shopping habits and addictions to clothing and fineries that she couldn't afford. I looked up at the tall white apartment building from the crowded sidewalk as people pushed past me. It was only a block from the heart of the city nestled over a chain department store that sold designer clothes and goods at discounted prices, and a block from the largest mall in the city and all of the best restaurants. *Location, location, location.* I rang his number from the door, feeling the flush rise up.

"Hey there, I'll be right down." His voice wasn't as deep as I remembered from the previous weekend.

"O.K., I'm wearing a purple sweater."

As I looked around at the people on the sidewalk passing me, I doubted that he would need the description. Most donned business suits and toted briefcases as they walked from the Statehouse at the end of the block. My sweater was purple, gray and black in a block pattern. I bought it on clearance from a high-end department store at the end of last season and still could barely afford it. It proved to be a wise purchase however, as color blocking was in style in all of the mid-range stores this season. I was just six months too late to be on the cutting edge of fashion. I turned my back to the front doors of the apartment and watched as a beautiful chestnut complexioned woman with long flowing jet hair was escorted out of the passenger's side of a new Audi across the street. She and a beautiful mahogany man, around six-two, wearing a perfectly tailored gray tweed jacket, designer jeans and black wing tips, walked hand in hand into the sushi bar on the corner. *Good for you brother-man and woman.* It was always refreshing to see a comfortable black man with a black woman. It would have been even more refreshing, actually, downright shocking, to see a comfortable black man with a black woman who didn't wear a weave that was worth more than I got paid in month.

But I smiled anyway and put a hand to my natural hair, arranged in locs that fell to my shoulders. Although the pretty, extremely low maintenance style worked for me, in my heart it didn't quite fit. Growing up, my mother didn't know a thing about hair and treated it as something to be dealt with rather than cherished and molded into a form of expression. She and I had been deeply cursed with some of the hardest to manage hair in the world. That's what my mother always said. That sentiment was deeply planted as a seed of hatred for the mess that grew out of my scalp. As a consequence, from the time I was three my hair was thrown into braids and hidden with extensions as often as possible until finally, in my late teens, I came across locs. Thank goodness the style had finally converged from the west and east coasts and now everywhere you looked in the Midwest, locs were being worn proudly. As I absent-mindedly turned to face the front doors again I saw him coming out of the elevator. *Damn!* I wanted to be facing the other way. So much for playing coy and slightly disinterested.

Breezing out of the door in a black, double-breasted, wool pea coat opened to a light blue dress shirt, dark jeans, and Diesel shoes he stopped in front of me and stuck out his hand. Even with my long legs in four inch heels, he towered above me.

"How tall are you?" I questioned him bewilderedly. *Shoot! Was that first thing I had to say to this man upon meeting him again? Way to keep it cool.* I always had a problem with my mouth, or rather its accidental conversion of internal dialogue into audible. I learned early on to own these inappropriate outbursts when they came rather than apologizing for them like a person with any measurable shame would have. Audacious is much better than socially awkward.

Cain bit his lower lip and smirked.

"I'm six-four." He said with confidence. "Don't you remember what I look like?" He was wearing frameless glasses that slid down his nose a centimeter as he stared at me. *Maybe I wouldn't have looked so dumb.* And the diarrhea mouth continued.

"You weren't wearing glasses last time I saw you." I said as I took his hand in greeting feeling like a six year old with a social dysfunction. *I need a drink.*

"No, I was wearing contacts. But you were wearing them, right? You look great with and without. Are you hungry? There's a Cuban restaurant I've wanted to try a few doors down." The words came from his mouth like butter. *Dang. At least someone knows how to hold a polite conversation.*

"That sounds wonderful." I smiled at him. "Let's go there."

"Great." He turned and used his long arm to direct me to the left.

I used the walking time to get my head together. Ok, *Myra. Please do not run this thing into the ground. You are charming and intelligent and beautiful. Act like it!* I tried to channel my grandmother's grace and walked on. Literally three doors down Cain stepped in front of me and opened the door. The restaurant was small and smelled heavily of pork and spices. The only aisle was lined on each side with four top tables all lit with glowing red orbs, candles flickering under them. A short man with black hair parted and slicked to each side stuck his head around the corner from the kitchen as we entered.

"Sit anywhere you like." He looked curiously at us for a moment and then ducked back out of sight. I chose the farthest seat after delicately removing my jacket and placing it on the chair closest to the wall. Cain sat across from me, stretching one arm across the back of the chair next to him and unhooked the top button of his shirt with the other. *He is really pale.* I bit down hard on my tongue to keep that observation silent. It stayed unsaid. *Good, girl, Myra. Atta way.*

"How was your day today?" I asked politely. As he spoke my gaze wandered from his eyes, hazel and round, to his long nose, to the stubble that shadowed his face, to his lips as they moved. They were thick, soft looking. Just beyond his lips were teeth that, while straight, had obviously never seen orthodontia. They were too natural looking to have worn braces. One of his front teeth was slightly discolored and seemed to have been chipped and then replaced with a cap, just like mine had been after an unfortunate bathroom stall incident. I silently praised myself for not mentioning his central incisor. He asked me about my day, I replied, and then we dove into the standard first date interrogation tennis match. I had to admit, after spending several hours with him the past weekend I thought that our reunion would have felt more comfortable. But nope, it was as awkward as any other first date with a stranger. Although we had spoken in great detail about ourselves, our families, our careers and hobbies, the large amount of alcohol consumed had had its way with our memories and left very little for us to sift through. I could feel my composure slipping again as I fidgeted with the large onyx ring on my index finger.

When the waitress finally appeared, I ordered a Corona Light with extra lime. Cain did the same and I served the ball again. I tried my best to ask him leading, open-ended questions that I hadn't already asked during our previous meeting and finding that nearly impossible to avoid. When he asked me,

"So where did you grow up?" I felt a bit better because we had discussed our upbringing in depth upon meeting. I answered his query and then returned the query. After he was finished we both remained silent. I watched him pick up the bottle in front of him and gently place it to his mouth, puckering his lips around the glass opening making a duck face. I laughed to myself then glanced around the room. The waitress had taken our dinner order fifteen minutes previously and had still not reappeared with the plates. Directly above Cain's head was a TV on mute with the news on. I watched a middle aged Middle Eastern man holding a little boy in his arms and pointing behind himself at a smoldering building. His house was burning- I gathered. It occurred to me that several minutes had passed and neither Cain nor I had spoken. In an attempt to prevent this date from ending up like the house in the news, I tried harder.

"What do you do for fun around town?" I asked him. He told me that he played recreational basketball and went to the gym a lot. *So he is a meat head. Great.* "That's fun!" I assured him, feeling a little judgmental. "Did you play in college?"

"Yes. I did. I loved playing." Luckily for me, I knew just enough about basketball to make him believe I understood twice as much as I did and we carried on about the city's NBA team and the local college teams until our food arrived. As we ate we continued talking about our interests. Cain was nice, but there was something about him that felt very superficial, much more uptight and stuffy than the happy and flirty man I had met while tailgating. This person was as bland as toasted bread. White bread toast, more specifically. I was bored.

The food we ate, on the other hand was deliciously entertaining and as each bite touched my pallet, I tried to discern the ingredients that were combined to make the dynamic flavor. I had the duck and Cain was quickly devouring the pulled pork. I noticed that his plate was lined with little blood red peppers.

"Is your pork hot with all of those peppers?" I asked, reminding myself silently that it would be rude to ask for a taste. He looked up for the first time in a few minutes and I gasped as I saw his face, which was covered in a layer of sweat from his forehead to the pool where his collarbones met. *Holy crap! Oh my God! Is he having a heart attack?* I stood up from my chair abruptly and flinched as it fell back onto the white and gray carpet. Ready to give the man across from me mouth-to-mouth resuscitation if necessary I took a step in his direction.

"Cain, you are perspiring severely. Are you feeling OK?" I had taken an emergency response class at the ambulance company where I worked. "I am going to check your heart rate and if needed I am trained to administer a defibrillator." Cain's mouth was full of food and slightly open as he stared at me in confusion.

"What are you talking about?" I could barely understand him. His eyes widened as I placed a finger on his throat. He swallowed, and then spoke, "I'm fine, really. I sweat a lot when I eat spicy foods. Not a big deal. It happens all the time." Cain put his hands up to ward me off and looked up at me as if I were insane. I stopped dead.

"Oh," I quickly removed my hand from his neck. "OK. Sorry, I just have never seen anything like that before." I backed back around the table. "It is actually pretty alarming." I said as I righted my overturned chair and sat back down, "I am sure anyone would have reacted that way." I mumbled to myself trying to justify my reaction. I picked up my fork and started eating again, staring at the red rice, slightly annoyed. I abstained from asking why he had chosen something that was clearly marked spicy on the menu if it turned him into a puddle like Frosty the Snowman at the end of the children's tale. *Two points for me.*

As the night continued, so did my intrigue. I could not reconcile the guy from the football game with the man sitting across from me. There was obviously a missing link. So when he asked me on a walk after dinner, I obliged. The sun was setting and cast a beautiful fuchsia light over the concrcte buildings. I walked next to him and explained about my promotion in the finance department of a local ambulance company. As I spoke, every so often, I would look over at Cain, and even though we were walking at a decent pace, he never took his eyes off of me. It was very intimate. I felt a strong urge to touch him. His large muscular hands swung delicately at his side and I wondered how one would feel wrapped around my own in the cold. Cain listened and asked the appropriate questions as I explained what I did on a daily basis and how my department, Contracts, fit into the company as a major source of revenue.

"So, if a car hit you right now and you needed an ambulance, would you want me to call for your company so you could get some kind of discount?" He asked seriously.

What kind of question is that?

"Well, yes I get a discount, but no! I would want you to get whichever ambulance was closest!"

"OK. But what if you weren't hurt too badly, then wouldn't you want the discount?" he prodded.

"What kind of injury are we talking about here?" I gave in with a sigh. We discussed the different levels of injuries that would warrant taking the extra time to call for my company. It amused me that he was level-headed enough to think about the ambulance bill in a potential crisis. It made me think about his emotionality, or lack thereof. He was bizarre. Extremely analytical, but silly as well.

The temperature had dropped considerably since we left the restaurant. I wrapped my fitted wool jacket around myself tighter and pressed my lips together. Cain talked about his work at the pharmaceutical company in town. We stopped at a light, waiting for the walk sign to appear and I caught a whiff of his cologne. It was musky. Cedar, amber and a trace of something else which left a sweet distinction in my nose. I took an intentionally deep breath and the fragrance filled me, warming me to the core. Onward we walked across the street and I listened on, determining that his voice was pleasant. Almost pretty. I wondered what it would sound like over the phone or spoken in a whisper close to my face. My heart began to quicken as I thought about his lips, and I felt flushed again. Before I had time to gather myself he stopped in his tracks. I looked around and saw my car a few yards away.

"Oh." I said sounding disappointed. "We're back?"

"Yep. We are back. It's getting pretty cold, huh?" Cain looked around unassumingly then dug his hand in his pocket for his keys.

This was the point where I was supposed to agree. Take his hand, thank him for the dinner he had purchased and had not allowed me to split with him, tell him that I had a wonderful time and walk to my car. That is not what happened. That is not what happened at all.

3.

How I got myself in this situation was something I pondered deeply as I lay fully clothed, passionately kissing a man I had just been on a first date with. *What am I doing?* The night was supposed to end downstairs, outside of Cain's building door. He was supposed to walk me to my car and then I would have gently kissed his cheek. Maybe lips, if the moment was right. Why, then, were my hands lightly resting on his broad shoulders and my lips being devoured by his?

In the flashing blue light of the television scene that played inches from where we sprawled in his downtown loft bedroom, there was no end to the desire that Cain displayed for me. He took handfuls of me everywhere he could, cupping my face in his fingers and staring deeply into my eyes. Shocked by the transformation of this previously sedate young man, I hoped that my previous assessment that he was not a psycho was correct. As he kissed me, thoughts of missing person shows on the Discovery Channel flashed through my consciousness. Stories aired of women who casually went home with men after meeting them and were never seen again. Viewers sat at home on their sofas, shaking their heads with a *"Isn't that sad? She had no self-respect."-* look on their faces. *Crap.* I was addicted to those TV shows myself, and if I had watched the scene playing out with Cain and me, I would have been yelling for me to jump up and run for my life. But there, in the quiet of his bedroom I didn't feel any danger. My cackles, which were finely-tuned thanks to the rowdy crowds at my university, were not standing on end, they were relaxed.

There was something volcanic about Cain, though, as he almost desperately clung to me. My eyes darted around the room searching for anything suspicious. Directly above me, was an abstract painting, unframed, of a man and woman kneeling and embracing in wide blue strokes. It was beautiful, sensual and made me feel desire, not physical but emotional. It made me want to experience love, to give it and receive it. I wondered what kind of feelings it invoked in Cain. The room was small, with barely enough space for the large bed where we lay, an oversized glass desk in the corner and a few other awkwardly placed items. *Why does he have such a large bed and desk in this tiny room? A double bed and a small wooden desk would work so much better here.* It didn't occur to me that his long frame would not be able to fit in a double bed or under a smaller desk without being uncomfortable.

I continued to scan the room. The walls were unpainted and mostly bare. There was a gym bag shoved in the corner by the walk-in closet with a sock hanging out, the culprit of the slightly musty smell of the room. A dress shirt and tie lay across the back of a director's chair in another corner and next to that was company issued laptop bag. I saw nothing to raise any alarm, but that could have been because there was no real space for anything creepy. I drove my attention back to Cain and the situation at hand.

Generally, first kisses, the first series of kisses, are awkward. It seems that no one is ever really sure how to approach the mouth of another person. I, especially, due to my large lips, have to be very careful not to overwhelm my partner. When Cain kissed me, however, it felt like the most natural thing in the world. He knew exactly how to take my lips into his own full ones and hold them. His jaw was neither too weak nor overpowering and the first time his tongue brushed mine I felt every cell in my body catch fire. The entire interaction felt as if we had done it hundreds of times before.

"God, you are so beautiful." He choked out. *Does he really think so?* I could only imagine the horror that was my eye make-up at that point, liner and mascara probably running due to the dry climate in the room, not to mention the dust. I opened my mouth to disagree with him. In my opinion, and I certainly was an expert, my hair was too unconventional, my lips were large and full, but not shapely, my eyes too dark brown, my chest, way too large for my frame, my hips and waist in a weird proportion, and my legs were thin and straight rather than shapely and muscular. I was average at best, but I had a hell of a sense of humor as far as I was concerned and I could dress my ass off.

Like most little ethnic girls in America for the past two-hundred years, I grew up exposed to images of "beautiful women" who looked nothing like me. In fact they looked quite opposite from me. Advertisements always told me what to purchase to look like these women but never mentioned that other traits were desirable too. And while over the years different looks and trends became the "IT" in relation to beauty, none of those images were ones I could identify with. Even when black women were featured, I still could not relate. My hair wasn't long or flowing, my hips and butt were not big or shapely enough, my eyes were not round and sparkling. I became prey to the media hype at an early age, and even though as an adult I fully understood the psychological angle taken by marketing companies to trick us into buying their products, the damage was already done.

This was not the time for a lengthy conversation about societal beauty with Cain, however, and I appreciated his effort to make me feel comfortable. He was sweet and I wanted to reward him for that. I was trying hard to focus on him. It should have been easy as he was breathtakingly gorgeous. I found myself mentally swatting away the gnats of insecurity that buzzed around my head. *God, I hope my breath doesn't smell. I can't believe I left my mints in the car.* I noted that Cain's breath wasn't the freshest. *Good. Maybe he won't notice.* I let my body relax into the memory foam mattress.

Cain's hand lay gently on my abdomen. Shockingly, it spanned virtually the entirety of my stomach. *How is it possible that he is this big?* I loved the way he dwarfed me, made me feel small and delicate in a way I hadn't experienced. I reached my hand to his and began to play with his fingers. Picking each one up and holding it and then putting it back down and grabbing another one. *His fingers are bigger than my thumb!* I was thrilled. Cain began to make small noises indicating that he was enjoying himself and I smiled at that. I hungrily tasted his lips, and although I knew that sleeping with anyone on a first day was an awful idea, I was having a hard time controlling how my body was responding.

My mother's voice echoed from somewhere in the dark. *No relationship ever lasts when you sleep with a man on the first date.* My mother was raised as an only child on a tobacco farm in southern Kentucky. She lived with her parents until she was eighteen and went to a University a few hours away where she met my father. I doubted my mother had ever seen another man's bare chest in person before my dad. I knew for a fact that she had never slept with anyone else. *How does she know that no relationship ever lasts when you sleep with a man on the first date? Hearsay?* I was beginning to doubt the validity of her statement, when it sounded loudly, forcefully in my mind. *No relationship ever lasts when you sleep with a man on the first date!*

Cain, apparently, didn't hear it and rolled on top of me, his boulder-like frame pinning me. I kept my legs firmly together straining against the instinct to wrap them around his waist. He began to kiss my neck and my thoughts floated away. I envisioned him, all of him, beautiful and muscular as my hands moved over his back and settled at his belt just before the round of his buttocks. My hands slid up and under his dress shirt and I dug the pads of my fingers up and down the smooth skin of his back. He exhaled sharply moved his head to look me in the eyes again.

"That feels good, baby." He growled and plunged into another passionate kiss. After a moment, his mouth left mine and moved to my ear lobe. I inhaled slowly, trying to gather myself. *No relationship ever lasts when you sleep with a man on the first date. No relationship ever lasts when you sleep with a man on the first date.* My resolve was fading.

I was no novice to sex, especially meaningless sex. I spent a lot of time in college with my best friend Ava reliving the 60's Free Love movement. Back then, I found it intoxicating how eager young men were to have me. Every weekend was like a game. What cute guy could I flirt with, convince to buy me drinks, and then go with to a midnight diner and come home with me? The following morning would consist of Ava and me lying on our couch, regaling the hilarious and sometimes horrifying stories of the previous night's sexual interlude. More often than not, we never spoke to the guy again. We weren't trying to form lasting relationships, we were trying to have fun and perhaps declare our sexual independence. I often thought about those days and how much had changed. I saw the world completely differently now. I saw myself completely differently as well.

As I got older, left school and started working, those kinds of activities died down to zero. I started figuring out what I wanted from men and my relationships with them. Most importantly, I started to understand the emotional implications that random sex had on the psyche and personal paradigm and decided that I wouldn't behave that way again. Laying there with Cain felt different from those wild and immature experiences. As I took all of Cain into my senses, I knew I wanted to see him again. More than wanted, I needed to. He made me feel awakened.

"Does that feel OK?" It felt better than anything I had ever experienced. I used all of my strength to push upwards on his chest, forcing him off of me and climbed on top of him, legs astride. He looked at me in surprise, smiling, bright teeth glowing in the cool light. I let myself down on him kissing his neck and cheeks. My tongue traced a line from his salty Adam's apple to his ear and a soft moan escaped him. My locs fell to the side like a curtain of tassels. With one large hand, he gathered them and gently ran his fingers through their length.

"I love your hair. It's so beautiful." I turned, head cocked to the side and looked at him incredulously. *OK! Now that is taking it overboard!* No man had ever called my hair beautiful. *Cool*, sure. *Awesome*, sometimes. White men usually thought of my hair as some kind of Rastafarian statement rather than an expression of style to be admired for its complex beauty. But there was sincerity in his face that filled me with endearment. I took his hand in mine and kissed his soft palm, then placed it under my sweater past my smooth stomach to my chest. He bit down on his lip as he molded his hand to my breast. Softly, almost imperceptibly, he grazed his thumb over the apex of the soft mound. I sighed loudly, leaned forward to millimeters from his face and touched his top lip with the tip of my tongue, smiling slightly to encourage him.

In a flash, he was on top of me again, hands everywhere. He rested his palm over the zipper of my jeans, fingers facing into me and began to massage. I moved against him, losing all sense of time and space. The last voice warning me of the implications of having sex with this man faded away and in its wake was only the desire to be as close to Cain as humanly possible. He thought that I was beautiful which made me feel provocative, charming, and desirable. He did all this during a first date, which, more often than not, is rife with awkwardness and unease. Generally, after a first date, it took me at least a week to shed the embarrassing feelings of oafishness that the date invoked before I could consider speaking to the man again. Cain had certainly performed a miracle. Grabbing the back of his shirt, I pulled it off and flung it across the room. I stopped dead, or at least I thought I had died. And gone to heaven.

"Oh my God!" I started. I felt like someone had hit me over the back of the head. Sure, I was expecting to see Cain's chest and torso, which, under clothing, seemed strong and firm. I was not expecting this. His body was perfect, large and thick, well defined with muscle. Staring, I fought the urge to laugh out loud. The perfection of him was absurd, almost too much to handle, and I felt a wave of insecurity wash over me again. I thanked God for the dark room which concealed my imperfections. My knee, scarred from a sports injury of my childhood, the pouch of fat right below my belly button that I just couldn't get rid of, the stretch marks that lightly traced the round of my bottom. As the images wandered through my mind and overwhelmed me, I wanted to retreat. I feared he would judge me for my imperfections. I was half considering fleeing the room when I felt his warm hand on my cheek. It directed my eyes back to his.

"Are you ok?" His voice was low and sweet.

"Your body is flawless." My face wore a look of pure intimidation. My instinct was to roll on my back, hands and legs in the air in a display of submission like a dog.

"Do you really think so?" He sounded unsure. "I need to do a lot of work and eat better. Probably stop drinking beer…" he faded out. I noticed that his posture was slightly protective, chest sunken down as if he were trying to hide himself. His insecurity about his body was palpable. *How could someone as stunning as you have any insecurity at all?*

"You are the most beautiful man I have ever seen." He scoffed loudly.

"Oh, well at least in person. At the very least you are the most beautiful man I have ever seen in person, hands down." He smiled and pulled me up to my knees where we were eye to eye and then he hugged me, stoking my hair as my head lay on his shoulder. No one had ever done that before either. Men were generally uncertain about to approach my hair and tended to err on the side of caution by means of avoiding it all together. Slowly, my confidence rose again. My gaze lowered to the perfect curve of his chest and I placed my hand on its smooth surface, tracing my fingers from top to bottom. A soft sigh escaped his lips and he nuzzled my ear and then kissed it. I continued, using my fingers to press deeper into his flesh. His breath intensified.

The amount of power I felt to make this gorgeous man so turned on was intoxicating. I wanted more. I moved in front of him and placed my mouth to his hard chest, tongue gliding over every curve. He let out a soft growl and held my head in place as he reached around my body to rub my neck and back. I felt his body begin to shake with excitement. I relented for a moment, and in one powerful motion he yanked my sweater up over my arms. I didn't even wince when I heard the fabric tear. Leaning back slightly to look at my lace covered chest as it heaved in the dark, his eyes moved to my face taking it in. He studied my chin, my lips, my nose and cheeks pumping silent admiration into each. He looked at me as if he wanted to both protect and destroy what he saw, he looked greedy and hungry and it made me uneasy.

Our eyes locked again and I felt it. A strike, deep in my chest. *Where is this coming from?* The amount of passion I felt for this stranger was overwhelming. I raised my finger to his mouth, softly pressing his swollen bottom lip. There was something so sweet, so sincere that radiated from him but the look in his eyes was one of a predator. He wanted me. Without thinking I asked breathlessly, "Will you make love to me now?"

I don't know what made me say that. He didn't love me. We had just met. There was no way he could make love to me. He could have sex with me for sure. He could do other verbs to me, absolutely. He could not make love to me. He pulled me close to him. I felt all of my weight being enveloped by his strong arms and then he laid me down gently, washing over me.

"Yes." He breathed, eyes were burning now. "I will make love to you." And even though it was impossible, that's exactly what he did.

4.

Well, well, well. Maybe the old adage about sleeping with someone on the first date isn't true. I looked down to see a text message alert from Cain. It was the afternoon after our first date. Smiling to myself, I allowed butterflies to dance in my stomach and picked up my cell phone from the desk to reply. I quickly put it back down. *I shouldn't text him back yet, I don't want to seem too eager or like I have too much free time on my hands.*

I was at work, and while my management position at the ambulance company only slightly aligned with my major in school and it paid my bills, which would satisfy some, I knew that my time there would be minimal. The building was sterile and cold, an old warehouse turned billing center on the south side of town. It featured one large room where all of the departments were separated by islands of cubicles. Every person that stood up could easily be viewed by their co-workers who were most likely texting on their cell phones, stuffing their faces with candy bars from the vending machines or slurping down the free fountain soft drinks that, I was absolutely certain, contributed to the rampant obesity that plagued the people who worked there.

I attempted to work on a new contract that had just landed in my inbox that morning. My mind, however, was focused on what I would say to Cain when I responded to his message, or, even more distracting, on what had happened the night before. Sure, I had been waiting for his text message since I left his apartment that morning at 2 a.m., my mother's warning about loose women chasing me down the hallway, out onto the sidewalk and into my car. Despite that, I made up my mind that, even if I never heard from him again, I had a lot of fun and was still glowing from the intensity and passion of the night. It wasn't until then that I realized how much I had needed a pick-me-up! I was now as perky as a NFL cheerleader on Monday Night Football. These were the things I kept repeating to myself to abate my nervousness until my phone lit up with his message and I was hit with a tidal wave of relief. *Thank God.* Images of Cain swept over me. His smooth and freckled skin, his precision trimmed and styled hair, his pillowy pink lips and where he placed those lips so sweetly.

"So what did you do last night?" Lilly, my co-worker and friend, popped her head over my cubical wall, startling me from my haze of lust driven disorientation. She worked as the manager in the billing department across the aisle and we had become friends over our mutual dislike of the automatic air freshener in the women's restroom. Lilly was completely cynical, which I adored, and she hated everyone who worked there except for me, which made me feel special. She took the ponytail holder out of her corn-silk blonde hair and allowed it to envelope her shoulders, shaking it out. I stared at her perfectly angled ends in amazement and wondered if my hair could ever look like that. Just the ends, not the color or texture. *Obviously. The only way I could have hair like that is if I took a field trip to the to the weave shop.* I could not begin to imagine what I would look like with straight hair past my shoulders. *Probably ridiculous.* A hand went to the end of one of my locks and I sighed dejectedly, and then spoke.

"I had a first date last night. With the guy I met at the football game last weekend. Remember?"

"Oh, yes! Excellent! How did that go?" I wasn't sure where exactly Lilly was from, but her speech pattern had the slightest twinge of a Minnesota dialect, vowels hard and elongated. She had two older siblings, but their differences in ages left her growing up alone with her single mother. Both brother and sister had moved to the east coast when she was only a toddler. She therefore assumed the air of superiority that no one but an only child could muster.

"It went really, *really* well." I could feel a toothy grin smear across my face. "So very well." As I spoke that last affirmation I looked up at Lilly and knew instantly I was caught. Her eyes narrowed back at me and she gasped dramatically.

"Myra, you didn't. You *didn't!*" She half yelled. I cringed into my shoulders and looked around guiltily. *Busted.*

"What are you talking about?" I tried my best to wipe away the smile and sound innocent, but the more effort I exerted, the more relentless my grin became. "I didn't do what?" I giggled. The look on Lilly's face was one of shock and disgust. For an instant, I thought I saw her mouth move up in a smile, but then it was gone. For all of her apparent alarm, she had to know me pretty well to guess that I had slept with Cain. Lilly and I had not been friends during my "wilder days", we had not yet met, but I amused her with the stories from time to time.

"Myra, I can't believe this!" She squealed. The jig was up. I smiled and hid my face in my heavy palms, peeking around them every so often as Lilly began her moral tirade which lasted the better half of three minutes, "…And moreover, I hope you didn't like him because he will never contact you again… ever!" At this, remaining silent, (I learned that silence was the best way to appear repentant while Lilly chewed me out for my various transgressions) I pulled my hands away from my face, picked up my phone and held it out so that she could see the text message alert. "Is that him? You haven't even read it yet?" she asked incredulously and snatched the phone out of my hand.

"Lilly, don't you dare! Give that back!" I shrieked, forgetting that we were at work and that I was supposed to at least feign professionalism. Co-workers surrounding us were beginning to look over in interest. Lilly clicked a few buttons on my phone and then, in her best surfer boy impersonation,

"'*Hey Angela, it was great seeing all of you last night, but I am moving to a remote island today and will not be able to contact you or receive your messages again.*' See? He didn't even remember your name!"

"Give me that!" I jumped out of my chair cursing myself for not activating the device's password feature and took the phone from her, heartbeat quickening as I looked down at the screen. *I had a good time last night (smiley face). I hope you have a great day.* I could feel my brow furrow as I read it over then looked up at Lilly, "I wonder what this is supposed to mean. Other than he had a good time, obviously."

My face fell. I didn't know what I expected the message to say, but this certainly wasn't it. After over eight hours of convincing myself that I was at peace with, even proud of, my lusty choices with Cain, the first slug of shame wrapped itself around the corner of my mind. I could feel the slime oozing down my temple. I liked him a lot, even after only two meetings. It hadn't occurred to me that sleeping with him so soon could dissolve any interest he might have for me. *Oh, wait.* My hand involuntarily went to my forehead with force and resulted in a slap. *Shit. No relationship ever lasts when you sleep with a man on the first date.* Had I really ruined the potential of a new boyfriend, maybe even husband,- I had done a lot of daydreaming in those eight hours- with an impulsive return of my former *college self,* a virtual child with little awareness of consequences, few scruples and an alcohol habit verging on destructive? "Well, at least I had fu…" *Fun.* My gaze dropped to the dull and dingy gray carpet. I couldn't even finish the sentence. Now that I had a witness to my indiscretion, I felt dirty and dumb. Lilly, who was several years my senior and quite intuitively maternal at times, placed her hand on my back,

"I'm sure you will see him again honey, and if not, at least he had enough respect for you to contact you again. Sometimes men don't even do that, you know?" Her face was suddenly soft and warm. "Hey, I'm ordering Chinese, you want your favorite? My treat." Bless Lilly's heart. She was truly a good friend. She knew that the only real way I had discovered to suppress stress, uncertainty, sadness, loneliness, anger and shame was with greasy take-out.

"That sounds perfect, Lilly-Pad." I perked up a little at the thought of chicken lo Mein. She hated when I called her Lilly-Pad but I loved it. Nicknames were my thing. Although the receiver didn't know it, a nickname from me was the mark that I loved them and every time I said it was like uttering just that. She stuck out her tongue at me, smiled, and then walked away.

Sitting on my couch that evening with a glass of cheap wine and a book stuck open to the same page I had begun on, I was on the verge of a panic attack. I stared at my cell phone sitting on the coffee table and then at the clock, it read 6:35 p.m. I still hadn't responded to Cain's message. I decided it was time. After Chinese with Lilly, I had thought about little more than what I would text back to Cain. I wanted just one more meeting with him to prove that I, in fact, was not a floozy and was actually a super respectable woman. Dinner, a movie and a PG good night kiss farewell. I could feel my self-worth hinging on whether or not he would agree to see me again. *And we have mutual friends! What is Henry going to think when he finds out about this?* Images of my college buddy, Henry- a man I had spent hours of my life flirting with flashed in my head. He and Cain had been friends for several years. *So instead of jeopardizing just one potential relationship, I have jeopardized two!* My thoughts went back to the limitless number of responses I could choose. One of them had to be the key to a second date. Would it be open ended? Should I just reply with *"you too"* and leave it at that, hoping that my apparent disinterest would reel him in? Finally I decided on my response. Picking up the phone, I sighed loudly. *How did I get myself into this and why am I acting like a pubescent fifteen year old?*

Hey there. I had fun. Have an amazing night.

My logic being that if he didn't respond I could text him back in a few days. If I would have left it open then the ball would have been in his court and I would have had to wait for him to reach out to me. I played the dating game under a fairly strict set of rules which was put together under the influence of HBO's "Sex and the City", all six seasons, and two movies, the movie "Two Can Play at That Game", starring Vivica A. Fox and HBO's "Entourage"-for the male insight. These guidelines had been road tested by not only me but my friends, and had rendered decent results at least fifty percent of the time, which was good enough for us. I had not explored why, if these rules were so reliable in establishing fruitful relationships, my friends and I were all currently, and, in some cases, chronically single.

I tossed my phone on the cushion beside me and tried to focus on the novel in my hands. *Now for the dreaded waiting game. Jesus, I need a cigarette.* I had engaged in smoking throughout my years in college and partook every once in a while now, usually when copious amounts of alcohol had been consumed or a stressful event occurred. I looked at the bare walls of my apartment with distaste. I had spent several hours in the past week flipping through home magazines trying to nail down exactly *what* my interior design style was, and had put each magazine down more confused than I was after reading the last. I was never the "home-maker" kind of woman. My bathroom towels were disgusting and old, I did not own a paper towel holder and there were books everywhere. Everywhere, except the antique bookshelves I purchased upon moving in, which held weird and tacky knick-knacks. There was absolutely no distinguishable color palette. Picture frames of gaudy glass and bronze sat next to wooden figurines of African art. I had read that a person's home reflects their personality. If that was true then I was clearly some kind of schizophrenic. I had a very defined taste in fashion, so where was it in regards to decorating? I promised myself that I would pick out paint colors during the coming weekend, which was the same promise I had made to myself every week since moving in six months ago.

I looked back at the phone and checked for messages. *Nothing.* It had only been three minutes. I could hear the cigarettes calling me from the other side of the apartment. Promising that it would only be one and that I deserved something special due to all of the unfair stress I had put myself under, I leaped off the couch and strode to the hall closet around the corner, feet feeling refreshed as they made contact with the cool tile floor. I opened the door and stooped to pull out the small step stool hidden in the corner under umbrellas and scarves. I climbed on and reached to the back of the top shelf, feeling around for a soft plastic covered pack. My fingers made contact and I opened the box, slid a firm white stick to freedom as well as the lighter that was stashed snugly alongside, tossed the package back and jumped off the stool, which jiggled. Replacing the stool, I closed the door, grabbed a sweatshirt out of the laundry area, tucked my feet into my slippers and made a b-line for the sliding glass patio door.

The cold air stung my nostrils as I put the cigarette to my lips, looked around to make sure no neighbors were around to witness my shameful habit, flicked the lighter and inhaled. I always felt so guilty when I smoked. I hated how judged I felt, even when there was no one around to see me. In my experience, smoking meant so much more than you had an unhealthy habit. Somehow, people linked smoking to social class. No one was ever snubbed or looked down upon for eating fast food every day or never exercising or pumping their face full of Botox or drinking a bottle of wine a night. All were unhealthy, but there was a stigma to lighting a cigarette. *"What's wrong with cigarettes?"- Carrie Bradshaw, "Nothing, they are fabulous." – Stanford Blatch.* A favorite Sex and the City quote of mine. I smiled, began to feel more relaxed and stared up at the sky.

While it lacked in night life, living in the suburbs had its advantages in natural beauty. I picked out the few constellations I could distinguish and wrapped my arms around me, letting my thoughts wander. *Orion's Belt, Cassiopeia, and the Drinking Gourd.* In my mind I zoomed out from the city I lived in, out of the state, up hundreds of thousands of feet into the stratosphere. Turning to the east, I flew over the valley and mountains to the coast in the crystal night looking over the little circuit board cities as I passed. I approached a diamond lit city and zoomed in to Washington, DC. I felt my heart looking for someone. Someone that I missed. I couldn't see him but I could certainly feel him. A helicopter flew over my apartment heading for the airfield a mile north of my apartment and I was brought back to my balcony.

My ex-boyfriend Ralph and I broke up after dating for two years. Five months out of the twenty- four were good. He was living in Manhattan at the time, attending school at NYU and I was taking a summer course at Columbia University. We met at a cafe he worked at when he spilled iced coffee down the front of my white cotton dress, and then had the gawky inclination to try to wipe the mocha off my chest with a dishtowel. Standing at the counter, it took me several seconds to stop him as I was most concerned with not allowing the sticky brown liquid to penetrate the cover of my overpriced laptop. When I finally realized that a complete stranger with coke bottle glasses and a sparse mustache was fumbling with my chest, I grabbed his wrist and stared him in the eye wordlessly.

"I am so sorry, Miss. Really, I didn't mean to spill… and then wipe… Oh, God." His voice was deep and raspy, a contradiction to his thin frame. He seemed so absolutely flabbergasted and pathetic that I couldn't help the laughter that rose from my throat. I heard snickers and giggles from behind me and turned to see that we had the full attention of the ten patrons in line. I let my head fall back, continuing to laugh with short locs swinging, and placed a hand over my shiny and now sticky cleavage.

"May I please have a wet, hot towel when you get a chance? I would like to clean up. I'll be in the restroom." I said, smiling brightly. He seemed taken aback as if he expected me to yell at him and was surprised by the sweetness I displayed. His reaction elicited an explanation from me. "This kind of thing happens to everyone. Don't worry about it; I am just glad it wasn't hot. "

A few minutes later, there was a knock on the wooden bathroom door and I opened it to coffee shop worker, Ralph. He had several hot towels, a new iced mocha and a piece of lemon coffee cake in his hand. His face wore an awkwardly tense expression as he handed me the towels.

"I will keep this food out here for you." He said quietly, eyes down.

"Thank you. Very much." I stared at his face almost stooping to get a closer look, hoping he would raise his gaze to mine again. He didn't, only shut the door as he backed away. I cleaned up the best I could which wasn't very well at all. My white dress was now transparent and stained, bright blue bra easily visible through the fabric. I walked down the hallway into the main shop trying not to convey the mortification that I felt. Ralph was sitting at a double top watching me approach. I sat down across from him. He looked embarrassed, unsure and curious. I caught him sneak a double take at the top of my dress and then try to disguise a laugh as a cough. I moved the piece of cake that lay on a napkin towards me and broke off a little piece then popped it into my mouth. "So." I said matter-of-factly. "What do you do for fun? Other than enter unsuspecting women into wet tee-shirt contests?" His face went blank and all color drained from it. My humor is often lost on people on first meeting, so I helped him out the best I could. "Well at least answer me this. Did I win?" A look of sweet innocence on my face. He looked at me; face unchanged, tilted his head to the side and said,

"Of course. Why do you think you got the cake?"

Over the next few weeks while I finished my class and he worked and did a summer session at NYU, we spent part of everyday together. I would sit for hours with him in the café and he would sneak me food and coffee, which were greatly appreciated on my student stipend. At night, we would lie in his un-air conditioned apartment have incredible sex and talk about our lives and all of the things we wanted to do with them. I wanted to start a non-profit for urban high schools implementing a program that would teach financial literacy, and he wanted to travel the world and create art from the lives of poverty-stricken cultures and communities. I knew from the first time we kissed that I would have to be careful with him, that he was going to fall head over heels for me and that I could break his heart, even if I didn't mean to. I hadn't meant to for sure, but I did. The night air stung my face where two tears had fallen. *Love is so beautiful in the beginning. And then, it's nothing.* After ending things with Ralph in a yearlong breakup, I was filled with so much excitement when it was finally over. I had been emotionally alone for so long I couldn't wait to find someone who would be perfect for me. But after a couple of painful dates I decided to take a hiatus from the *single-and-ready-to-mingle* world and go into hiding. My date with Cain had been my first step back out there and, considering the outcome, perhaps I was a little too vulnerable. Perhaps I still wasn't ready. The glow from my cigarette died out with a huge gust of wind. I sighed and threw it over the railing. Interestingly enough, I felt guiltier about smoking than I did about sleeping with Cain, a complete stranger. *Funny how that goes.*

5.

Fifteen unread emails? In the last twenty minutes? How is that even possible? Confused, I checked the clock at the bottom of my screen. *10:45 a.m.* It had been an hour and a half since I had last looked at the clock and I was fifteen minutes late to a manager's meeting with my director. *Shit!* I scrambled, grabbing my agenda and reports out of my daily folder. I snatched the pen off of my desk, shoved it into my mouth, leaned over my keyboard and typed. *Into a meeting! See you later!* I exited into the hallway through the double doors, almost knocking over an elderly worker.

"Sorry, Delores!" I called without looking back. I thought I heard her mutter something rude in response but there was no time to check her on it. Being a young African American woman in a managerial position at a billing center in a predominantly white, blue collar side of town had proven to be interesting. My capacity for tolerating the ignorance and bigotry of others directed towards myself had been stretched far past what I believed possible. I was not well received by everyone, especially the older crowd, and I knew beyond a shadow of a doubt that was because of the color of my skin and nothing else. Both of my parents were executive level business professionals and they taught career advancement at a steady pace was crucial to survival in the industry. If you weren't accelerating, you were slowing down; there was no standstill in the business world. I understood that as a minority in management I had to play both sides of the fence-making both the boss and the employees feel that I was exclusively behind their interests. Using charisma, grace, intelligence and raw business savvy, I had to win everyone from all sides. Of course, there were some people who wouldn't like me just because they were hateful, but I made a point to never give them a reason that they were aware of.

I approached the door to the conference room where the meeting was being held and peeked through the rectangular glass. Inside, a round table discussion was in progress with several of the center's managers, my director and the director of operations- the Big Dog. I took a deep breath, opened the door quietly and walked in smiling. All conversation came to an icy halt. My director glanced up, brow raised, looking very displeased.

"Please excuse my tardiness," I rushed in, "I was speaking with the CFO of Howard Hospital about a possible addition to our contract." That was a bold-faced lie. I didn't even know the name of the CFO of Howard Hospital. A thought that crossed my mind when Cody Marsh, our director of operations a.k.a. *The Big Dog*, straightened up.

"Oh, really? Good work! *Excellent work!* Stay on top on that one, Myra. Kevin Brothers is a tough business man. Howard Hospital has not had a rate increase in ten years. Find out what he wants and let's make a deal." *Well, I guess I know his name now and have acquired a new contract negotiation assignment.*

"Absolutely, sir. I sure will." I sat down across from Lilly who gave me a skeptical look followed by a roll of her eyes. Clearly off the hook, I settled in and began to take notes and follow the discussion.

The purpose of the meeting was to discuss the potential for a change in software that would limit billing errors which caused insurance denials leading to loss of productivity and revenue. The new process had been pitched to the billing clerks in all departments and the managers were relaying the general response- which was negative- to our directors. This didn't particular pertain to me. My department was small and the team was young, technologically inclined and actually relieved to be getting rid of the current archaic system with its black background and blinking neon green font. Due to my overall lack of interest in the griping of the older "stuck in their ways" population of the billing center, I gave myself leave to daydream about what had quickly become my favorite topic. Cain.

Today's tardiness had been no isolated event. For the past six weeks, the majority of my time at work had been spent in constant conversation via instant messenger with Cain. He was funny and clever, and I found that he made me feel funny and clever in return. Entire workdays went by in a flash, such a flash that, in fact, I often had to make up work at home to compensate for the fact that I wasn't doing it while in the office. Cain and I talked about music, family, sports and daily life, and at the end of each day he would send a final message "Have a wonderful evening, gorgeous."

Back in the meeting, I was smiling at an interesting and incredibly hilarious subject that Cain and I had just broached before I had realized I was late for this snooze-fest meeting. Suddenly my conscious snapped back to the room I was in. I had just been asked a question by the Big-Dog. *Crap, what did he just ask me?* I shuffled through my papers to buy myself a moment as I squeezed my brain, trying to remember what had just been said. Something dripped out: *"Ms. Knight, what do you think about the general trend of negative reaction towards the new system." OK, got it.* And I went into business driven auto-pilot.

"Cody, the truth is that the majority of our employees in this billing office are fifty years of age and older, only thirty percent of which have earned degrees from an institute of higher learning. Statistics show this group is less technology-secure. Not only does it take them longer to understand and master new technologies, but they also are less inclined to do so. In an ever changing market and with the current economic recession, we absolutely cannot afford to lose money where it could be saved, just to keep employees happy in their technological ineptitude." *Ew, was that harsh?* I continued anyway. "The benefits of implementing this new system far outweigh the cost of not only the software, equipment and training of our current employees but also the training of new employees if the ones with us now cannot or refuse to learn a system that is best for the growth and sustainment of our corporation." *That was definitely harsh.* I smiled, tight lipped and confident, hands folded and delicately placed on the table in front of me. I knew that most of the managers would think that I was being a hard-ass, or maybe even a kiss-ass, but most of the managers there didn't understand that the Big-Dogs of the world didn't care about the feelings or inclinations of their employees at the bottom of the barrel and the best way to move up was to put big business above every single one of them.

"I couldn't agree with you more Miss Knight." He smiled brightly at me then turned to his second in command, my director, eyes narrowed, in shark mode. "Go ahead and start the conversion process over to the new system. Six months from now, I want total immersion within the office. I also want a system skills test created, tested and administered to the employees here in eight months."

About this time, I was beginning to worry that word would get around the office that I had thrown the opposition to the new system under the bus. That wouldn't likely help my image. The attendees of the meeting started to shuffle their papers and belongings in preparation to get back to their desks.

"One more thing, team." We all looked at Cody, some with distrustful, resentful eyes, some with admiration and reverence, and me with all of the objectivity I could muster. After all, I wanted to be his colleague in the not so distant future, "The conversation as it happened here is completely confidential. No one is to mention the details of our discussion or who was supportive of what outcome. Any violation of this will be met with discipline." He glanced at me and his left eye twitched slightly. *Was that a wink?* The managers glanced around nervously. "I will make the announcement of the change in a few weeks. That is all! Have a good weekend."

Well that solved that. I knew, after that not so subtle warning, that no one would be spreading the fact that I rather ruthlessly championed the new system. The last time a warning of this kind was given to us by the director of operations, a manager spoke of the meeting's specifics to one other person. *One.* Well, the director found out about that *one person* and the blabbermouth was walked out of the office carrying a company box of her belongings a mere three hours later.

The group filed out of the dim conference room and back towards our designated sides of the building. I felt a rumble in my stomach which brought the realization that I hadn't eaten breakfast that morning, an awful habit that I couldn't quite get under control. A warm, soft arm circled around my shoulders as I crossed the cafeteria. "Hi there, Lilly-Pad!" I said cheerfully without turning to look. "What do you want for lunch?" She started right in, not giving me a break in the slightest.

"How is it, I would like to ask first, that you come in twenty minutes late,"

"Fifteen minutes late!" I interrupted.

"Twenty minutes late," she continued, "blatantly daydream for the duration of the meeting with mouth agape, smiling to yourself like a lunatic and still manage to give a witty and eloquent answer to the Big-Dog's question after being snatched from your reverie?"

"My mouth was certainly NOT agape!" I squealed, laughing. "Thank you for calling my answer witty." I said coyly, nudging her as we continued walking side by side to our departments.

"You're welcome, sweetie." Lilly and I had the relationship of sisters for sure. There was a lot of teasing and egging on but I felt the love beneath it all. We had been friends for just over a year since I began working for the ambulance company, but she was one of my very best friends in the world. "Oh, I brought chicken stew and French bread for our lunch!" Lilly called back to my desk and she continued moving past. "Meet you in the cafeteria at about 12:25!"

The topic of discussion at the lunch table was about one thing and one thing only. The fact that, finally, Cain and I were going out on another proper date. *DDD*. Dinner, drinks and, dancing. Lilly and I chatted about where we would go, what I would wear and if we would spend the night at my apartment. I had only seen his thus far.

After our rather infamous first date, I had been invited over for dinner several times, usually once a week. In the comfort of his bedroom, or even sometimes the living room if his roommate wasn't home, we would lounge around, flirting and laughing as we got to know each other. He would tell me about his workdays, his friends and annoyances with his roommate, while I smiled and did and said anything that I could think of to be supportive and loving. There was something about Cain that seemed distant, not simply to me but to the world as a whole, despite his seemingly blossoming social calendar. He seemed disconnected, lonely and sometimes even a little sad.

My very first trip to see him had been on a Thursday and then again I visited on the following Wednesday. Cain was very busy with work and then with his recreational basketball league in the evenings so he rarely had the time or energy to go out during the workweek. Because of that, I traveled down to his apartment after he got home at around 10:00 p.m. This was not ideal, but I wanted to be flexible. Like usual we chatted for a few minutes, ate Hamburger Helper, and then went to his bedroom to "watch a movie".

The first time we went to "watch a movie", I had mixed feelings. We walked into his room and Cain shut the door behind him. I stood rather awkwardly in the crowded space and sat on a director's chair in the corner. Cain crawled onto the unmade bed, propped up four pillows in stacks of two, and looked at me expectantly. "Why are you over there? Get in here, crazy girl. Geez." I shyly kicked off my shoes, slid as gracefully as I could over to the pillows he had stacked for me and looked at him with an uncertain smile. Sure, we had already had sex, and on our first date no less. Therefore, it made sense that Cain would expect that we would be having sex again and again from here on out as long as he chose to date me. That didn't stop me from being extraordinarily nervous. I had been nervous as I got ready in my apartment that evening, nervous as I drove the thirty minutes to his apartment, nervous as I rode the elevator up to the seventh floor of his building, nervous as I walked down the open hallway of the 1920's department store turned luxury apartments and subsequently that nervousness had persisted to that very moment, mounting to an all-time high. I had promised myself that the next meeting after our first date would be very traditional. Dinner, a movie and then a quick kiss goodnight. I did not plan on being in his room and I certainly did not plan on being on his bed.

My heart raced like a herd of gazelle escaping a hungry lion as he turned on the T.V and pressed play on the DVD player, then turned to me. I stared straight ahead. *Maybe if I don't look at him he will get the hint and we can just watch the movie.* I realized then that I did not want to have sex with him. I wanted to be the respectable woman that I had grown into over the last five years not the overly enthusiastic girl I had accidentally turned into the night of our first date.

It was very clear to me at this point that Cain was the kind of man that I could absolutely seriously date. He had the education, the career, the lifestyle of travel and fun, the looks, not to mention the fact that I was drawn to him in a way that I was unfamiliar with. It was rare that he wasn't in my mind in some capacity. Just as the length of time that he stared at me became awkward, I felt his massive hand cradle my chin and the side of my face, turning it towards him. Our eyes met for a second. His were odd, dark amber with flecks of green and I looked down.

"Hi there, brown eyes." He said in almost a whisper. I knew that this was it, that he was coming for me right at that instant and that now was the time to tell him that I wanted us to slow down. I needed to tell him that I wasn't this kind of woman that I didn't feel comfortable and I was leaving immediately.

I took a deep breath to speak all of these things, but in a rush of air Cain swooped in, covering my mouth with his, full lips completely devouring mine. Initially, I wanted to pull away, but as the heat rose to my face I couldn't deny him. As our mouths worked together, just as they had the night of our first date, I found myself sliding away. I floated above my body just below the ceiling again and looked down at two people on the bed.

Cain's hands moved to hold my face, supporting my neck which had grown weak with the pulsing of blood. At first I sat perfectly still, not sure how to proceed, but Cain's passion was infectious and my hands were the first to catch. My palm glided over his cheek, which was covered in a fine stumble, and moved down to his neck, as I let each finger trace a lane like swimmers in lap pool. He groaned and pulled me into him. My mouth was the next to become infected. Rather than following his lead in the kisses, my lips began to play their own game, first with his bottom lip, sucking it's warmth into my mouth and then releasing it and again and again. Next, I moved to his top lip, letting my tongue tease its smooth surface.

I could feel his breath spurt out of his parted mouth. His hand softly moved up my back, the fabric of my sweater separating his touch from my skin. *This is OK. We haven't crossed any lines here. We are just kissing. Just kissing. I won't let us go any farther tonight.* His strong fingers reached the nape of my neck where they massaged as his mouth deserted mine to find my jaw. From there, his tongue traced a country road, twisting and turning, curving over the slight hills and valleys down my neck to my collarbone, which he kissed passionately. His hands had moved to the back of my thighs, kneading and grabbing, inching closer to my behind. My head fell back as he made the road trip back up my extended neck and detoured to my chin then my lips, gently kissing them, one by one. I pulled my head down, level with his. He stared at me, hands frozen centimeters away from the fleshy rounds of my backside, his chest heaving in anticipation.

OK! This is it! The perfect stopping point. Go ahead and tell him that you have to leave for the night. Kiss him softly once more, slide off the bed and run. Run as fast as you can out of this place. I opened my mouth but nothing came out and my body didn't move. I tried again but it seemed I was stuck in place. System overload. *CTRL+ALT+DEL! CTRL+ALT+DEL!* But again, it was too late. I felt his long fingers graze the soft skin of my stomach as his hand moved under my sweater. His eyes never left mine as his warm flesh moved slowly past my belly button, gliding past my rib cage and settled on the front of my new boutique bought bra. The weekend before I had decided that now that I was entering a potential relationship, my four year old under garments would no longer suffice. I thanked myself for the investment as, evidently, it was about to pay off. I still couldn't move, couldn't speak, and could only think about what was going to happen, powerless to stop it. I recognized the moment

Cain realized that the clasp to my bra was at the front. His eyes widened like a child's discovering a new toy, cheeks raising his lips into a smirk. I figured that he would be direct, unclasping the garment quickly, in which case, I may have been snapped out of my trance long enough to tell him no, re-hook my bra, grab my shoes and make a b-line for the door.

I would have looked psychotic, for sure, but this date was going nowhere close to the second date of a nice dinner, hand holding and a walk through downtown I had planned out in my head. *Perhaps I should have filled him in on the agenda.* I was well aware of the repercussions of starting a relationship in this way. It could quite possibly stamp the words *Booty Call* in bright red permanent ink on my forehead and I wanted more than that, so much more. Cain was far from an amateur, however, and knew how to take his time. He moved both hands to the mounts of my chest and used his thumbs to gently slide over the broad surface left to right, his eyes never leaving mine. He was so powerful. So in control. So sexy.

My body didn't stand a chance, I just hoped that my heart, dignity and self-respect did. A voice spoke out from the corner of my mind. This one, unlike the night of our first date, was soft and encouraging. It told me to give in, to let go and to listen to my instincts. What did my instincts tell me? *To rip off this beautiful man's clothes and have the time of my life giving him every piece of me for the next hour and a half and taking every single piece of him in return.* My instincts told me that I wanted him, had wanted him from the moment I saw him, and that I had been lying to myself to preserve some false image of who I wanted to be. I had slept with other men in the past quickly and without a second thought because I didn't care if I ever saw them again. I wanted Cain, body, heart and soul and I was afraid of that.

The jig was up. If I walked out now, Cain would think I was playing games with him and would probably decide that I was a waste of time. If I stayed, there was a chance, a huge chance, that he would never see me as anything more than a sexual object. *Damned if I do, damned if I don't.* I felt my face lift into a cringe, brows furrowed, teeth clamped on the side of my bottom lip. *Here goes nothing.* With an audible sigh all restraint left and as I inhaled, red hot desire filled its place. I held his face gently in both my hands and leaned in close, resting my forehead against his own for an instant, and then took his mouth deeply with my own. After parting, I slid slowly from the mattress, standing before him.

I had been told by more than a few that I was an amazing lover. I intended to show Cain the very best of what I had to offer in that department. I lifted my sweater from my body and dropped it elegantly on the floor. Positioning myself so that he could view the profile of my body, I turned my head to face him, holding his gaze while I unbuttoned my pants and moved the dark blue denim down, rocking my hips side to side as they slid. My forest green bra matched the forest green thong I donned and when he caught sight of the lacy forms, desire left his mouth in the form of a moan from deep in his throat. I stepped out of my jeans and turned to face Cain. I moved to the fastener of my bra and in an instant it was unclasped. Cain's jaw was protruding from the intense pressure he was exerting to clench it. I lowered my arms, letting the green fabric fall away and onto the floor.

"You are the most beautiful thing I have ever seen." He said, eyes enveloping my body. I walked slowly to edge of the bed and stopped, telepathically telling him what to do next. To my amazement, he slid forward to the edge putting one knee between my legs just as I had silently commanded. Bracing myself with his shoulders, I climbed into his lap, straddling his broad thighs and waist, breasts just below his chin. He looked up at me grinning widely, and slowly took each cup into his mouth flicking the buds with his tongue. A sharp sigh escaped me. The place where his jeans met my open legs ached and demanded more.

My hands dove under his polo and found the muscle that made an imprint through the cotton fabric. I found two firm masses which responded compulsively as I pressed and squeezed them. As I did this, my fingers grazed his nipple, causing him to shutter and jolted in pleasure. I smiled, lifted the hem of his shirt up over his head and arms and placed it on the bed. I lowered my head to a symmetrical pink nipple and gently encompassed it with my warm, wet mouth. Cain stiffened as I let my tongue play there for some time, Cain's hand cradling the back of my head holding my mouth in place the whole time. My one unoccupied hand reached down from its perch on his chest to the inseam of his jeans where I massaged his inner thigh moving slowly inward. I was over six inches away when I felt his hard mass laying against his leg. My hand moved over the denim covered extension and started to massage there as well. Cain placed his hand under my chin and guided my lips back to his. It felt like coming home as we kissed, lips dancing and Cain moved his hips, forcing himself upon the inside of my palm harder and harder. Abruptly, he stood on both legs, me still attached to his waist, holding me in the air.

"You're driving me crazy," he kissed me quickly, panting for breath. "You know that though, don't you?" he asked, voice raspy. I nodded and smiled, cheeks burning. "Well let's see if I can return the favor." Cain placed both hands under my behind and lifted up, raising me higher and higher until his arms were shoulder height then slid my thighs down onto his biceps where they rested, his forearms extended up my back, face confronted with my core. I squealed and laughed from nine feet in the air as he walked over the door to stabilize me against the wall. *What the hell kind of kinky porn did I land myself in? So this is why he works out so much!*

A paranoid thought about professional women having their careers ended after secretly made sex tapes of them were released on the internet crossed my mind as Cain kissed the inside of my thighs. I had never been comfortable with men using their mouths to please me and I definitely wasn't OK with what was happening now. However, as I looked around the room from my new vantage point, I was truly amazed by the feat of pure strength that Cain had just displayed and was not about to ruin it by asking him to stop and put me down. I was looking around for cameras when Cain's soft tongue found the root of my passion for him and began to investigate through my forest green shield. All cohesive thoughts seized and I relaxed, pinned to cold gray painted drywall.

"Do you like that, Myra?" Cain stopped and whispered. "Tell me that you like it or I am going to put you down." He was teasing me and I loved it.

"Yes, I like it. I like it, please don't stop." *This is insane! This is unreal... this is AMAZING.* Cain had figured out a way to remove the barrier that was protecting me from completely losing my mind. When I felt it, his tongue on my most sacred flesh, everything but a bright burning light left my mind. I didn't care if I ever saw that abnormally strong clown again. I just didn't want him to stop. And he didn't, bless him, until I had experienced two heavenly releases while sitting atop that glorious perch.

Two hours later we lay, gasping for air, thoroughly tired and satisfied, passing a room temperature bottle of Gatorade back and forth. I couldn't remember the last time that I was so happy. I wanted to sing! I wanted to dance! I wanted to profess my love to the man lying next to me filling my nostrils with his sweaty scent in the dark room. The alarm clock on the desk told me it was 1 a.m. on a Friday morning. I mustered up enough strength to roll over to the side of the bed and stand. Drunkenly, I located my underwear by the door and went to pick them up.

"What are you doing?" Cain asked sleepily.

"It's really late, I need to get home." There was silence from the direction of the bed for several seconds.

"Do you want to stay?" I wasn't sure how to respond. I didn't know what the proper protocol was, or if it was too soon to spend the night, or if this fell under extenuating circumstances.

"Would you like me to?" I asked awkwardly.

"Yes. I would. Get over here and for God's sake do *not* put those panties back on." He feigned exasperation.

"OK." I whispered. I walked over and moved my naked body back to his.

"Would you like more Gatorade?" He asked softly.

"No, thank you." He turned on his side facing me, slid his massive arm under the pillow beneath my head, grabbed my waist with his other hand and rotated me, sliding me back until he was spooning me, my bare bottom against his bare stomach.

"Good night gorgeous." he kissed my shoulder then covered it with a blanket. I laid there, eyes open in the dark, trying to understand the feeling that was surging through my body. I was tired and yet had more emotional energy than I had ever experienced in my life. *I am in love with this man.* The thought crept into my head. I shook it off. It was absolutely ridiculous I had only known him for a month. It was lust I was feeling, silly schoolgirl infatuation. *I am in love with this man.* It was impossible. I couldn't love him. I barely knew him. I closed my eyes and relaxed into his warmth behind me. I could love him one day. I would love him one day. My mouth opened as my breath became deeper. As I drifted away one last thought popped into my mind. I didn't have time to correct it before I was gone, asleep and, helpless to it; *I am in love with this man.*

6.

Hot water raced down my back. I tried to relax. I was the epitome of stressed out, riled up, uptight and frantic. It was 5:30 p.m. on Friday and I was thrilled at the chance to get back on track to having a relationship in which I was courted and dated properly, outside the confines of Cain's cramped bedroom. His basketball league had finally ended and I was certain that from here on out, an exhausting six weeks after our first date, we would spend a great deal more time together. Steam filled the bathroom and condensation formed on the glass of beer I had taken with me into the shower as I prepared for our date. I took a few gulps and stuck my head under the warm stream. My neck strained as my hair took on water like a sponge. I knew that my locs wouldn't be dry by the time Cain picked me up a few hours later. They wouldn't be noticeably wet, just fresh looking and smelling like honey and lavender thanks to the overpriced shampoo I purchased from a new salon down the street. Relaxation came as the alcohol seeped into my system, intensified by the heat. *I should have gotten a new outfit.*

I closed my eyes and ran a fashion show of the five outfits I had laid out on my bed in the next room. My sense of style was considerably established for a twenty-three year old. My family's discriminating taste in fashion was inherited from my paternal grandmother who was never out-dressed, anywhere. The outfits I chose were ordered from most to least conservative. As a rule I always tossed out the outliers, but it was nice to have them there as visual references. Another gulp of decreasingly cold beer and I continued to work on my body. I ran my razor under the near scalding water and applied shaving lotion to various sections of skin. Cain was four, almost five years older than me and while I didn't want to look too conservative, I didn't want to appear like an immature, tactless college girl by showing a lot of skin. I wanted to make a good impression. We had only been out in public together once on a date thus far. At this point, Cain's imagination was my closest ally. *Something that will do just enough to peak his interest without summoning up thoughts of promiscuity. Which, sadly, has been a running theme in our interactions.*

I had no idea why Cain drummed up such inhibition in me. I had never felt anything like the passion that spread from the tip of my head to the bottom of my feet every time I even thought about him. I was growing very attached to him rather quickly. I found myself rushing to work every day to get logged in and wait for Cain to message me. It was like a standing date, and I loved every second of learning about him and his life. Cain was the younger of two sons from a small, *small* town in the country to the south west. He had chosen his college based on the fact that it was only twenty minutes from his family home. While he was there he engaged in the usual college activities, joined a fraternity, played basketball, had a girlfriend and did very well in his studies. The few times that he had mentioned his parents, I got the impression that he was either a mama's boy, or his mother was overly attached. I hoped that the latter was true, though both were red flags.

Cain was a health enthusiast. His cupboards were filled with a veritable grocery store aisle of protein shakes, health bars, energy shots and B-Vitamin complexes. He spent a lot of time in the gym and was quite zealous about working out at least two hours a day. I had the misfortune one evening to visit him after he had missed a workout. He was tense, cold and unfriendly. No matter how good Cain looked, he often commented negatively about his body. He would state that he needed to work out more or ask me what I thought about his stomach, chest or arms. I always told him that he was completely gorgeous, which was my personal truth but he never quite seemed convinced.

I drank deeply from the now warm glass in the shower, holding it tightly to keep its wet surface from slipping through my fingers and continued preparing my body for the night. *It has taken far too long to arrange this date.* While I never brought up my displeasure to him, I was disappointed that Cain didn't feel more compelled to date me under normal circumstances. The romantic in me hoped for a long and intense courting process. I wanted flowers sent to my work and candy sent to my home with a card scribbled with messages of adoration. Unfortunately, none of those things had happened. *Maybe tonight is the start of an entirely new relationship for us.* A voice laughed in the back of my head but I shook it off. I had invited him over to my place several times over the last month and a half, tried to tempt him with dinner, dessert, "a movie", but his responses always ended up including *"I cant. I'm sorry... I have plans."* I was getting annoyed with his apathy when finally he agreed to spend a Friday evening with me.

I threw the remaining golden liquid into my mouth, breathed deeply and reached for the shower facet. *Tonight is the night. Everything has to be perfect. Everything will be perfect.* I smiled as I climbed out of the porcelain den, wrapped my towel around me and started to apply liberal amounts of lotion to every inch of my skin, while fantasizing about Cain falling head over heels for me before the night was over. Perhaps the hot water calmed me down, or the beer, or both, but the fear and anxiety had melted away from my heart and pure excitement was shining through. *In a mere* (checking the steamy clock on the wall) *two hours I was going to be with Cain again!*

I pulled the iron stool from under the vanity seat at the sink and sat down. *Merlot, Rose Pink, Deep Amber.* I was awful at painting my nails. Absolutely awful. But I didn't have time to get them done professionally. I picked up the Warm Amber and shook it furiously. *I wonder if we will stay here or at his place.* The thought struck me for the first time. I thought about my kitchen, the floor needed swept and mopped. The counters were littered with pots and plates. In the family room, papers covered the coffee table and glasses were scattered on window sills and lamp tables. *This place is a disaster!* I put down the nail polish, grabbed my plush robe from the back of the door and scurried down the hall towards the closet that the cleaning supplies called home.

An hour later, I laid on the couch, face sticky with sweat, hands reeking of Comet and Mr. Clean, in desperate need of a nap. One of the many obsessive traits I picked up from my mother was cleanliness. If I was the only one witness to my small messes and slight disorganization, I could cope just fine. The thought of someone else witnessing these things, however, was enough to send me into a broom welding panic attack. I looked at the clock and sighed. I was going to need another shower for sure, and another beer. I stood, stretched, dropped my robe to the floor then strode into the kitchen and liberated another cold bottle from the case. I finished the bottle in five long stretches of my throat and tried to contain the belch that rose from my stomach behind my hand. *Ok. One hour until Cain comes to pick me up. It's go time.* I gave myself a quick nod then sprinted to the bathroom like a mad woman for round two.

After another forty-five minutes I was refreshed and a little tipsy. My make-up was expertly applied in deep earth tones, the night's first layer of lip gloss shone from my plump lips and I was donning the perfect second date outfit, a fitted black cotton blazer atop of a cream silk blouse that dipped just low enough to see the roundness of my breasts. My wrist and ears were adorned with brass bangles and dangling chandeliers. Midnight Blue skinny jeans hugged my legs slimming down into a new pair of cognac colored riding boots. Staring into the full length mirror in my room, I smiled. *Damn, I look good!* I sprayed my favorite perfume in the air three times and ran and twirled through the mist in celebration. I felt absolutely beautiful and on top of the world, ready to conquer anything. *This is going to be an amazing night!* After a small victory dance I heard my phone buzz. *That must be him! He must be on his way!*

I jogged to my purse on the bed, packed with everything I would need for the evening, dug my hand inside and felt around. My fingers brushed a cold hard cover. Pulling my phone out, I saw Cain's name across the screen and shrieked with joy. My hands shook with adrenaline as I opened his message. He would probably be there at any second. My eyes locked to the words on the screen:

Hey. I think I am going to hang out with some friends tonight. Maybe some other time.

My eyes traced over the message again and again. *This must be some kind of joke. Ha! Ok, he's kidding.* I tried to smile and laugh, but the giggle got caught in my throat. I prepared to respond via text, hands spasming so violently the phone almost dropped.

You're not being serious, right?

I didn't believe it. It was a joke. A tacky-ass joke but that could be forgiven. No human-being would cancel a date with a woman a mere minutes before he was to be at her home. *Please God, let this be a joke.* I put the phone down on the bed next to me, glancing at it every five seconds. I continued to pray that a message validating that Cain was not a prick would come to my phone instantly to dissolve the feelings of disappointment, anger, and foolishness that I was drowning in. My phone vibrated, and before it had finished, I was staring at another message from Cain.

Yea. Sorry. Have a good night.

A sharp cackle rose from my throat. I dropped my phone on the soft down comforter beside me and began to laugh, not a chuckle but a deep release, full of irony and fire. I looked to the left where I saw a beautiful woman sitting on the bed. *All dressed up. And nowhere to go.* I couldn't believe it. The rage started to build. *Inconsiderate. Selfish. Scumbag.* I hit the bed beside me with my fist. Then a different emotion rolled over me. *Did I do something wrong? What happened?* I ran through the conversation we had over instant messenger that afternoon mere hours before. I had relayed how excited I was, he told me that he would pick me up at around 7:30 p.m., I sent him my address, he confirmed that he received it and then we said good bye. Nothing happened that would explain this sudden change of heart. And then a sad voice spoke out. *This is because I have been sleeping with him. If I hadn't slept with him so often, or at all, for God's sake, he would have been here. He would take me seriously.* My mother's voice rose from somewhere below me. *No man is going to buy the cow when you are giving the milk away for free.*

"God damn it!" I screamed out. That was certainly what I felt like, a damn stupid, used up cow. I stood up from the bed, paced a few times thoughts racing through my head. *Maybe I should call him… But what the hell would I say?* I felt utterly helpless, powerless, there was nothing I could do to will him to live up to the plans we made. I began to take out my earrings then stopped. *No. Maybe he will text me back, apologize and then we will go out as planned. He has to know that this is fucked up right?* He certainly wasn't an idiot. He had to know that I could never see him again if he went through with this. That I would be forced to ignore his texts and instant messages and the feelings that I had grown for him. As long as he texted me in the next hour my pride and self-esteem would allow me to go out with him. *Everyone makes mistakes. Please God, make this asshole text me before an hour has passed.*

I stormed out of the room and into the hallway to the closet by the front door. I ripped the small stool from the corner, climbed on top, clawed at the back of the shelf and, before I knew it, was outside on my balcony smoking a cigarette. I purposely left my phone inside so that I would not torture myself by looking at it every couple of seconds. I also found a bottle of beer in my hand. This was my third in two hours. *Desperate times call for desperate measures.* I stood in the cold air looking out over the rows of apartment complexes. I felt like I had just come down from a drug induced high, and it was painful. So many endorphins had flooded my system all afternoon and now I was left with withdrawal. How intense my elation was worried me as I took a long draw from the stick in my mouth. *Why do I give him so much power over my happiness?* After I smoked as much of the slim cigarette as I could and stomped it out on the concrete of my balcony floor, I went inside and sat on my couch. It had been seven minutes. As calmly as I could I retrieved my phone from the bedroom. *No new messages.* Back on the couch I picked up my beer and drained it, then slammed it back onto the coffee table. I turned on the television and pretended to watch a nightly entertainment show as the feeling of anguish spread. I felt absolutely desperate and sick to my stomach. *I need a drink.* I looked towards the refrigerator which held the remainder of my beer. *Something stronger than beer.* The reality was sinking in that not only was this man kind of a jerk but he was a jerk who had no real interest in me.

7.

"Ooooh, girl! Oh, hell no! That is so messed up!" I looked across the glass table top at two beautiful, deeply familiar faces with mouths open, eyes wide. Earlier that evening, after spending twenty minutes sitting on the couch in my apartment, staring at my cell phone, the realization dawned that there was going to be no text from Cain apologizing for his abominable behavior. I quickly sent a picture of myself, dressed ready to go out for a night on the town, to my closest male friends, Lucas and Harper, with a single message. "SOS." They both responded within minutes to the distress call and we agreed to meet at their favorite gay-friendly cocktail bar in an artsy downtown neighborhood.

"Honey, you have to let that little boy go." Harper was appalled. "He is so clearly not worth it! *Oh. My. God.* Having you dress up, looking all cute and stuff and then he's gonna stand *MY* baby up? Oh, hell no! Hell no! What did he say again?" he took a long drag of his purple cocktail.

"He said," I pulled at the extra dirty double vodka martini that was glued to my hand, *"I think I'm going to hang out with some friends tonight. Maybe some other time."* I stated then reattached my mouth to the wide brimmed cocktail glass.

"See, that's just rude. He could have at least said he was sick or something! Blatantly standing people up. Clearly, homeboy has no tact!" I sat silently staring at the table and nodding in agreement to each of the enthusiastically stated observations. "He better be glad that you aren't some crazy chick," Lucas continued. "Because a lot of girls I know would have done some serious damage over that."

"Preach, baby!" Harper echoed, egging Lucas on.

"I'm just saying. This situation would warrant keying a car, slashing a few tires, maybe even a brick through a window for some women."

"I've seen worse!" Harper cried out, now swaying like a grandmother in a pew of a Baptist church.

"I know, right? I clearly can never speak to that fool again." I said dejectedly.

"Clearly!" shouted Lucas.

"Never!" cried Harper.

"Right!" I added, not quite as earnestly as my friends. The loud music and strong beverages of the sushi and cocktail bar were the perfect antidote to what I had just endured. The stark white walls were made iridescent by neon purple and pink lights bouncing across their surface. My two friends and I were tucked into an extra-large booth covered in smooth, cold white, faux leather in the corner. Freezing air seeped through the glass sealant at my back. I shivered and pulled the black blazer tighter around me. My eyes zoomed across the large open room, scanning the packed tables and bar. *Maybe I'll run into him tonight.* I couldn't keep the thought at bay. I had no idea what I would do or what I would say to him, but one of the reasons I didn't crawl into bed and pull the covers over my head in shame was the possibility that I might see him out. He would look at me and how fabulous I was in my new riding boots and fall to his knees, begging for forgiveness, then swoop me up in his arms and carry me off towards the direction of his apartment. I sighed quietly as I was hit with how pathetic that dream was.

"What does this asshole do, anyway?" Lucas' emerald eyes shown as he picked up his vodka cranberry and puckered his lips around the tiny bright pink straw. My friend was drop dead handsome. Large eyes, thick curly brown hair, olive skin and plump firm lips, courtesy of his Venezuelan mother and Caucasian father. I had been in love with him since the day that I met him, which was ten years prior. Unfortunately for me, and every other straight woman on the planet, he was on our same team. The one which was attracted to men. So my romantic fantasies turned into platonic admiration.

I explained to my two friends what exactly it was that Cain did, and his high level career on a fast track to the top of the largest corporation in the city. When I was finished they both sucked their teeth loudly and looked at each other.

"Well damn, girl." Harper threw his hand in the air dismissively. "That may be worth a little crazy." Lucas looked at him in disgust and smacked his hand playfully.

"No, but really honey. You are far too fabulous, and I have put far too many droplets of blood, sweat and tears,"

"*Tears,* honey!" Harper piped in.

"Into raising you to see you plunge your affections in less exalted grounds than you truly deserve." I smirked at Lucas who was a mere year older than I. The sentiment was sweet, but did nothing except bounce off of my increasingly alcohol affected shell. Cain, with all of his credentials, was the best catch I had ever come close to reeling in, true, but the very strong feelings I had grown for him as a person trumped that over and over.

"Well Myra, besides all that security stuff, which is very important," Lucas spoke softly.

"Very, honey!" Harper chimed.

"Yes, very important," continued Lucas glancing at Harper in annoyance, "what else do you like about him? From what you have said he doesn't seem like he is even all that nice to you. "

My head tilted at this. I thought about it while staring at the last of three blue-cheese filled olives skewered by a toothpick in my glass. "He has made my life an exciting place to be." Cain's face came to my mind and I was instantly warm. "I never get tired of talking to him. When we are together, my biggest concern is how much longer I have with him and dreading the moment when it comes to an end." I continued, feeling lighter and lighter headed. "I always wish I was with him. There is nothing that I wouldn't drop if he texted me and asked to see me. Absolutely nothing." I knew for a fact that was true. If he texted me right then I would be out the door before I could say a proper goodbye. "I know that we have only spent a small amount of time together but, you guys, I feel so perfectly right when he is around." I closed my eyes. "And when he takes me into his arms it's like there is no one else in the world." My eyes opened and I sighed. Harper and Lucas were staring at me, looks of concern on their faces.

"So what's happening with bedroom the activity?" Harper was never shy about getting all the juicy details.

"I can't even begin to describe the exquisiteness." I said solemnly.

"And the equipment?" Lucas couldn't resist.

"More, much, much more than ample." I flashed a smile. Lucas let out a sound of approval and raised his hand to me in congratulations. "Cain is just so big in general."

"How big, baby?" Harper was leaning on the table towards me, getting very interested.

"He is six-four, one hundred and ninety pounds. So muscular. Like the statue of David, girl." Each breath I took was filling me up with pure bliss as

I visualized Cain's body. "Large hands, large feet. Large everything." Harper let out a hoot. "And when he holds me, I feel completely surrounded, like I just melt into him. When he holds me I feel like there is nowhere in the world but right there. It feels like," I stopped abruptly. As I listened to myself, I heard words far past admiration, I heard adulation.

"I sound obsessed don't I?" I couldn't hide the disgust I felt for myself and hung my head again.

"Everyone gets a little obsessed now and again honey," Harper spoke softly, placing his soft hand on my arm. "The good news is that you realized it early and can adjust accordingly!" He finished his sentence with more enthusiasm and slapped my arm. I glanced up at them and read all over their supportive faces what I already knew. That I wasn't done with Cain. No matter how badly he had messed up tonight, no matter how embarrassed I was or how much I deserved better. We all knew that this incident was not the end of him in my heart or my life. I could see in their eyes an acknowledgment of my feelings, like they had both been there before, and were sorry for what I was about to go through. I dug in my purse and pulled out my phone. *No new text messages.*

"To Solomon's?" I asked weakly to which both gentlemen lifted the remainder of their drinks in agreement. Solomon's was our favorite dance spot in the city.

"Ok baby doll," Harper said resolutely, "I'm gonna go get your coat and then we are going to go twirl our asses off." I watched as Harper sashayed away and felt Lucas's warm hand cover mine in support. I lifted his soft skin to my lips and smiled. Harper returned with my coat a moment later and handed it to Lucas, who stood behind me and placed it on my shoulders.

The techno music of the club, which could be heard across the street from the building where we parked, was bone shaking. The drinks were lethal and the bartenders were muscle rippling, glitter dusted objects of pure desire, for me and the other five-hundred men in the establishment to drool over. Solomon's was such a wonderful place, my favorite place, to throw all of the burdens of life away, get lost in the rhythm and movements of my own body and watch hundreds of attractive men do the same. I loved men, all men, of every race, shape, size and sexual orientation. There was nothing quite like being on a hot dance floor full of sweaty, testosterone filled men who had absolutely no interest in looking at me or any of my goodies. It was liberating to be able to dance and twirl and vogue walk up and down the floor without feeling judged by myself or anyone else. To be able to be my authentic self. My authentic self who was past the verge of intoxication and headed to the bar again for a fourth round of killer drinks.

I danced my way, stumbling through the crowd to singer Robyn's *Dancing on My Own,* to the bar and leaned up against it.

"I'm in the corner, watching you kiss her. Oh!" I turned and sang to a fellow patron who smiled at me and winked.

"Hey, what can I get you?" I turned my head to a beautiful brunette bartender with a chiseled chest, smiled at him and kept right on singing.

"I'm right over here! Why can't you see me? OH!" at the top of my lungs. The bartender raised an eyebrow. *"I'm giving it my all, but I'm not the girl you're taking home. Oooh! I keep dancing on my own!"* with the end of the chorus I threw my arms in the air and twirled. The others at the bar were looking on in amusement. A few clapped supportively.

"What can I get you babe?" The bartender's voice had a slight edge of impatience.

"Alright, alright," I slurred. "I will have three. No! Wait, wait, wait! Don't rush me! Four! Four vodka cranberries." The bartender opened his mouth to do what seemed like cut me off, then closed it again as the considerably more sober Lucas landed next to me at the counter and put his arm around me.

"Hey bud, how's it going?" Lucas addressed the bartender. "You alright, darling?" he whispered in my ear. I wrapped my arms around his waist and pulled him closer.

"Oh yeess. Yes, yes, yes!" I nodded emphatically. I grabbed Lucas's beautiful face and kissed him softly on the cheek. "I love you. Thank you for rescuing me tonight."

"You are welcome my love! What are friends for? You just needed a little fun to get your mind off of things."

"Will you yell at him for me?" I looked deeply into Lucas's eyes which were doubling from my skewed vision.

"Who, baby?"

"Cain! Will you tell him to stop being mean to me? You are a man, he will listen to you!" I propped myself against Lucas's warm body. "This is the best idea ever!" Out of the corner of my eye I spied Harper approaching us, sashaying again. "Mama!" I clapped my hands in celebration as he ended his journey next to me, facing Lucas.

"Harper, it may be time to take Myra H-O-M-E." Lucas spelled out. *I can still spell, Lucas! I am getting out of here. I am not going home yet!* I turned back over to the bar where our fresh drinks sat and got the bartender's attention to continue my performance.

"Somebody said you had a new friend..." I sang sassily. *"But does she love you better than I can?"* My voice rang out. I was now incorporating movements featuring pointing at the bartender and making kissing faces. He stared back at me, looking a little scared. I cut right to the chase. He was sexy and although everyone in the bar knew it, I needed to articulate it. "Look," I stared right back at him. "I am going to be honest with you. You have the most amazing abs I have ever seen. I want to lick them. Is that weird?" His face went completely blank, I thought I saw his right eye begin to twitch. The seam of his mouth formed a straight line.

"Well, can I lick them?" I asked nicely. "Please?" His eyes widened in shock. It dawned on me through the haze that was my mental faculties that I could be kicked out and banned for sexual harassment. I mentally surveyed the room for an exit in case he called for security, then stared at his unchanging face for what seemed like an hour. "So that's a no?" I took a step back from the bar, an uncomfortable look splayed on my face. His form in my vision split into two, which was pleasant, and I began to feel dizzy, which was not.

He shook his head, looked down at the ground, back up at me and then he threw his head back in laughter. As he roared, his whole body shook. Lucas and Harper gathered by my side and looked at each other puzzled. "Is that a yes?" I stammered taking a step forward, eyes half closed. I held myself up on the bar with the side of my body.

"Hey guys, I think it time to take your friend home." Mr. Amazing Abs said, still chuckling to himself.

"I think you're right." Lucas said quickly.

"Wait! What about our drinks!" I shouted, sounding disgruntled. I looked over at the bartender and shoved out my bottom lip in my best drunken pouty face.

"They will be here for you the next time you come. I promise." And he smiled at me. It felt a little flirty. Somewhere between my serenade and his great jawline I had begun actually flirting with him. *Talk about having an addiction to unavailable men! Shame on you Myra for flirting with that hardworking gay bartender.* Suddenly I felt very self-aware. Like all of the overhead lights had been turned on, and I was standing in the middle of the dance floor surrounded by all of my exes, naked.

"OK. Thank you." I said in a much smaller voice. I turned on my heel and power walked towards the door.

"Bye Marcus! We will see you later baby!" Harper called back to him over his shoulder as we exited the dance floor, walked through the bar and out into the cold night.

Oh my God. It felt as though the fist of Zeus was crashing down with horrific force on my temple. The bright white of the room seeped past my eyelids and I ducked my head under a pillow for protection while full consciousness came to me. *Why is it so bright in here? It is like being inside of a refrigerator. Shit!* Apparently I, or whoever had helped me into bed the night before, forgot to shut the plush curtains that hung beside the double paned windows of my apartment. *What happened last night?* I racked my brain trying to pull out bits of information, flashes of memory. I saw Lucas and Harper and felt immediately better. I was confident that they had not let me get into too much trouble. At least one of them surely had the situation under control at all times. As I came into awareness I wiggled my toes under the down comforter and began to stretch my back by making small arching movements with my shoulders. The general feeling I was left with was one of happiness, and so I was left with no other choice, or memory, than to conclude that I had a good time. I rolled from my back over to one side, pulling the cover over my shoulder. *What time is it?* I didn't actually want to know. Slowly, I moved my head from the darkness of under the pillow and opened my eyes. In front of me, sitting on the nightstand, was a glass of water, a bottle of ibuprofen, and my phone with a pink sticky note attached. *I have the best friends ever.* I slid up in bed and noticed that I was wearing a matching set of pajamas I had acquired as a Christmas present from my parents the year before. I was sure that Harper had picked them out, and laughed at the ridiculous pink flannel covered in three scooped ice-cream cones. I reached for my phone, changed my mind and redirected my hand to the tall glass of water, draining it in one serving. With considerable effort, I launched myself out of bed, from under the covers and I walked to the adjoining bathroom. Although I tried not to look, I started as I caught sight of myself in the mirror. My black eyeliner was running and smeared all over my face, eye shadow had somehow reached my forehead and only traces of my raspberry lip liner remained. *Jesus, I look like I was hit with a bus.* After refilling my glass with tap water and crawling back into bed, I picked up my phone. The sticky note read- *See video message inside.*

"This should be good." I said to the ibuprofen bottle. I started the video which cut on abruptly.

"Good morning sunshine!" Both Lucas and Harper screamed from somewhere in my family room. I winced at the volume and immediately turned it down. Harper was donning a sunhat and a pair of Gucci sunglasses he found in my closet.

"We had a blast last night!" Lucas beamed.

"Unfortunately, your faded ass only lasted until midnight," Harper started in, "like some kind of broke down Brandy Cinderella! But that's OK!"

"We are going to brunch tomorrow, well actually today, so if you get up before 1 p.m. call us!"

"We love you!" The pair shouted together and then the feed ended. *I only stayed out until midnight?* I shook my head and smiled reaching for the bottle of pain killers. The clock on my wall told me that it was eleven-thirty. I wanted to crawl back into the bed and hide under the covers for another couple of hours. Suddenly, and without warning, a rapid secession of thoughts flicked through my mind like a movie on an eight millimeter reel. Cain, the horrid text message he sent me the night before, the awful feeling associated with it and the reason I was with Lucas and Harper the night before rather than on the date I had planned for.

"Uggh!" I screamed and threw myself back, landing in a pool of pillows. *Why can't men just act right? What an asshole.* Any other weekend morning I would have been content to waste the day away in a state of happy hangover wandering around my apartment pretending to be accomplishing something, but I knew that if I stayed in that house I would surely torture myself thinking about Cain, and I refused to let him be the centerpiece of my Saturday after the tomfoolery he had displayed. I rolled off of the bed and made a b-line for the bathroom.

By the time I made it out of the shower I was famished and in severe pain. It occurred to me that the drinks were not only strong at Solomon's but made with dirt cheap alcohol. *I would be in better shape if I would have drank a liter of moonshine.* I dried off, moved to the kitchen, made myself a bowl of cereal with soy-milk and sat on a bar stool, beginning to pout. Not only was the guy I had been sleeping with, I winced, an asshole, but I was completely hung over. *The guy I had been sleeping with.* I echoed to myself. Not even someone I had been dating, just some random I had let in my pants. I couldn't believe that I had been dumb enough to think he actually wanted to be with me. *Am I really that naive?* All of the signs had certainly been there. The unavailability, the apathy towards any part of me except what was between my legs. I doubt he even felt badly.

8.

An hour passed and my body began to feel better thanks to the small mimosa I had fixed myself after cereal. I didn't have any orange juice after filling a flute with champagne, so I added a drop or two of lemon juice. It did the job. The hurt in my heart and pride, however, was steadily increasing. Laying on the couch with head and feet propped up with my laptop on my stomach I went over the instant messenger chat history between Cain and me over the previous month. *There just has to be something that I am missing for him to treat me this way!* I noticed that there were quite a few instances of asking Cain if he wanted to go to the movies, dinner, a basketball game, and he always declined. *That is quite a hint actually.* Seeing them all in a row in that way was a wake-up call. I felt like an idiot.

Buzz... Buzz... Buzz. I popped my head up from the couch. My phone was ringing from somewhere in the kitchen. I stood cumbersomely and walked through the dining area and past the refrigerator. *Buzz... Buzz... Buzz.* Glancing around I spotted the origin of the call on the counter next to the loaf of bread that had been left out overnight. *Damn! I just bought that.* I was bad at leaving food out to spoil or get stale. Picking up the cell, I read an unfamiliar number across the screen. *Who in the world is this? On a Saturday? I don't think so!* I clicked the side of the smartphone, turning off the ringer and hopped up on the counter next to the sink.

My rule was to not answer phone calls unless I knew exactly who it was on the other end. If it was someone I wanted to talk to, they would leave a message and I could call them back. If they didn't, I probably didn't want to talk to them in the first place. I propped my elbows against the cold faux-granite counter top and leaned over the stainless steel sink faucet to pick a deep red apple from the large basket of fruit I always kept stocked. As I bit through the crunchy, sweet flesh my thoughts wandered back to the night before. Throughout the morning, bits and pieces of the evening's events had come back to my conscious memory. I was more than a little embarrassed by some of them, but happily remembered the care and love that Lucas and Harper had shown me throughout the night. I looked over at the neon green time on the microwave and wondered if it was too late to meet up with them for brunch, as I certainly didn't want to be alone much longer. *Buzz… Buzz.* My phone's screen showed a missed call and a voicemail. Intrigued, I pulled up the message and brought the phone to my ear. A deep voice came through the speaker and startled me.

"Yea, hi Myra. This is Marcus. The bartender from Solomon's. Last night you left your wallet on the bar top. I looked in it and found the *if lost, please return to:* card. So I am calling you. I will be here for the next few hours. If you would like to come get it, and maybe have that drink you were so excited about, you are more than welcome. Talk to you later." The call dropped. In disbelief, I jumped from the counter top, and found my purse sitting on the dining room table. After rummaging through it for a few minutes and coming to the conclusion that my wallet was not, in fact, present, I shook my head, scolding myself for always leaving things places. I walked back over to my phone and selected the message again, this time turning on the speaker phone. I listened as I walked to the back of the apartment and rummaged through my closet for something to wear for the afternoon.

"I will be here for the next few hours. If you would like to come get it, and maybe have that drink you were so excited about, you are more than welcome."

His voice was deep, very sensual. *Is he asking me to have a drink with him? Or is he just telling me that I can have a drink while I am there?* I pulled the image of Marcus from my memories and cringed as I remembered the scene I created serenading him with club music. At the time I had thought that Marcus was gay. He had a beautiful, well chiseled face with a slight coat of brown stubble, a thick head of brown hair, broad muscular shoulders, and muscular arms. Muscular everything. Not to mention that he is a bartender at one of the most popular gay clubs in town. But then again, there had definitely been an awkward exchange between Marcus and me. I felt a warm tingle rush over my body and then I cringed again as I remembered my ridiculously inappropriate comments about wanting to lick his abs. *Oh, my God. How shameful!* In social situations I was often my own worst enemy especially when alcohol was involved.

I continued shuffling through my closet. *Was he flirting with me?* I was almost positive he was. Not that gay men couldn't flirt with straight women but he had made me nervous when he did it, and after listening to his message the answer to the riddle of Marcus' preference was even less clear. *He is probably just being nice.* Even so, I picked out a cute, tan, off the shoulder sweater with a tapered waist, and light wash skinny jeans that accentuated my small, but not unfortunate backside. After applying day makeup and pinning my locs into a sweep that left them resting on my shoulder I grabbed my keys and purse, sans wallet, and left the apartment.

The club looked a lot different in the light of day. There was a sparse splattering of patrons around the circular bar and every man looked up as I walked through the solid oak doors only to drop their heads quickly back down. The disappointment that I had lady parts was palpable. I glanced around for Marcus and spotted him bending behind the bar displaying what I imagined was a very firm backside which was covered in tight medium wash designer jeans. He emerged with a bottle of Jameson in his hand. The smell of hard alcohol and beer bluntly hit my nose and I shivered, feeling uncoordinated and uncomfortable, hangover still lurking. I was desperately unprepared to try to impress Marcus, even as a friend. Still, I shrugged my sweater a little further down to show more skin. I walked over to the bar and stepped up, taking a seat on a stool several spots down from where my wallet's protector was standing, serving a customer. He was even more handsome than I remembered. Today he was wearing a white tee-shirt that hugged his arms and chest, chatting with an older gentleman who was drinking what looked like a Pina Colada. The customer said something and then reached over the bar and covered Marcus' hand with his own. Marcus flashed a brilliant smile which bore deep dimples and didn't cringe away from the personal touch of the man. *He doesn't seem to mind that kind of attention at all.* I glanced the other way afraid I might be invading a personal moment.

"Hey, Myra." Marcus was right across the bar from me a moment later. "How are you feeling today?" He held a smirk that told me he was mocking my intoxicated show from the night before. I was fixated on his eyes which I hadn't noticed before. They were bright aquamarine. Large, round circles like tropical whirl pools spinning towards dark pupils sucking the air right out of my lungs. He assumed a confident posture, strong as he leaned on the bar towards me. I opened my mouth to speak, but nothing came out. He lifted one eyebrow and licked his lips. His mouth was small and round, bottom lip at least twice the thickness of the top, both framed by a strong square jaw. *Damn! He is gorgeous.* Several moments passed and I hadn't managed to even acknowledge that he had spoken to me. I was just staring and beginning to look like a lunatic. I was nervous, embarrassed and wanted to hide. *OK, Myra. Snap out of it.* I swallowed hard and pretended to cough. Generally people were a lot *less* attractive in the sober daylight due to a phenomenon called *Beer Goggles*. The affliction when alcohol makes people look more esthetically pleasing to the onlooker. "You OK, Myra?" Marcus was beginning to look concerned. *"MYRA!"* I screamed to myself. I shook my head. And opened my mouth. This time something came out.

"You have really beautiful dimples." *Damn it! What is wrong with me?* I clamped my mouth closed.

"Jeez, Myra. First you complement my abs and now my dimples? You better be careful or you are going to give me a big head!" Marcus laughed deeply. "Let me grab your wallet." He walked away. I dropped my head. I was ready to go. *I am clearly too hung over for this.* The mystery that was Marcus paled in comparison to my desire to get the hell out of there and to stop making a fool of myself. I knew if I stayed it would only get worse. Marcus approached with my Michael Kors wallet. As I watched him, his powerful legs visible beneath his jeans, I suddenly didn't want to go anywhere. I promised myself to act like a sane human being.

"Thank you so much for calling me." I reached out to him. "I had no idea it was even missing." He placed the wallet in my hand and looked at my face. I moved my gaze down quickly.

"No problem, at all. That was a really good idea you had."
What was a good idea? Did he think that I left it on purpose to trap him into calling me? "Oh, no. You don't understand. I didn't leave it so that you would have to contact me. I was pretty drunk last night and must have just…"

Marcus looked at me with another puzzled expression then interrupted, probably trying to save me more embarrassment. "No. I meant to have the *If found, please return to… card."*

I laughed to keep from crying. My headache was coming back with a vengeance. "Oh yea. This kind of thing happens to me all the time." *And now I look like a forgetful ditz. Perfect.* Marcus looked over to the other side of the bar where he was being summoned.

"I'll be right back." And he was gone. I picked up my wallet and glanced inside. Everything was there, including the hundred dollars in cash that I had taken from the ATM. I was relieved. I looked up and Marcus had his back to me. He turned toward his customer and lifted his right arm to open a bottle of craft beer. On the inside of his bicep was a tattoo in stark black ink , the silhouette of a nude woman lying on her slightly arched back. The mystery intensified. I pondered the tattoo for a moment and he was back,

"So, what can I get you?" He addressed me. Upon arriving, I was intent upon not drinking, but after the more than awkward behavior I had displayed, the increasing pain of my blood through my veins made me decide to indulge.

"Johnny Walker Black, please. Neat." He looked taken aback.

"Oh, wow. So you are a whiskey girl, huh?"

"Yes. I get it honestly. From my father and brother." I smiled.

"Fair enough," he turned around to get the bottle. "So what do you do?" He reached for a bottle above the bar and his chest moved and flexed. My first inclination was to simply sit and watch the magnificent sight before me, but with much effort I went on to give a three minute run down of my job. After placing my drink in front of me, Marcus leaned across the bar listening and nodding interestedly, flashing that bright smile several times.

"How long have you worked here?" I asked. I had taken a few sips of my drink and could feel my nerves unwrapping a little and a new daring creep in. *Alright, I am going to get to the bottom of Marcus. Now.* A giggle escaped my lips as I realized that I had just referenced Marcus' bottom. Marcus looked at me, eyes darting left to right, as if he had missed an obvious joke and then started talking. I looked down. *God, I am so weird!*

"This will be my second year, next month." Marcus explained. "This is my uncle's shop and he needed some help covering the weekend day shift, so I stepped in." I consciously fixed my face to hold the pleasant smile I was wearing. "It's good money and I am in school, so I don't really have too much time for a normal Monday through Friday. Ya know?" His story was getting good.

"Sure! That makes a ton of sense." Marcus looked to be about twenty-eight or twenty-nine. *What is the back story here? Why is he so old and still in school?* Not that there was anything wrong with that, but I was interested. "So what are you studying?" I asked casually, glancing around the room.

"I'm in my last year of med school." My eyes zoomed back to him.

Myra, do not react. I took a sip from my glass as nodded. "Oh nice. What area of medicine?" My voice was only slightly higher than normal. *Please be straight. Oh man. Please be straight.* My friends and I were not the money hungry, gold digging, doctor hunting kind of women, but a nice, extremely attractive straight doctor? I very well may have been looking at the Holy Grail.

He smiled largely. "Gynecology and Women's Health." I couldn't control myself. A smile spread across my face as my eyes widened. I felt my head fall back and I laughed for a couple of seconds. "What?! What is so funny, Miss?" Marcus grinned at me and crossed his arms, pretending to be offended.

"You are quite an enigma." I shook my head. "You work at a gay club, topless sometimes, you have a tattoo of the silhouette of a naked, top heavy woman on your arm and you are going to be a gynecologist." He was awesome.

"What can I say? I like the job here, I am a people person and, well, I love women. I figured I would learn how they work… at least physically. I am still trying to understand the emotional side."

"You and every other man on the planet, honey." I rose my glass to him in a toast. I noticed how fluidly this conversation was going and I went in for the kill. Before the wild fantasies started, I needed to know my chances with the extraordinarily attractive man standing across from me. "So, just so we are clear, because single ladies everywhere want to know." I spoke slowly, intentionally, as to not offend. "You are,"

"Straight." He finished the sentence as if he had been expecting it. Shooting me a stare that burned into me. "And yes, what is happening here is my attempt to get to know you a little better. Your performance was compelling and I couldn't help but wonder what you were like sober." All of the sudden I was nervous again. *So what is this, some kind of date interview?*

"Oh," I started offensively. "I am not exactly sober right now." Marcus shook his head and laughed.

At that moment, because God is good, Marcus was called away from me to the other side of the bar which gave me a little time to regain my composure. I yanked at the sleeve of my shoulder to show a more skin and pulled up my posture from slouching. By the time Marcus returned, no more than three minutes later, I had begun daydreaming about our future mansion, our weekend sports car and our twin greyhounds. *I have serious issues.*

"Sorry about that." He motioned with his head towards the direction from which he came.

"No problem at all. You are technically at work." I teased him.

"So now that you know everything about me, tell me something about you. What do you do for fun?" He looked at me again with those tropical eyes and plump lips and suddenly all anxiousness was gone. Like a calming wind had just hit me, his presence swept away my self-consciousness. I relaxed my posture back into the stool and answered him.

"I love to go out. Out to eat, out dancing, out drinking. I am pretty recently single, so getting a grasp on what that means and how to find myself again has taken some getting used to. But I am enjoying myself for the most part." I grinned up at him. *Wow. That was candid.* I didn't care. It felt right to be honest with him

"Do you find that you enjoy being single?" he asked me, eyes still fixed on my face.

"I am not sure yet." I hoped that was an OK answer. We continued talking for the next hour. He was an avid hiker, biker, runner, basically anything and everything that had to do with the outdoors.

"Oh yea, there is nothing like camping out in the early spring down in the Smokey Mountains." He was beaming, "The night sky is so bright. My friends and I plan a couple camping trips every year. They're a lot of fun."

"I have never been camping, but I would try I think. My friends' idea of camping is a night at a Holiday Inn Express."

"Oh, I bet you could manage just fine." Marcus was rocking back and forth, arms crossed over his broad chest. I looked down at my phone as it vibrated next to my purse on the counter. It was almost 4 p.m.

"Wow! Time flies when you are having fun! I have to get going. May I have my check please?" I started to shuffle my things around. I needed to get back and catch up with Ava about the night's plans.

"Of course, let me get that." Marcus walked over to the register and started fiddling around. He pulled off a receipt that printed, wrote something on it and then slid it across the bar. I picked it up and read it.

May I take you out sometime? (Smiley face).

I looked up at him and laughed. He was intentionally looking stoic and in the opposite direction.

"Yes," I addressed him, "You may. But you don't have to pay for my drink, Marcus." *He is sweet.* "How much do I owe you?" I appreciated the gesture.

"Hey, my uncle owns this joint, remember?" He rested his elbows on the bar and leaned towards me. My face felt hot. "Besides, I just had the best afternoon at work I've had in two years. So thank you for that." I felt a strong desire to touch Marcus to ensure that he was real. I brought my hand over the bar and rested it for an instant on his arm.

"You are very welcome. Thank you again, and please have a wonderful night. I am excited to talk to you again soon." I scooted off of the stool and gathered my coat and purse.

"Me too, Myra. You got everything? Try not to leave anything else purposely so that I have to call you." I stuck my tongue out at him and made my way towards the door and out of the dark building.

9.

Cold wind sliced through the sheer lace stockings wrapped tightly around my legs. The lightweight purely ornamental, cropped sailor jacket with large brass buttons hanging over my shoulders did nothing but hold in the smoke smell from the loud club behind me. Of course, the jacket was dry clean only. It amazed me that smoking was still allowed in public bars and restaurants when it was banned in most of the rest of the country. Nothing was worse than waking up the morning after going out and smelling like stale cigarettes. And this assertion came from an occasional smoker. This unpleasantness nothing to stop me from visiting these places, however, so I kept my complaints to myself. Vision slightly blurry, I scanned the sidewalk looking for a tall head of blonde hair. The last text I had received from Cain told me that he was waiting in line but he was nowhere to be found. It was currently 2:16 a.m. The bars would close in less than an hour.

After meeting Marcus at the bar earlier that day to retrieve my wallet, credit cards and dignity, I decided that that night was no time to sit at home and sulk. After all, even if Cain didn't want me, a hot med school bartender did! Potentially. I called Ava and asked her to go out with me, to which she happily agreed to do. We went about hatching a plan of how we were going to convince Stella to go out with us. Stella was the third and most stable leg to our best friend tripod. A self-declared homebody who preferred staying home and completing a puzzle to venturing out to the crowded, smoky, obnoxious bars, when she humored us with an outing, raucous times were inevitable. Apart from her company, the added bonus of Stella's presence was that she was undeniably and classically gorgeous and an unintentionally relentless guy magnet. She would flip her long blonde hair and bat her large amber eyes and men of all ages and ethnicities would turn into puddles of beverage buying goons. Ava and I loved to be right there to catch all of the free shots and cocktails flung in her direction. On the dance floor guys couldn't resist us all together, a Neapolitan delight: Stella the blonde vanilla, Ava the redheaded strawberry, and me the brunette chocolate. So Ava and I decided the best plan would be for me to come over to their house with everything I needed to go out and then we would beg her to join us.

At around 8:30 p.m. I arrived at Stella's white three-bedroom ranch with all of my gear in one hand and a bottle of wine in the other. Her giant evergreen bushes swayed delicately in the breeze beside her immaculately trimmed hedges, as I stepped up onto her fully furnished covered front porch. *When did Stella get a rocking chair?* How it was that she owned a home when I was just seeing the finish line of paying off my car that I had for five years was a mystery to me. It was just another way that Stella was leaps and bounds ahead of me in the "adult" department. The heavy door opened and Stella, in her pajamas, with pale hair in a high pony tail, stood backlit in the entrance.

"Hello, my dear!" I sang with a broad smile. "You look lovely."

"Hi honey. I was gardening and doing yard work all day." She replied begrudgingly as we embraced. I walked into her home and removed my shoes onto the cream marble floor then continued passed the perfectly pedicured family room and dining room. Stella had always had a very thorough sense of interior decorating design, which I greatly envied. Matching frames hung on her walls filled with pictures of her loved ones and a gilded mirror glistened atop her fireplace.

Ava was getting set up in the bathroom, heating up straightening irons and laying out makeup and I shouted her a greeting and headed with Stella to the kitchen to pour three glasses of wine.

"I made cookies. They're on the oven." *Of course you did.* I smelled them immediately upon entering but had assumed the heavenly fragrance came from a candle. I should have known better. I was secretly waiting for the day when Stella would legally adopt me so I could stop hoping to be like her and just enjoy the fruits now, before the afterlife. While I indulged in not one, but two double chocolate chip cookies Stella and I chit chatted about her parents and two brothers. Growing up in the same neighborhood meant that she, Ava and I were in and out of each other's family homes houses daily, becoming surrogate family members.

In the white granite bathroom, Ava and I were at the double vanity while Stella sat on the edge of the large soaking tub, sipping her Chardonnay and watching us.

"So Myra, time to spill. How did your long awaited date with Cain go?" She asked excitedly. I kept both of my friends updated with minute to minute alerts of my interactions with Cain since first meeting him. They knew all of the juicy details word for word. All of the details except the ones of the previous night. Those were too gruesome to relay via text message. I sighed loudly, shaking off the ebb of embarrassment that rose with the thought of sharing the tale. I stopped applying the bronzer I was using to make my cheekbones more defined, turned to both of my best friends and then hopped onto the counter. They stared at me in shock and disbelief as I explained to them how Cain had waited until just moments before he was supposed to be at my home to ruthlessly blow me off. After I finished the recount, I jumped down, faced the mirror and started applying makeup once more. I didn't want a pity party and just I had feared, retelling the story made me feel the hurt like it was brand new, especially as I read their faces. There was nothing but silence for about twenty seconds. I assumed my friends were trying to figure out to say, other than the obvious.

"Oh, my God. Seriously? Wow. Just wow. That is fucking horrifying." Ava broke the quiet first, shaking her head as she spoke. Stella appeared in the mirror behind me and wrapped her arms around me.

"What an asshole. He is such a loser. Honestly, Myra. Don't spend any more time on him." She kissed my cheek and then walked out of the perfect bathroom and down the hall towards her room.

"Where are you going, Stella?" I called after her giving Ava a knowing smirk.

"To find something to wear. I am coming out with you." She said in an exasperated tone. I smiled to myself. I hadn't even had to ask. "What an asshole!" She added. I couldn't tell if she was more upset at the fact that Cain had hurt me, or at the fact that now she had to take off her sweatpants and go out in public with us. Either way, I was satisfied. Ava and I slapped hands as quietly as we could and continued getting ready for a night of fun.

An hour and a half later, Ava, Stella and I were all dolled up and made the short journey from Stella's Southside home to an area just north of downtown, where the streets were lined with bars and clubs. We started at a sports bar. The clientele was twenty something fraternity type guys and the girls who loved them. We sat alone at a table eating fried mozzarella sticks, pointing out cute guys and laughing at most over the loud pop music for wearing different variations of the same exact polo shirt in twenty five different colors. About an hour passed and we progressed to a lounge down the street. The room was filled with gray leather sofas and sectioned off by sheer curtains for an intimate ambience. Cool blue lights gave the place an almost extraterrestrial feel. We sat in a corner shielded by white fabric, and were approached by a group of thirty something men who wanted to buy us drinks. We stayed for half an hour, Stella skillfully dodged giving her number to the gentleman who had purchased our beverages, and we made our way out the door and onto our next destination. Next was a large bar with a DJ. It was a dark, dingy, strobe light lit club with a sticky floor and bodies grinding together on a dance floor that took up the entire room. The music was traumatizing, both in decibel and lyric as hip-hop artist after hip-hop artist assaulted our senses with raunchy rhymes and callous beats. After about two hours, two song requests to the DJ and four rounds of shots, all three of us were beginning to slow down. We were standing next to the bar, talking to group of men who, I was informed by Ava, were brothers. I opened my small clutch and reached inside for my lip-gloss, after catching one of the cuter of the men staring at me, when a light shining from the bottom of the bag caught my eye. I picked up my phone dubiously, sure that my mother had sent a message checking up on me or asking me to come over the following day, only to find that I had seven missed text messages. All were from Cain. My heart jumped into my throat with such intensity that I almost coughed. I fumbled through them, hands shaking.

Hey. How is your night going? Twenty minutes later, he had sent another.

I am really sorry about last night. An hour and a half later.

So you are really pissed, huh? What can I do? And then another hour.

Where are you? May I please see you tonight?

That's what your evil ass gets for treating me like shit! I was elated, just barely stopping myself from doing a victory lap around the dance floor. I tossed my phone back into the bottom of the clutch and then spun around, picking up my drink, feeling more than smug. I forcibly focused my attention back to the group and the very cute brothers, but my mind kept being interrupted. It was like a little bug was buzzing around my ear whispering Cain's name every few seconds. I didn't want to reply. I was having fun and he didn't deserve to see me ever again, let alone tonight. Regardless of what I knew, I couldn't stop the urge. After ten minutes I was speeding towards panic. *What if I don't respond and he never contacts me again? What if I wait too long and he decides I'm not worth it, that he doesn't want me? This could be my only chance. What if he meets someone else tonight?* In a sudden outburst of seemingly random hysteria I grabbed

Ava and Stella away from their audience and showed them the text, catching looks from the men as I did it

"OK! What do I do?" I asked them frantically hands framing my face in distress.

Ava squealed loudly, "Text him back and make him come out here!" That was exactly what I wanted to hear and I reached towards Stella to reclaim my phone, but she disagreed.

"After everything that jerk did to you? I would ignore him for the night. He doesn't deserve to think he is even on your radar." I looked discouraged at this.

"But I want to see him! I miss him! What if he gets mad at me for ignoring him?" I whined.

"Oh, you mean like he ignored you last night when he *stood you up*?" She rebutted. I reacted to that bit of cold, hard truth with a sagging of the shoulders and a pained expression. Stella looked at me like a disapproving aunt, and then flung her arms in the air. "Fine! Do what you want! Text him and have him come here."

Ok. I am on my way. I will text you when I get there.

"Holy shit!" I cried as a feeling a nervous excitement washed over me as I looked down at the instantaneous response on my phone. I showed the phone to Ava and Stella. They cheered and jumped up and down like schoolgirls.

"Thank God, because I am so ready to go home!" Stella yelled. The group of guys behind us had disbursed but none of us showed any signs of disappointment. We headed to the dance floor for one more twirl, anticipation and excitement flowing freely through my veins.

I'm here in line. It looks like it will be another twenty minutes before I can get in. Are you hungry? We can get some food instead.
I was, in fact, famished after the night of dancing and drinking and my friends were ready to hit the road, so rather than making him wait to get into the crowded club I kissed Ava and Stella good night and left the steamy dance floor.

I'll be right out.
It wasn't all sacrifice on my part. As I walked onto the cold concrete sidewalk, my feet, strapped into five inch Nine West black suede platform heels, were on fire. Even the numbing effects of alcohol could not soothe the sharp pains that were beginning to stab at my arches and toes. I

alternated putting my weight on the left and then the right as I stood, looking for Cain. *Where is he? Is he trying to stand me up again? I will literally murder him.* I drew my mouth together in a line, and just as I contemplated going back inside to sit down, I saw him. Face red with cold, glasses on, hands shoved into his pockets, shoulders shrugged up to his ears, looking miserable. A warm sensation of relief and satisfaction filled me. My stomach started to dance and tie itself into bows with the same feeling I experienced every time I saw him or even thought of seeing him. *Thank god, he's here.* No matter how excited I was, I reminded myself, this is the man who stood me up. I turned my head from his approaching direction to gather myself, taking deep breaths to calm down. It took every bit of my restraint to keep myself from leaping into his arms. I counted from ten.

"Oh! Hi, Myra!" The voice was directed at the back of my head. I twirled around, making sure my hair whipped a bit and locked eyes with Cain. A cool smile spread across my mouth.

"Hello, Cain." The people standing in line outside of the bar looked at us with interest. Cain leaned in to give me a kind of awkward hug. *Yuck, he just patted my back while hugging me. What is he? My uncle? Back patters are the worst.* We released each other and stepped back. I watched his eyes move from my face and hair downwards to take in my outfit, his lips stretched into a smile as he glanced my shoes.

"Sorry, I had to move my car before it got towed." He stopped suddenly, "You look really…" he was probably not sure what the best, non-offensive word choice would be. I chose not to let him off the hook.

"Really, what?" I looked at him, blank eyes in a harsh stare, which he returned unflinching.

"Amazing" The way his lips moved when he spoke brought the warmth to my cheeks. I flushed and looked down as that heat spread to other areas of my body. Areas, which, all of a sudden, wanted his attention.

"Thank you." I said quietly, much less self-righteous than I had been moments prior. "Where would you like to grab a bite?" I wanted to get moving. The adrenaline from seeing Cain was wearing off and my feet were beginning to speak to me in angry tones again. A few doors down was a late-night burrito bar. Cain agreed and we walked side by side down the storefronts.

The bright lights of the restaurant were harsh, and I squinted as I passed through the door held open by Cain. Inside was like a slutty Sesame Street episode, featuring rainbows with girls in every brightly colored short skirt, dress and tall heels imaginable all standing in groups of three or more or beside their male escort for the night. I looked at Cain and smiled at him then gestured toward the clientele, mocking them. He smiled back and shook his head.

"You look like them you know," grin widening. "Only a lot hotter and a little less skanky." I let out a short hoot at the underhanded complement. *A little less skanky is still pretty skanky.*

"Well, thank you, kind sir!" I retorted sarcastically. Cain snatched me closer to him and kissed the top of my head. I swatted at him and pushed at him playfully. My stony resolve, supported by rejection and hurt, was slowly crumbling. He made me laugh, and it was hard to stay angry while giggling. When we were together, it was so easy to forget about how imperfect our relationship, or lack thereof, was, and to drown in how amazing everything felt.

Waiting in line, my feet hurt so badly I wanted to sit down on the dirty floor, or take my shoes completely off and be "that girl". I very well may have had I not been with Cain. I tried not to wince in pain and took deep breaths while Cain asked me about my night. I explain in a delightfully dramatic fashion, over exaggerating all of the best parts and forgetting to mention any dull or undesirable aspects, how I had been on a whirlwind adventure with my best friends to some of the city's best bars and clubs. I wanted him to understand how amazing my life was and that he was lucky to have captured any of my time at all.

"Oh that's cool. Yea, I've had a pretty good weekend myself." The comment stung me. In a flash, the anger that I had for Cain erupted to the surface. *I am so happy that you had a wonderful time standing me up last night.* I didn't say a word, but turned and put my back to him ending the conversation.

I didn't speak as we collected our food, and as we made our way to a table in the corner, a tiny seed of agitation took root. By the time my rear-end hit the sticky plastic seat I was fuming. *This fool hasn't even apologized for last night. He hasn't even brought it up. Who does he think he is?* When I agreed to meet Cain out I had imagined him remorseful, pensive and visibly distraught about the disappointment, unease and hurt he had inflicted on me the night before. As I looked into his face I saw nothing of the kind. He was digging into his eleven-dollar burrito without a care in the world. I wasn't having it.

"So, Cain, what the hell is your problem?" My head was slightly tilted to the side, my arms folded and resting on the blue speckled linoleum tabletop. My anger, definitely fueled by the several tequila shots I had participated in, dared me to jump across the table and strangled him. His head lifted quickly with a look of being pulled out of a trance. He glanced side to side in confusion and opened his mouth to speak. I dove in.

"Do you generally stand women up whenever you feel like it because you find something *better* to do?" My tone was sharp, sharper, I'm sure, than he had ever heard from me. "I was excited to spend time with you, Cain. I have been asking you to do so for about two months now and you always tell me that you have plans and then finally, when you promise to get together, you *stand me up?"* Involuntarily my hand flew into the air signaling for him to pay attention. "I looked fucking fabulous. Fabulous!" The last shot at the bar had taken hold. A tiny voice in the back of my head warned me to reel it back in and under control but I raged on. The volume of my voice rose, I couldn't stop it.

"I was ready to show you the best time of your life! YOUR LIFE! Is this how you generally treat people, Cain? Because if so it's bullshit." I held my face in an expressionless stare that I had learned from my mother. It was truly terrifying. Cain looked on as if he expected me to continue, and I almost did. I had spent the previous twenty-four hours creating a beautiful oration for just this situation, but I held off. I asked him a direct question and I found myself wanting to know the answer. *Does he generally treat people like this?*

Is he really just an asshole? He continued to look on. "That wasn't rhetorical, Cain. Please answer it." I said more softly. He swallowed his food, eyes shifting around, scooting around in his chair, visibly uncomfortable as if he wasn't used to being called out on his crap.

"No." He said defiantly, rolling his eyes at me. He must have seen my reaction to the tone of his voice that said, *Really Cain? Are you going to get an attitude with ME honey? I'm a black woman and will cause a whole scene. And I'm drunk? Don't test me.* So he amended, "No," much more gently. "I felt really bad afterwards. I knew I messed up for sure. "He looked down at his burrito like he desperately wanted another bite. I picked up mine in response and took a large vengeful mouthful,

"Continue." I probed, full of beef and lettuce.

"I like you, Myra. I really do. But I don't want a serious relationship right now. I just got out of one four months ago that lasted five years and it was terrible." *Terrible? Wow that's a strong word.* This was all news to me. Neither of us had shared anything about our past relationships. "But I really like hanging out with you. You are sweet and funny. Most of the time." He smiled a bit. *So, he doesn't want a serious relationship, but he thinks I'm great.* I let this sink in. *He doesn't want a serious relationship. But maybe, after he gets to know me better, he will! How could he not?* It was settled in my mind. I would make him want me.

"Cain that's fine. You don't have to want a serious relationship with me, but you could have communicated that and treated me with a little respect. I like hanging out with you too and, like you, I too am just out of a long relationship so I don't necessarily want to jump back into anything." I was on a roll. It felt good to finally speak my truth and stand up for myself. I didn't want to stop and with this kind of momentum and the help of liquid courage surging in my blood, I decided I would confront all of the issues I had right there in the smelly over-priced Tex-Mex shop with bad florescent lighting. "But that doesn't mean that I want to be your fuck buddy, Cain." He looked a little taken aback. "I am not OK with you only contacting me when you want me to come *watch a movie* nor am I OK with not being courted a little. I don't think us going to a movie or to dinner once in a while would qualify us as being in a relationship." As I spoke, Cain's mouth moved down. He was grim and a look of detachment slid across his face. I could tell that he was shutting down. *Maybe he has heard this conversation too many times before.* I stopped talking to see if he had anything to say. We sat for a few minutes in silence. I continued to eat my burrito even though I didn't want it. My stomach was in knots. *Why isn't he saying anything at all? My only request was that we go out a couple of times! He's acting like I asked him to move in!* A few more minutes passed without a word and I started to panic. A black pulse of regret crept its way into my consciousness. *Why did I have to have this conversation now? I should have waited.* My mind was searching for anything to say to reverse the effects of my words as I watched Cain eat his food, eyes roving around the room to anything but me.

"How is your burrito?" I asked him when I couldn't bare the silence anymore.

"It's good. How's yours? " He answered disinterestedly. I couldn't
believe how he was responding. He was completely disengaged and I was
at a loss at how to handle it. I searched for something to say, but was afraid
of making the situation worse. We wordlessly finished our food, threw
away our trash and headed to the door. As we walked down the street, I
stopped mid stride.

"Oh, Cain. I don't have a car downtown. You will have to take me
home." *Adding insult to injury.* I was sure this was not going to help my
case.

"Oh right, you were out with your friends. That's fine. I can take you.
Would you rather go now or in the morning?" he took out his phone,
presumably to look at the time.

"I can take a taxi. Don't worry about it." I was stretching out of my way
to not look like a burden. "It's no big deal." I turned and stepped towards the
street to look for a cab. There were several parked outside of the bar and I
cursed them for being so available. There was no way I wanted to pay the
sixty dollars it would cost to take me the twenty minutes home. I bluffed
and stuck my hand halfheartedly into the air to hail one of the drivers.

"Myra, stop. Don't be silly. I am taking you home. It's fine." *Phew,
thank God!* One of the drivers had just noticed my flag.

I spun around and walked back to him. "Thank you, Cain." He gave me a
quick nod and walked ahead of me down the sidewalk.

By the time we reached his car, I couldn't feel my toes and was pretty
sure that I was noticeably limping. Once I managed to open the door, I
practically fell in head first. Cain entered the car, still silent and started the
engine. *Alright Myra. This is it. You can either turn this thing around
before you get to your apartment or be prepared to never speak to this guy
again.* I was disgusted with how he was reacting, but not ready to chalk up
the situation as a loss just yet. Growing up, my mother always complained
about how hard-headed and stubborn I was. When I wanted something, I
went after it, even if everything crumbled around me in the process. I took a
deep breath. I was afraid of what he might do or how he would respond. I
had never seen him this way before and I couldn't tell if he was temporarily
annoyed or completely turned off. I had a feeling that while words and
conversation may not be able to help, my sensuality and our severe sexual
chemistry was not something that he could deny easily. Slowly and as
delicately as my alcohol-filled system could manage, I moved my left hand

toward the back of Cain's head and placed the tips of my fingers softly at the base of his hairline. He had liked this in other situations and I took a shot. I slowly began to run my fingers up and down his neck, incorporating my nails to scratch softly occasionally. He didn't object, so I continued moving my hand down to the top of his shoulders. Within a minute, his shoulders relaxed and a soft growl escaped him. I was filled with relief and continued gently massaging him.

"That feels really good." His eyes wandered over to my lace covered thighs then up my body and landed on my lips covered in a thin layer of gloss. I scooted as close to him as the car's console would allow, leaned in, and spoke gently.

"You know, I didn't mean that we can't still have sex. I will never want to stop doing that. I love doing that." Another one of my personal truths. He sighed but didn't say a word. "I would just like to incorporate more time getting to know you. We have fun together, right? That doesn't sound so bad does it?" I gently kissed his ear and then moved my mouth over the lobe and took it into my mouth. He didn't answer me but moaned and removed one hand from the wheel of the car and buried it between my lace-covered legs sliding, roughly, up towards my core. A sharp ache stung inside. I hated it. I wanted him desperately but I knew my desire would not be satisfied with sex. Not this time. I needed an emotional connection with him which was, I knew, completely out of reach for me at that time. I settled with manipulating the hell out of the situation to break down whatever boundaries I could. I leaned in to him passionately kissing at his neck and jawline. My hand moved down to the swollen mass in his jeans. With clinched jaw, Cain moved his hand from my shorts to my breasts, grabbing each one roughly.

"Fuck." Cain snarled. From my head buried somewhere below his jaw I felt the car turn once, suddenly then once more and then stop. I removed my mouth from Cain's stubbly jaw to look out the window that was already fogged up.

"Where are we?" I was breathless.

"A park entrance." He answered. He grabbed my face in his hands and covered my mouth with his, tongue searching for mine, wet and wild. His seat belt unclicked and then mine. "Take off your shorts." He demanded raggedly. Sobriety came to me for an instant. *Is he serious right now? Is this really what I want to be doing after we just had the "fuck buddy" conversation?* I looked at his face and then down at his already exposed member stiff and red. Again, I didn't want to have sex with Cain. Especially in this car that smelled like an old gym sock. Fear rose. *What if I refuse him and he never speaks to me again? I don't want to hurt his feelings or make him feel that I don't want him. What if this rejection is the last straw?* I took off my shorts as he watched and then, wanting to die of embarrassment, peeled off the lace tights. I moved to remove the thong underwear I donned.

"Leave those on." Cain reached over with both strong arms, grabbed me and lifted me over to him. I raised my knees so that I could be positioned on top of him, straddling his massive legs. I leaned forward to kiss him again and he grunted, holding my head in place as our mouths worked together. His hands moved to cover both of my breasts. Finding the opening of my blouse, he savagely pulled it apart, tearing off buttons in the process. Shocked, I screwed my face up in objection. *Really? This was a three-hundred dollar blouse! Sure, I got it on sale for seventy-five, but it's Chanel for God's sake! Have a little respect!* Before I could mourn my shirt, Cain pulled at the front clasp of my bra and it opened, exposing my bare chest which he took, one at a time into his mouth. This was by far the most aggressive sexual act I had ever been involved in. Everything was rough and I felt dominated, and only mildly concerned with how much it turned me on. I cried out as he unexpectedly bit down on my nipple, inflicting cruel pain and covered my hand over my breast defensively. He smiled looking up at me, mischief on his face. *This guy is just fucking with me. I'm just a toy to him.* The anger and hurt that had plagued me the night before, and earlier in the restaurant, reared, coupled with the loss of my blouse. I raise my hand slowly and, before I knew what was happening, smacked him with reasonable force across the mouth. His eyes widened in shock. I shocked myself. I loved it. I raised my hand again and moved to come back down but he grabbed my wrist stopping me mid-swing. I smiled as he looked at me, jaw set. I had clearly crossed one of his boundaries but I didn't care. I leaned in close, took his bottom lip into my mouth and let my tongue bounce around its surface until I felt him relax. Then with piercing force, I bit down quickly. He jumped.

"Ah! Damn it, Myra! That hurt!" I laughed loudly then shushed him.

"Oh, I'm sorry baby." I cooed, "Let me make it better." He shifted away from me to protect himself. I lifted my hand slowly to his face and cupped his chin. "I'm sorry." I said smiling, insincerely. I kissed him, deeply and passionately and moved my hand down to his hardness. He moaned and kissed me back, filling my mouth, taking my breasts into his hands. He put his lips to my chest our bodies beginning to slowly move together. In one quick motion, he lifted me with one arm, moved my underwear to the side and placed me back down right on top of him, all around him. A sharp gasp escaped both of us as he entered me, his head resting against me. I felt like I was going to burst apart from the number of emotions pouring into me. *I hate him.* He was a horrible asshole who was just using me, and I was the stupid twit who was letting him. *I want him so badly.* I didn't care what the price was. Nothing had ever felt so amazingly right and terrible wrong at the same time. As we moved together, I felt myself inching towards heaven. I was so close, but so far. I was afraid of the man below me and orgasms have little to no tolerance for fear. *I don't trust him.* There was someone hiding behind the mask that he wore, and I wasn't sure if that person was good or evil. I looked down at his face. It was softened. He stared up at me, wonderment in his eyes, hand delicately placed on my cheek then leaned towards my sternum and placed a kiss, his hand moved to support the back of my neck.

"You are so beautiful, Myra. I want you to come for me. Let's come together." It was so sweet. His voice sounded as if he really wanted nothing more in the world at that moment. I leaned into him, wrapping my arms around his head and holding him close to me as I worked with his body to do what he requested. I lifted my face towards the ceiling of the car. My body was beginning to glow and tingle, toes contracted, back stiffened and I took one final breath before I fell all the way back to earth from the climb. During the free fall, my mind could understand one thing. *This man is one dangerous drug.*

10.

I stayed on top of Cain for a minute and a half counting to ninety in my head. I didn't want to get off of him too quickly. I didn't want to get off of him ever, but I definitely didn't want to overstay my welcome in the now steaming hot car. As I moved, he put his hands on each side of my waist and lifted me, helping me back to my side of the car where I tried to figure out the most subtle and lady-like way to put back on my clothes. As it turned out, there was no way to appear subtle and lady-like after having sex with a man in a car in a city owned parking lot. An article I read in a local newspaper came to mind about a private foundation granting two-million dollars to increase park visitation. *I wonder if this counts towards their goal.*

I wanted to declare: *That was amazing!* But I wasn't sure it was, so I stayed quiet. Cain was remaining silent as well but when I stole a glance at him his disposition had completely changed to relaxed, almost cheerful. I cracked my window to help with the defogging progress and then drew a tiny smiley face on the cool glass with my finger. The glass beneath my skin squeaked back softly.

I was wrestling so many feelings I thought I would accidentally scream out in the silent car for *everyone* to shut up. I was scared and saddened by Cain. I wasn't sure that after the tense last hour or so I would ever see him again. It was abundantly obvious at this point that there was something not quite right about him, but to me the electricity was worth the risk of being shocked.

"You are going to turn left in two lights onto Buckford Boulevard." I said quietly. His large hand was lying on his knee and I wondered how he would respond if I reached over and held it.

"Mmk." He answered. We traveled for a few more minutes, the radio just audible above the bumping of the tires on the road. We entered a commercial area glowing with bright lights and signage when Cain put on his left turn signal.

"Oh, no. You stay straight on this street." I warned.

"I want a milkshake," he nodded at the twenty-four hour burger joint on the corner, "You want a milkshake?"

"Sure." I answered slowly. I wasn't actually hungry. Not only had we just eaten burritos but my stomach was still unsteady with nerves. He pulled into the drive-thru. It was 3:45 a.m. and yet there were five people in line ahead of us. We sat in silence for a few minutes as the bright light of the restaurant dining room shone through the windows, illuminating our faces.

"So what else did you do tonight?" This was the first attempt that Cain had made at conversation in over an hour. Increasingly confused, I picked up where I had cut our earlier conversation off, describing the music and the general crowd. *What is going on? Are we just going to pretend that nothing happened and that I didn't say anything about our relationship and then receive the silent treatment?*

"Cool. My night was pretty good too. Had a few drinks with some friends and then headed home early." *Yep! We are totally going to pretend that none of those things ever occurred.* "Why were you ignoring my texts?" Cain asked slowly as if tiptoeing around a sleeping Kodiak bear. "Because you were mad? You generally answer my texts pretty quickly." I made a note not to respond as promptly, it made me look desperate.

"Actually I didn't even see them until I wrote you back tonight." Cain made a grunting noise, indicating that he had heard me but was not quite convinced, and pulled the car up a few feet as we moved up in the line.

"Did you dance with a lot of guys, get a few numbers?" he tried to come off playfully but there was a slight edge to his tone that let me know he cared about the answer.

"Oh, ya know. Not too many." I replied coyly, trying to establish some mystery. We pulled up to the microphone.

"Fine. Be that way." He turned to his open window, "I will take a medium mint chocolate chip and a medium chocolate milkshake." He turned to me, "Is medium OK with you?"

"Um, yes. That's fine." I was unsure of why he didn't ask me what flavor I preferred. The speaker gave Cain the total and we pulled forward.

"You told me that mint chocolate chip was your milk shake and ice cream flavor, remember?" I racked my memory, and did recall remarking at a commercial we saw while in his bed one night as we watched Comedy Central.

"Uh huh. I remember. Thank you sweetie." I didn't mention the fact that while more often than not I chose mint chocolate chip, right then a strawberry milkshake sounded better. A few more moments of silence and then we pulled to the window to collect our desserts. I hated how awkward I felt sitting next to him. One part of me wanted to be as far away from him as possible and the other part of me never wanted the car ride to end. He handed me both of the cups as he paid, and I placed straws in both. Cain quickly pulled out of the parking lot and back onto the main street. He looked down at the cup holder.

"Thanks for putting a straw in mine, babe. May I have some of yours?" I hadn't even tasted mine yet but my straw was already two inches from him lips so I agreed. "Oh, that is good. I can see why it's your favorite." I remained on my side of the car trying to mute the thoughts crowding my head. This guy had gone from aggravated silence, to aggressively passionate and dominating, to chipper like a kid on the first day of school. I sucked at my straw and stared at the dark trees zipping past, listening to Cain comment on songs that came on the radio and a few restaurants he had visited in the area. Slowly, with the consistency of his new mood, I relaxed.

"May I try your shake?" I asked sweetly. I was less interested in the shake and more interested in sharing something that was his and putting my mouth somewhere his had just been.

"Sure."

I picked it up and put my lips to the straw. A dry slurping sound resulted. I brought the cup down from my face dejectedly.

"You drank it all already?" I was shocked. "And then you had the nerve to act like there was some in there for me to try? That's messed up!" I laughed and slapped at his knee.

"Sorry." He retorted, chuckling to himself. "I thought maybe some more had gathered at the bottom by now." We continued talking and teasing and I gave him directions until we pulled into the parking lot of my apartment complex. The development consisted of ten large white stucco buildings, each five stories high. Their red clay tile roofs were vaulted lowly and each of the windows leading into the apartments was arched. In the middle of a field of usually dead grass, the development almost accomplished the architect's goal of looking like it was in the middle of a south-western desert. Almost. Cain flung his car into a spot designated for visitors and put it in park.

I reached down to the floor of the passenger's side seat, grabbed my clutch and unbuckled my seat belt.

"Thank you for dropping me off, Cain. It was really nice to see you." I turned towards the door and opened it. The last few minutes with Cain had been pleasant and if I never saw him again, I was happy with our final interaction.

"Whoa, Myra! Hold on." His voice was surprised and I turned back to his puzzled face. "It's three a.m. I bought you a burrito, gave you an orgasm, got you your favorite milk shake, and drove you home in the middle of the night and I don't even get a place to sleep?" His tone was scolding. "Aren't you going to invite me up?" A smile spread across his face causing his eyes to sparkle. I was caught off guard. After everything, I certainly didn't expect him to want to stay.

"Of course, Cain. Please, come up." I buzzed briefly with happiness. I was tired, like I had been at an amusement park all day enduring ride after jerky ride. He shut off the ignition, rose out of the car and followed me to the entrance of my building, which I unlocked, and started to ascend the stairs. It wasn't until we were a flight away from my door that I remembered.

Oh dear, God. My apartment is a mess. I hadn't anticipated anyone, let alone Cain coming home with me that night. In my wildest fantasies, I ended up with Cain tonight, but at his apartment making passionate love- not mine. My mind raced and feet slowed as I tried to figure out what to do. *I can pretend that I lost my apartment keys.* Cain had seen the huge key ring I used to open the downstairs door. *I can tell him I forgot that my aunt is staying for the weekend.* That excuse sounded lame and unlikely. There was nothing to say except the truth.

"Cain, my place is a pit. I wasn't expecting anyone to come home with me tonight or I would have picked up a bit." I didn't look over at him while I spoke, fearing receiving a disapproving or judgmental eye.

"That is fine, no big deal at all." He sounded pleased, perhaps at the idea that I hadn't planned on sleeping with someone I met out. I led him down the long, gray, sterile hallway to my apartment.

"This is not at all what I expected." His voice bounced off the walls.

"What do you mean?" I looked over at him.

"I expected you to live somewhere a bit more, organic." He glanced around at the harshly lit hallway that buzzed from the halogen lamps above us. "Somewhere older, with more character."

Well, you are going to be very surprised at my poorly decorated apartment with clothes and dishes strewn everywhere.

"Hm! That is interesting! I have to admit, this place is lacking something. But it's fine for now. I will probably be here for a while though because I *HATE* moving." I unlocked the door and stepped in taking a deep breath. I prayed that it didn't smell like trash. *All clear.* The apartment smelled lovely thanks to an Apples and Spices air freshener in the kitchen. I removed my heels in the entry hall, thought I may have heard my feet cheer with relief, walked in the dining room, plopped my clutch and keys down on the table, and grabbed a hair tie laying there, pulling my locs up and out of my face.

"Can I get you anything to drink? Water? Wine? Beer?" I had already begun swooping around the apartment picking up dishes and glasses and shuttling them into the kitchen, flipping light switches as I went. Cain had made his way from the door after closing it, shoes still on, and was standing by the dining table looking down at an open book.

"Uh, yea," he called distractedly. "What kind of beer do you have?" He glanced up and moved towards the kitchen.

"Oh no! Stay there! I'll bring it over." I called to him through the opening between the cabinets and the countertop. From where he stood near the table, he couldn't see the pile of dishes that were stacked on the counter.

He laughed. "Oh, OK. I'll just sit here and try not to look around, if that would make you more comfortable. Should I close my eyes?" he continued. "That might make drinking the beer a little difficult at first." I could hear the humor in his voice.

"Look. I don't usually have guests over when my apartment is a disaster like this. It has been a drunken past two days and I haven't had the energy or the caring to clean." I made the comment hoping that he would pick up on how his cold actions the previous night had affected me. I glanced towards the hallway leading to my bedroom remembering the catastrophic state my bathroom and bedroom were in. Clothes and jewelry were scattered all over my bed and floor. *My mother would be so ashamed… at not only the fact that this man is here in the middle of the night, but even more so at the fact that he is here and seeing this mess.* My mother was the perfect housekeeper. Laundry, dishes, dusting, and vacuuming. I still didn't understand how she could clean so immaculately. I could never make a bathroom shine the way that she could. She would have never been in that situation. At my age she already had two children.

11.

I fixed myself a vodka tonic and delivered a beer to Cain, then continued cleaning up the kitchen. Just as I unloaded the last dish from the dishwasher and prepared to load the counter full of dirty dishes into the racks, Cain spoke.

"You know. I really don't care about the mess. You've seen my place, which is usually a shit hole." He was walking around, taking in the titles of books and faces in frames, and then stopped at one of my bookcases, where odd knick-knacks lined the shelves. "But what the hell is this?" He picked up a wooden frog and held it out to me from the palm of his hand. The frog was stained dark brown and held a large stick in his mouth. On its back were five ridges of varying height. I smiled widely and strolled over to Cain, taking the frog from him and sliding the stick out of his mouth. I lightly ran it over the raised ridges, creating a deep, hollow reverberation. Cain looked down at me, and placed his hands lightly on my shoulders.

"This is a Cuban Call Frog." I explained, noticing that now Cain's eyes were green as opposed to their earlier gray. "I have one and so do the other members of my immediate family. When one of us needs something that we don't know how to ask for, we play it and someone will respond."

"Oh, really?" he looked skeptical. "And does that work?" he placed his hand on my face, brushing his warm thumb over my cheekbone. I smiled.

"Well, I can't remember the last day that I didn't speak to at least one of my family members. Whether I played the frog or not. We are very close. So yes. It does work." And set the frog back in its place on the shelf. Reaching up, I placed my hand on the back of his neck and rose to my toes, getting as close to eye level as I could then kissed him on the chin softly. His breath brushed my face as he exhaled. He sighed very quietly then wrapped his arms around me and pulled me into him, hugging me hard. I tossed my arms around his neck and held on for dear life. I felt light headed, his body pressing against mine, nearly my entire weight taken over by his strength. I could feel my insides tingle. Forget butterflies, this was an electrical storm, pops and bangs so intense my legs almost gave out from under me. Cain buried his face into my neck and breathed deeply, rubbing his hands along the length of my back.

"You feel so good. It feels so good to hold you like this." My chest burned white. *I am not going to be the first to let go.* In slow motion I felt Cain's arms loosen around me. Each muscle shifted away from me like single stitches being pulled out of a garment. Before he had completely detached from me, Cain bent down and rested his lips on mine, his jaw still. It wasn't seductive or perverse, no tongue probing or teeth teasing, just the quiet of the air exiting his nose above me. His lips trembled after he pulled away, hovering just centimeters from mine.

Cain bent his knees and then his back, slid his arm to my lower legs and lifted me into the air.

"Where is your bedroom?" *Shit! It is a disaster.* Holding on to Cain's shoulder I pointed around the corner.

"It's back there. But Cain...,"
Cain smiled.

"Yeah, I know. It's messy back there. I don't plan on looking at anything except for you." And with that he spun around and jogged to the back of the apartment, me squealing in his arms the whole way.

Cain drew an invisible line from my lips down the front of my throat, through the valley of my chest to the bottom of my rib cage. I was laying, propped up on pillows like a goddess staring at the ceiling, wrapped in bliss. After Cain carried me back to my bedroom he laid me down on the bed and kissed me sweetly and slowly. He crawled next to me on his side and stroked my hair and cheeks and deeply explored my entire person, head to toe, for what felt like hours. Initially, I was concerned. *Is there a reason he is not being more aggressive?* Cain would usually have been inside of me by that point, taking his fill. I looked at him and he met my eyes while he took each of my fingers and placing them on his lips. I came to understand that what he was doing was more intimate than anything we had done previously. He began to move his hands around my body deliberately, as if he were testing for my reaction, trying to figure out what I liked best. He was getting to know me. Soon after we made love for the very first time ever.

While Cain was deep within me, moving to and from my body with delicate power, I gave up on hiding anything from him. I was overcome with the passion I felt for him, a blinding high that did not dissipate even after our bodies left each other. His naked body sat up and began to rub my legs, like he wanted to continue to show me all of the attention in the world. I closed my eyes as Cain's hands and then lips moved down to my knee.

"What happened here?" he asked softly.

"I tore my ACL in high school." I answered, eyes still closed.

"Ouch. Does it still hurt?"

"Only sometimes when I do a lot of lifting." I hated the scar on my otherwise beautiful legs. They were my mother's, only longer.

"I am going to get some water. I'll be right back." Cain rolled over leaving the sheet on the bed.

"Wait, no! I'll get it." Still ashamed of the state of my home, I sprang up, too late; Cain had already run out of the bedroom. I collapsed back on to the pillows.

"Oh my God! It is disgusting in here!" Cain shrieked in a feminine voice from the kitchen.

"Shut up!" I called after him playfully.

I rolled over to the edge of the bed and stood up towards the bathroom. As the door closed behind me I flipped on the light and found me naked, makeup smeared all over my face, smiling and glowing brighter than a million watts. I was happier than I could ever remember. *I could be with him every day for the rest of my life. I know that I could.* Grabbing a tissue to wipe my eyeliner back into place, I gargled some much needed mouth wash and exited back into to the moonlit bedroom. Cain was sitting on the edge of the bed holding something.

"You and your siblings look identical. Especially you and your sister. I had to take a second look." He was holding one of my favorite family photos taken a few months prior.

"My sister is eight years older than me! I hope we don't look identical." *Damn you cigarettes and alcohol.* I sat next to Cain and laid my head on his shoulder. "What is your family like?"

"My brother is," he paused, "my brother." He finished solemnly. "We get along fine I guess. My mother is very loving. My dad is very quiet." I waited for more. None came

"Do you look more like your mother or your father?" This was the first time he had ever spoken of his family.

"Oh, I would say my father, definitely. He's a stud." He looked at me and winked. I slapped at his knee then climbed past him onto the bed. He followed behind me as I laid down, arms enfolding me again. Unexpectedly he continued softly speaking next to my ear as he held me.

"My mom is very emotional. She had a lot of trauma very early and I think it affected her ability to handle her feelings well. My grandma also lives with my parents. She was sick as a young adult and has been in a wheelchair ever since."

"Wow." I tried to envision the family dynamic that had cultivated the man behind me.

"Did I tell you I also have a nephew? My brother's son? He is four and his name is Dyson."

"Like the vacuum?" I said happily, unable to help myself.

"Yea. He is great. I thought that I would never want kids until he was born. He is just so amazing. I love him so much." Cain continued with a story of how he had taken Dyson on a walk near his family's home and the funny things his young mind had come up with as they talked about the different animals they saw. My back to Cain, I affirmed him with passive responses so he knew I was interested. I was shocked that he was telling me so much about himself.

"My dad is retired and sometimes works at a grocery store in town. My mom doesn't work so that she can take care of Grandma and Dyson." I nodded my head into the pillow. "Based on my brother and his sometimes strained relationship with my parents, I think that I am the one who is going to have to take care of my parents. So I am preparing myself for that." I turned over towards him.

"That is a very noble and loving thing to do." I placed my hand on his cheek and then turned back around so he could hold me again. He kissed my shoulder.

"You have the softest skin I have ever felt, Myra. Really." I giggled then was silent as I gathered my thoughts. There was something very particular that I wanted to talk to him about. It had been on my mind ever since earlier that night at the restaurant.

"So, Cain. You said that you recently got out of a relationship? What was that like?" I held my breath, hoping that he wouldn't shut down again or ignore me altogether.

"Her name is Myra."

"Whose name?" I was startled. *Clearly he doesn't mean what I think he means*!

"My ex's." *Son of a bitch. His ex-girlfriend and I have the same name?*

"Oh." Was literally the only thing that would peep out of my mouth.

"It lasted several years. I met her in college. She's a lawyer." *Great.* "She has her own house." *of course she does,* "and I still love her." *Of course you do.* In my mind I pictured a Swedish super model in a Chanel suit and six-inch heels. I wanted her dead immediately. "Things just fell apart. She…" he stopped.

"She what?" I helped him along. I hated this. I hated thinking about her and about them as a couple but I hated the thought of not knowing everything about her even more.

"She refused to have sex with me. Well, most of the time. We hadn't had sex in several months when we broke up." As he spoke he hugged me a little tighter. *That bitch!* Sympathy filled me for Cain. *Well, at least there's that. She may be a lawyer and undoubtedly better than me in every way. I am sure she is even an amazing decorator but she is a cold and frigid bitch who mistreated Cain terribly. I am kind and loving, that means so much more.* I soothed my own ego and convinced myself that there were more important things than being wildly successful.

"Well, do you know why she didn't want to?" I asked, not sure if I should but there was no holding me back.

"We had a couple of issues…," he started in then changed tone drastically, "But that is why I am not interested in starting a new relationship right now. I just want to be single for a while, is all."

I bit my lip, "Yea. OK. I guess I can understand that." *Note to self: I must never deny him sex.*

"So what about you?" he moved from behind me and guided me onto my back so he could look at my face. "What about your ex?" I went on to talk about Ralph and how we met and how we separated. I didn't mention to Cain that I recently heard that Ralph was coming into town for a few months from a mutual friend. After I finished we stopped talking for several minutes. Cain laid his head on my chest and I scratched his head.

"I find it fascinating," he broke the quiet, "that you always know exactly how to touch me." I smiled down and kissed the crown of his head. "I've never mentioned that I love to have my head scratched like that, from front to back. But here you are, doing it."

"That is very interesting." I hadn't even thought about that fact that I was doing it a certain way, it was instinctual.

"My aunt used to always do that to me. It made me feel calm and happy." A few more moments passed laying in heaven. I was trying to stop myself from falling asleep, eye lids getting heavier by the second. Cain yawned.

"I feel so comfortable with you, Myra. You are really awesome." I cringed as I realized how many times he had spoken that name in a setting as intimate as this but with someone else. For five years. And then I felt it again: *I am in love with this man.* This time I didn't fight it. I let the feeling wash over me and take me off into a dream.

12.

I decided that the best course of action would be to just leave my phone on my desk rather than continuing to take it in and out of my purse every couple of minutes to check for new text messages. It was Wednesday, and I hadn't seen or heard form Cain since he crept out of my apartment at the first light of day three days before. I had rolled over Sunday morning to an empty and cold bed next to me after being kept warm by him all night. Cain's body temperature was perpetually radiating from him like a space heater. *Too bad his demeanor is the exact opposite.* The utterly confusing thing was that on Saturday night he had finally let down some of that frosty shield and opened up to me, and as I fell asleep I felt closer to him that I ever had, and happier than I could recall. All day Sunday I had expected Cain to reach out, but he never did, and still hadn't on that morning as I tried desperately to finish a report for Saint Josephine's Hospital. After not getting a text from him all day on Sunday, I had reached out to him that evening.

Hey you. I had a lot of fun. Thanks for bringing me home. I was sad when I woke up and you were gone. I hope you are OK. No response. For the first two days of no contact I was indignant. *What kind of person sneaks out of a woman's apartment and doesn't contact her for days?* Waking up that Wednesday morning with no word from him I felt concerned. *Is he alive? Did he get hurt?* I checked the city obituaries. *Nothing. So, that bastard is still alive. Unless he is in a ditch somewhere. Should I report a missing person? What would that call be like? "Yes, officer, a completely aloof guy that I have been sleeping with left my apartment in the middle of the night and I haven't heard from him since."* That would give the precinct a laugh.

Wednesday had become the one day every week that we saw each other. It had become a kind of habit. He would text me that evening and then I would go down to see him. *Is he going to contact me tonight like he hasn't been ignoring me all week?* I almost wished for that, as dysfunctional as it would be, just so I could see him and talk to him about what was going on and why he felt it was acceptable to ignore me. As the hours stretched on I decided, again, that he was an asshole, a big one, and potentially a crazy person. *This is humiliating.* So much so, that I hadn't told anyone, not even Ava or Stella. They had both contacted me and asked me how everything went, and I told them it was wonderful and that we finally connected in a real way. I hadn't told them that he went missing. I decided that I wouldn't subject them to the emotional roller coaster I was now riding.

I glanced at the clock on my computer screen. Eleven thirty. *What a creep. Regardless of what he says to me, when he says it, I am not responding.* I started to think about the real possibility that I may not ever hear from him again. My stomach dropped. For the seven-hundredth time I reran Sunday early morning in my mind. I tried to think of anything I might have said that would make him run away like this. My mind drew a blank. I thought about how much I would miss his sense of humor, ridiculous and sometimes crude, but always enough to make me laugh. *He really is sweet when we are together and alone, at least usually.* I thought about how he held my hand when we were sitting on his bed watching television, stroking the top of my fingers with his thumb. I pictured his body and shivered. Again, I looked at the clock. It was noon and I hadn't gotten a thing done on the report in thirty minutes.

"Hey you! Ready for lunch?" Lilly came around the corner and leaned up against my desk. I hadn't seen her since that morning upon arrival. I looked up at her in obvious misery. "What is wrong honey?"

I shook my head, "Can I have a cigarette?"
Lilly knew immediately that something big was up. I had only smoked a cigarette at work one other time, and that was when my boss was laid off and I feared I was next. We stood outside in the cold January air as I lit my cigarette and inhaled deeply, then expelled the smelly smoke away from me.

"So what's up buttercup?" Lilly reached for her lighter from me and lit her own. I began to explain the truth about the last weekend which I had hid from her for three days. On Monday, I told her all of the best parts of my time with Cain the past weekend, omitting the Friday incident all together. On Tuesday, when she asked me how he was, I told her that he was fine. I knew that I would feel her wrath from keeping this from her for so long, but surprisingly she stood quietly and listened supportively. I began at Friday with the standup and then told her about Saturday night, all of the gruesome and wonderful details.

"And when I woke up he was gone, and I haven't heard from him since." I looked at the ground, mortified, and flicked the end of my cigarette.

"But you usually talk to him every day, right?" Lilly inquired. I nodded in silence. "Well honey, I think it is time to move on. And to be honest I think it is for the best." This wasn't making me feel any better. "I have witnessed you and Cain for a while now, and he has never really risen to the occasion. I mean, this was the very first time that he had even seen your apartment, right? That is unacceptable." I nodded quietly again. I knew she was right. Whatever was happening with Cain didn't feel good the majority of the time. Since meeting him, it was only when we were together that I was without some feeling of frustration or longing. And that was always very short lived. There was something very wrong with our interaction and I felt like I was the only one being injured by it. I took a deep breath of clean air and then spoke.

"To tell you the truth, a really big part of me doesn't want him to contact me ever again. I want to find someone who is going to treat me at least a little bit the way I want to be treated." I didn't mean it. But I wanted to. I didn't want anyone else, regardless of how Cain treated me. I looked timidly at Lilly.

"Then why don't you, darling? You can. You are amazing." She took my empty hand with hers and placed the thin white stick back to her lips.

"Honestly?" I asked her. She nodded, so I continued. "I am afraid that I will regret it. Cain does something to me, invokes something in me that I have never experienced before. I am afraid that if I give up now, if I don't keep trying, even just a little longer, I will miss out on a relationship filled with the most exquisite love I could imagine." I shocked myself with that statement. I had just verbalized something that I had never consciously understood about myself. *Is that really what I am waiting for? Wow. That's deep.*

"I don't know that I have ever felt anything like that, Myra." I wasn't surprised. This obsession that I had with Cain was way past normal and healthy. I felt ashamed. Lilly had a long time boyfriend whom she loved dearly. "But what I do know is that no love is worth sacrificing yourself and how you should be treated. You have standards, my love, and you should stick with them regardless. If you are supposed to be with Cain then standing up for yourself isn't going to stop that from happening."

The words struck like a cord. I knew that there was no way I would put up with this from anyone else. As we walked back to the building, I thought about why I was letting myself be punished via Cain.

At my desk after lunch I put my phone in my purse for good. I knocked out the report that I had been struggling with, and two others, before it was time for me to go home. I stopped by Lilly's station on my way out of the building. She was on the phone and I sat in the pastel chair across from her, playing with and then dropping a Disney Princess figurine from her desk. She shot me an eye bullet and I quickly replaced the toy and folded my hands in my lap like a child, smiling largely.

"I saw you drop that," she began with a stern look after replacing the receiver. "So what are you going to do about Cain?" I paused, thinking for a moment. I had been considering my options since lunch.

"I am going to try to not respond. Or respond evasively and then start pulling away completely. You are right. I can do better." Lilly nodded sharply and then stood, walked over to me and bent low to give me a hug, her pale hair swinging in my face.

"Call me or text me if you need any moral support." I left her desk and the building feeling strong. Determined to begin the long and hard journey of separating myself from Cain. It was incredible how intensely I had bonded myself to him over such a short period of time, I didn't understand why but there was no denying it was there.

I turned off my phone the moment that I crossed the threshold of my apartment and placed it out of sight on the top of my bookshelf. Taking off my clothes as I walked, I grabbed a beer from the refrigerator and headed to the bathroom for a shower. A wonderfully relaxing forty minutes later, I emerged from the steam filled room, put on faded pajama pants and a ten year old softball shirt, and started cleaning. I needed something to keep my mind off of Cain and everything that had happened the previous weekend. Talking to Lilly earlier that day had been like ripping off a fresh scab. I wanted to sit and sulk and perhaps cry but more than anything I wanted to reach out to Cain. I wanted to talk to him, to clear away all of the evidence that he was no good and just be with him again. *Maybe he will text me and ask me to come over just like every other Wednesday.* I caught myself in the middle of the thought and backtracked. *No! I don't want to go down there, I don't want to see him. I don't want to hear from him.* I continued faking it.

It was seven o'clock and my room, bathroom and closet were all spotless. I walked into the family room and plopped down on the couch, eyes wandering to the phone that sat atop the bookshelf. I whipped by head away from it. *No. I am not going to look.* I stood up and walked into the kitchen to start a pot of water boiling for my dinner of spaghetti and chicken. I leaned against the counter after getting out and seasoning the little strips of white meat. They were tiny. I turned my nose up at them as I poked the raw meat with a fork. I had fallen prey to the organic chicken craze that had hit the suburban area I lived in. *At least chicken on steroids could fill you up. I can't believe I paid ten bucks for this crap.* Cain and I had held several conversations about the ridiculousness of the organic food movement, and how it was a total scam, and, in most cases, how the much more expensive organic was no less harmful for you than the regular produce or meat. There alone in my kitchen, I laughed out loud at a comment he had made and allowed warm feelings for Cain to enter my body.

Those pleasant feelings were quickly extinguished by freezing anxiety. *What if he has been texting me all evening. Maybe he has a perfectly logical excuse for not contacting me all this time. What if he has already asked me to come down? I could have been there by now.* I was completely forgetting that Cain rarely invited me over before 8:30 p.m. *I could be in his arms right now but I am not because I am being stubborn and childish.* With that last delusional thought, I rushed over to the bookshelf, yanked the phone down, pressed the power button and stared at the screen, yelling every couple of seconds for the poor thing to hurry up. As the screen came on I waited, punched in my new password and then looked for text message alerts to appear. *I hope it's not too late, I hope that he hasn't already made other plans.* Two new message alerts came one the screen.

"I knew it!" I shrieked. I opened the messages, fingers trembling, walking towards my bedroom to get dressed for the trip to Cain's, then stopped in my tracks. One message was from my mother and the other was from Lilly. My shoulders dropped and I sat down on the floor right where I was. I opened Lilly's message.

Hey cupcake just making sure you are doing OK. Stay strong! I am here if you need me.

I selected the call function and put the phone up to my ear. Lilly answered.

"I need you." I started. I went on to tell her about the last few hours and everything that I was feeling. "This is going to be a lot harder than I thought. I would have been down there in a second and totally forgotten all about how much of a jerk he has been to me. I feel really ashamed and mildly concerned for my emotional well-being."

"You know what? I am really very proud of you for not reaching out to him. That would have solved a lot because I bet you he would have responded right back." Lilly said wisely.

"Really?" I said, hope in my voice. *Why don't I contact him then?*

"Yes, but remember, you deserve better than that, Myra." My face dropped back down,

"Oh, yea. OK." Lilly and I spoke for several minutes more, during which I picked myself off of the floor and continued fixing dinner. By the time I got off of the phone, it was ready to eat. Lilly and I said our farewells until tomorrow and hung up.

At the table I sat in silence and ate my food. I wanted to crawl into bed, better yet under my bed and stay there for several days. I felt a tear gather in my eye and glimpsed it fall into my glass of wine. *How pathetic.* I just wanted to be near him. Doing whatever he was doing. I took my half eaten plate into the kitchen, covered it with plastic wrap and placed it in the refrigerator for lunch the next day. Shutting off lights as I went, I took my glass of wine to my room, closed the door, and climbed into bed. After draining the wine, I shut off the lamp next to me and buried my head deep under the pillow. And there, after promising myself that no one else would know, I let myself cry. I cried for myself. I cried for the messed up situation I had gotten myself into with Cain. I cried for how little he thought of me. I cried for how badly I wanted him and finally I cried because I didn't understand what was happening to me or how to make it stop.

I woke up the next morning on time, by the grace of God. I had forgotten to set my alarm clock, and jumped out of bed with just enough time to wash my face, brush my teeth and throw on a wrinkled shirt and dress pants. Of course, I was participating in a panel discussion with the Director of Operations, A.K.A "Big Dog", and representatives from ten facilities we serviced. I sprayed myself liberally with perfume and ran out of the door after tossing my phone and a banana from the fruit bowl into my purse.

By some miracle I made it in to work on time, just to sit down at my desk and see an email from my director with a rush order on a contract revision for a nursing home on the north side, Horizon's End. *I can't think of a more depressing name for a nursing home. It may as well be named, Last Stop.* I was sure that whoever came up with it had been trying to be lyrical and witty. It was absurd. My panel meeting was at 2:30 p.m., and I felt desperately unprepared in material and emotional energy. I had another meeting with my team at 10:30 a.m. and several invoices that needed my review and signature had to go out to our attorney's offices in Phoenix, Arizona. It was going to be a long day. I dug into work, fingers tapping away like a woodpecker on the keyboard. About an hour later I heard a rap on the top of my cubical wall. I looked up to see Lilly holding a Starbucks cup with the name *Myra* scribbled on it.

"I have a treat for you! Hot soy chai tea latte for the special girl with the big panel discussion today."

"You are the best." I sighed, took the cup in my hand and sipped as she walked away, blonde hair floating behind her, "Mmm, that's perfect."

"You're welcome!" Lilly called back, "Good luck." I smiled to myself because I already had good luck- in attracting great friends into my life.

Fifteen minutes until show time. I had been a superstar all day. I had an extraordinarily productive meeting with the contracts department, had skipped lunch to finish up some contracts and send them off to Arizona, and now I was reviewing potential questions for the panel. I had expected the Big Dog to ask me for a meeting prior to and was surprised by his receptionist's reply that he had no such thing scheduled. I felt great. My confidence level was up to All-Star and knew that I would knock this meeting out of the park. I made a quick note on the agenda in front of me and reached for my cup of now cold, but still delicious tea, head on the paper before me. My wrist flicked an instant too early, the effect of nerves and too much caffeine, and slammed into the lightweight paper cup, knocking it with notable force in the direction of my lap. I jumped up, but it was too late. The white blouse which had finally stopped being wrinkly from that morning, was covered with dark brown chai.

"Shit! Fuck! Balls!" I screamed, jumping up and wiping desperately at my top. Co-workers stood up to look at the spectacle I was creating. "I'm fine guys, sorry for the commotion!" I called back to them as I jogged from my desk and through the double doors of the billing center and into the bathroom.

This is a God damned disaster. I glared at myself in the mirror. It looked like I had been holding a baby whose crappy diaper had leaked all over me. I ran the hot water and began shoving paper towels under the stream then swiping them angrily at my shirt in vain. I caught myself in the mirror and was reminded of Ralph, my ex-boyfriend. I pictured the first time we met after he poured coffee all over me. The sweetness turned sour as my mind went to the awful romantic situation I was currently facing. *Why doesn't Cain treat me the way that Ralph did?* Frustrated with life, love, and stained apparel, I began to cry, still feverishly rubbing away at my ruined blouse. A moment later I heard the door open behind me and I wiped away the tears from my cheeks.

"Oh, honey! What did you do?" Lilly appeared in the mirror next to me. I looked at her, then down at my watch. I had five minutes until I was supposed to be in the large conference room. I raised my head to meet Lilly's eyes and burst into tears again.

"Honey, no." Lilly grabbed my shoulders firmly and turned me around to face her squarely. "Everything is absolutely fine. I have a sweater at my desk. You will put it on and button it up as far as it will go. No one will ever know. While I run and get it, you pull yourself together. This meeting is a huge deal and a great opportunity, which you deserve." Lilly was going for the pep talk of the year as I stood, face wet and red nodding silently. "By the time I get back I want you to be ready to go in there and kick some ass. Splash some cold water on your face, fix your eye makeup," I turned my head to see my black eyeliner running down my face. *I have to invest in some waterproof makeup!* "Saddle up!" With that Lilly patted my shoulder, turned on her heel and sprinted out of the bathroom. *She is right. I have to get it together, right now! I can do this. I can do this!* I gave my best fake supermodel smile as I wiped under my eyes with harsh, low quality paper towels. Lilly reappeared in two minutes with a cardigan and all of my notes and meeting materials. Wordlessly, she kissed me on the cheek, gave me a hug and herded me out of the bathroom, swatting at my butt as she passed by me on her way back to her desk. I walked to the end of the hall and looked through the glass windows of the double doors to the conference room. It was packed with people. At the front of the room was Cody, the Director of Operations, sitting behind a long table filled with what I assumed to be the other Directors who had flown in from all over the country. Next to him was an empty seat. My seat. I placed my hand on the door, took a deep breath and pushed.

13.

The seat behind the steering wheel gave way as I plopped down hard into the leather. *9:37 p.m.* I sighed, exhausted but happy with the completely successful afternoon and evening. Pulling out of the parking lot of the high end steak house on the south side of town I pointed my car in the direction of the north-bound highway. My nerves unwound slowly as I headed home.

The panel discussion that afternoon had been a grand slam. As the contract manager, I answered all of the questions about my department thoroughly and directly. It was almost like someone else, a much more precise and self-assured orator, entered my body and spoke for me. There was a large population of our current clients in the audience, many with questions of why their rates had increased. I quickly defused any tension and explained to them why the necessary increases were made and how it would ensure a more complete coverage package for them. I tossed in several charming smiles, hair tosses and witty jokes, and they were eating out of my hand. All of the facilities present increased their coverage, even those who had been on the verge of ending their contract with us altogether. The golden egg was the reaction from our Director of Operations. He looked like he could have kissed me, his huge red face grinning as he shuffled me around the room to mingle with the clients like a proud papa for an hour after the discussion was over.

"Myra! That was a bang up job! A truly bang up job!" He patted me hard on the back several times.

"Thank you, Cody! I really appreciate that!" I smiled back at him as we exited the conference room.

"All of the directors and I are going to Luna's Steakhouse tonight. We would be thrilled if you would join us for a little bit of business talk and a lot of good food and great scotch. Do you like steak and scotch?" Cody walked with me down the hall towards my department.

"Absolutely!" I answered. "More than most, I would say." He gave me a quick nod.

"Excellent. We will be heading there at around six o'clock!" With that he veered off into another small meeting room and closed the door behind him.

The dinner had been a lot of fun. In the fifty year old steak house filled with deep mahogany tables paired with burgundy leather booths and chairs, the lights barely illuminated the room enough to see the organic Angus on our plates. The brightest lights came from the bar with ornate trimming and brass fixtures. I rarely went out to eat on the south side, but I loved this place from the moment I stepped in. It smelled like cigars even though smoking was no longer allowed inside. I imagined at some point in history the place had been one large cloud of Cuban smoke.

There were twelve of us at a large table, I the only female and the youngest by ten years at least. Sitting quietly, contributing when appropriate, for the most part I listened to the conversation. You would have thought these men ruled the free world rather than running an ambulance company. Each one was more self-important than the last. A few of them had a couple of questions for me and how I ran the contracts department. As I spoke, I glanced over at The Big Dog who was pointing at me from the other side of the table and speaking quietly to a gentleman beside him. Then nodded and winked at me when he saw that he had my attention. *Peculiar.*

Several hours of appetizers, wine, steak, dessert and then at least two rounds of scotch, and I had every reason to be content. I turned on the radio and settled in for the thirty minute drive home. My cell phone had remained in the car while I was in the restaurant and I leaned forward to reach into the glove compartment and pulled it out.

One new text message

My thoughts immediately jumped to Cain, heart quickening, stomach lurching. I opened the message and read a number and a message that I was not expecting.

Hey Myra, It's Marcus. I hope you are having a great week so far. Mine has been hectic. I'm sorry I didn't contact you sooner. I was hoping that you would like to have dinner with me? Tomorrow night?

I wasn't as excited as I should have been but my spirits did get a lift. I waited until I had exited the highway on the north side and was sitting at a stop light to respond.

Hi Marcus! My week has been just fine! I am sorry your week has been crazy but I am really happy to hear from you. I would like to have dinner with you very much.

By the time I climbed up the three flights of stairs to my apartment, I barely had the energy to put on my pajamas. I stood in front of my bathroom mirror and took off Lilly's black cardigan to reveal my ruined white blouse, stained in deep brown. I laughed out loud, covered my face and thought of how Lilly had come to my rescue when I was on the verge of an emotional breakdown. *Sweet Lilly. I need to take her out to dinner this weekend or something.* I removed my clothing down to my underwear and shut off the light. The last thing I remembered was hearing my body make a soft thud onto the mattress.

Work flew by the following day. I felt on top of the moon after my stellar performance with the center's director. Midday, Lilly and I jumped around the parking lot and danced in cycles as I retold all of the glorious details.

"Great job, honey!" She cheered, cigarette in hand. "I knew you would knock them dead. You really are a terrific public speaker!" I was sure I was not, in actuality, but I appreciated her support.

"Thank you Lilly-Pad! I would not have been able to do it without you!" We hugged and giggled and I went on to tell her about the text message and dinner invitation from Marcus.

"Oh, wow. That is really exciting." I had already filled her in on the time we spent together at the bar while he worked. "Are you nervous?" I looked around at the cars in the parking lot while thinking.

"I'm not sure. I don't think so." I spoke slowly.

"Do you think that your excitement has been stifled by Cain?" I made a face like something smelled awful and flipped my hand dismissively in the air.

"Yea, probably."

Lilly tossed her cigarette onto the ground, reached for me and placed her arm around my shoulders.

"You know, it's like my mom always said," she paused while we walked through the building's doors, "the best way to get over someone is the get under someone else." I scoffed at her, pretending to be appalled, then continued through the cafeteria and down the hall to our desks, seriously contemplating the validity of that adage.

Hello, Myra. I will be leaving my apartment in about five minutes which will put me at your house in about thirty- five. I can't wait! See you soon! I looked at my phone and continued to put on my makeup, satisfaction arising at his excitement for our date. In a magazine I had read earlier that day, I saw a tutorial on how to best apply makeup to make brown eyes stand out. I was doing a pretty good job of recreating the technique. My burgundy blouse was tucked into a brown structured pencil skirt. Marcus had not specified where we were going, but it was always better to look over-dressed than under. Another lesson from my grandmother's book. I had done my best all day to not check my phone for a text from Cain. It had been five days of radio silence and I decided that if I didn't hear from him today, I would delete his number and never speak to him or of him again.

With the extra twenty five minutes before Marcus' arrival, I touched up my nails, polished the tan knee high boots that I had decided were essential to my outfit, and cleaned out my purse. I was just looking in the mirror to touch up my lip gloss when my phone rang from the other room. After pressing my lips together and turning off the light, I jogged to my phone and picked it up.

"Hi, Myra! I am downstairs!" Marcus sounded very chipper.

"Hello, Marcus! Wonderful! I will be down in three minutes." I shut off the phone took a deep breath, gathered my purse and coat and walked out the door.

The most challenging thing I had to do all day was maintain composure after I breezed out of the building and was confronted with the spectacle of Marcus, dressed in a dark gray tweed sports coat on top of a black dress shirt, dark denim and shiny black leather loafers, standing next to a red Porsche, no more than two years old, holding a single pink rose. If I would have been a star of a 1940's movie, I would have fainted for sure. *Play it cool. Just be cool.* I walked with confident strides towards him; the sidewalk had never seemed so long. The clicking of my four and a three quarter inch heels sounded like a drumroll. The closer I got, the more I noticed how uncomfortable Marcus looked. He ran his hand through his hair several times in a row and smiled, relaxed his face and then smiled again. As soon as I got within ear shot he called out to me.

"Hi, Myra" moved forward to meet me, closing the ten yard gap. He took a few steps and caught his foot on an area of uneven cement. His strong legs were moving him with such inertia that he flew right at me. Quickly, I sidestepped him and caught him under the arm, helping him regain his balance.

"Oh, God, I am so sorry. Are you OK?" He straightened up quickly and ran his hands through his hair again. I giggled.

"I should be asking *you* that! I'm fine! I have great reaction time." I said smiling, trying to hold in my laughter. He nodded quickly then smiled.

"Hi." He reached in and gave me a hug. He smelled spicy like clove. The sun was setting directly to our right and reflected beautifully off of his olive complexion. "You look absolutely stunning." He stepped back and looked at me, then handed me the rose in his hand. "This is for you." I looked up at his eyes and felt a quick shock like static electricity from a doorknob and glanced away quickly. I stared at the spot right between his eyebrows instead. They were thick and shapely. *I wonder if he waxes them.*

Thank you, Marcus. This is really nice." He took my arm and my eyes found the car parked in front of us again. He walked me around the front of his car and instinctively I stuck out my hand to graze it across the hood, the texture of the smooth paint invoking a sigh. My escort opened the door for me and I stepped down into the beautiful German work of art, heart racing. It was the first time I had ever been in a Porsche. I took a deep breath as Marcus closed my door and walked around to the driver's side, enjoying the new car smell. The interior wasn't nearly as tiny as I had imagined and there was quite a bit of leg room, which was how Marcus and his large stature were able to fit.

"So! Where are we off to? Nice car by the way." I couldn't resist acknowledging what felt like the pink elephant in the room which brought up a lot of questions. It certainly blew Marcus' struggling bartender/med-student image out of the water.

"We are going to Rouge. It's a Belgian restaurant. Do you like mussels?" I sat up a little straighter. Rouge was my absolute favorite restaurant in the city and I told him so in excited tones. "Perfect!" He smiled, dimples deepening. He turned over the engine and I let out a joyful

squeal which made Marcus jump. *Oops.* He laughed and turned to me. "You like cars, huh?"
I was an absolute enthusiast.

"I do! Very much so. I have actually always wanted a Porsche. I promised myself a few years ago that if I am still unmarried by the age of thirty-two, I am going to buy myself one."

"That sounds like a great idea!" Marcus pulled out of my apartment parking lot and onto the main road and I held on to the side of my seat as the car hummed below us. "I noticed you reached out and touched the hood as we walked by," *Busted.* Marcus voice was very somber. "Men have died for less, you know." Uncertain how to proceed, I started in slowly,

"I'm sorry Marcus, it's kind of a thing I do. Using sensory memory I mean." I decided to stop talking before he thought I was a weirdo. It was true, whenever I found myself in a new situation, I liked to use as many of my senses as possible to creative vivid memories for later.

"That is very interesting!" Marcus sounded sincere. He took his eyes from the road and shot me a sly grin, "And I was just kidding. I don't mind at all. You can touch anything that you want." *What?* "Oh, um. Yea." Marcus stumbled a little after realizing how his last remark could have been taken and then continued, "This car was a gift. I respect it and take good care of it, but maybe I would be more protective if I had purchased it with my own hard earned money." It was very insightful of him and I verbalized that. "Thanks. I try to keep a solid head on my shoulders." He smiled softly and then patted my arm playfully.

Upon entering the car, I had crossed my legs at the ankles, however, as I got more comfortable, I crossed my legs at the knees towards Marcus. My mother had always taught that crossing at the ankle was the proper etiquette while in the company of unrelated men. Marcus stole a glance and I used my hand to cover the scar on my knee self-consciously. We continued our conversation about foreign cars. He was a huge fan of the Ferrari and all things Italian.

The twenty minutes it took to reach our destination flew by. Finding enough things to talk about on a first date could be tricky, but Marcus and I were sailing smoothly. I asked questions about his job at the bar and he asked me about my time at college. It was all very easy and I felt the nervousness of first date jitters melt away into the premium Italian leather seats.

"Let me get your door." Marcus had just parked, quickly turned off the engine, and was out of the car in a flash. Apparently, chivalry was alive, well, and making me feel uncomfortable. He was at my door in an instant. *Did this man just jog around the car?* My door opened and in my best red carpet tribute, I swung my long brown legs out of the car, toes pointed, and placed my heels on the pavement. Ever so delicately I placed my hand on Marcus' extended one and rose from the car. Marcus was beaming like a prom date as we proceeded towards the restaurant. I felt on display. Marcus was adorable, and any woman would have been thrilled to be with him. I was no exception. But all of the ceremony had me wondering who it was all for.

"You smell really nice." Marcus spoke, leaning into me slightly as he pulled open yet another door for me. I smiled at him weakly. I thought back to if I had remembered to put on perfume that evening. More often than not I neglected the quite large and growing collection of scents that lined my bathroom shelf in brightly colored glass bottles. He looked away for an instant and I discreetly passed a wrist in front of my nose and detected a trace of cocoa. A small smile lifted the corner of my mouth. It was one of my favorite fragrances my father had brought back from one of his business trips to Paris. I had worn it for years. Marcus excused himself to check us in and I let my eyes wander around the open room. The restaurant specialized in traditional Belgian fare: mussels, frites, crepes, and of course beer. Large leaded glass windows spanned from floor to ceiling on some walls and other areas were covered in smoky colored antique wood panels. Industrial looking lighting fixtures swung ever so slightly from the ceiling, their light reflected from the polished concrete floor. I was so taken in by contrasts of the textures and colors that I didn't notice Marcus trying to get my attention. I was turning ever so slightly in a circle after noticing an etching weaving its way around the room where the ceiling and wall met, when I felt the lightest touch on the base of my spine. I turned quickly to see Marcus standing next to me, staring up as well.

"I have never seen that before." He pointed with the hand that didn't rest on my back. Warmth started to emanate from where he touched me. "They can seat us now. Are you ready?"

"Of course." I found the hostess standing next to the entrance to the dining room and moved towards her, shoes clicking with sharp echoes. We followed the ebony clad waitress, winding through tables and the hum of dinnertime conversation to the far corner of the building and into a small room off the main dining area. The door to the room was completely composed of elaborate stained glass except for its frame. It depicted a milkmaid sitting on an emerald hill with blue skies and clouds behind her. There were three tables in the room, all empty of guests and arranged with the intention of privacy. The farthest table from the door had a pink rose on the place setting facing the window. It occurred to me as we continued towards it that that was my seat. I looked at the rose, then at Marcus, then back at the rose.

"Oh, is this for me as well?" *Of course it is. When the hell did he put that there?* "Thank you so much, Marcus. You are so incredibly sweet." And I kissed him on the cheek because I felt obligated at that point. I hadn't known the side room existed and it was very obviously reserved for special guests. The walls were covered in original paintings and art pieces. This space, darker than the large room, was lit with ornate steel and glass hanging fixtures. Even the plates and glasses were different and more upscale than the ones we had passed in the dining room. If there was such a thing as a Belgian mafia, which I had no idea if there was, and that mafia had a large membership there in the city, I was sure that this was the room they plotted in. Marcus moved behind my chair to pull it out and then back in as I sat, which I was horrible at. I could never quite get the flow of when to sit down and I always ended up having to awkwardly scoot my seat up against the table. This time was no different.

I had officially reached my tolerance of romantic gestures which apparently wasn't very high. So when the waitress came by and offered us a wine list, I quickly declined. The last thing I wanted to do was to sip wine and attempt to be delicately enchanting.

"Actually, I love the beer here. May I take a look at your list of drafts?" Marcus looked a little disappointed.

"So you are a whiskey and beer girl?" Marcus leaned back in his chair after we had each ordered craft brews.

"I am." I smiled brightly at him. "I also love sports…"

"And cars!" He cut in. "Yes, you are quite a …enigma? Isn't that what you called me the other day?" I laughed.

"How so? What makes me an enigma?" I questioned, interested in how he saw me.

"You have a very sweet, down to Earth demeanor. You don't seem high strung or pretentious. I have heard you laugh about ten times already tonight. You seem completely relaxed." At that moment I was leaning on both elbows towards him. My grandmother was probably rolling over in her grave. "Look at you! Completely at home on a first date."

I tried to pull up my posture a little bit without him noticing. I certainly had been raised with manners and to display them in public but there was something about Marcus that made me extraordinarily comfortable. After I got over the initial shock of how show-stopping dashing he was, that is. He was right, this was a first date! I should have been nervous and bumbling. Instead I was as cool as a cucumber. "But you are totally uncomfortable with romantic gestures. I noticed with the car door and the roses. It's like you aren't used to them. Have you not been exposed to that very often?" I opened my mouth to answer him. The fact was that I had not, actually, been romanced like that in the past. I cleared my throat and tried to speak, but Marcus started again, "It seems to me that someone like you shouldn't settle for anything less than being swept off your feet. Hence, the enigma."

I was amused. *Someone like me? You just met me! Ok, who is this clown? Take it easy, smooth talker.* I looked at him suspiciously, trying to detect any bullshit that he may be trying to sell me, and received a sweet smile in return, his eyebrows slightly raised. He looked like a cherub. From somewhere deep in my stomach I felt a lurch. A kind of spasm that began to creep up my stomach and I noticed that my hand was lying on the table across from his. At the same moment, his eyes glanced down at my long fingers. *Oh, no. Is he going to try to hold my hand on this table?* Fear struck me and mixed with the nervous feeling that had spread north and south to my throat and legs. I tore my eyes from his face and saw, to my horror that his palm was beginning to lift off from its cream linen launch pad. I had no idea why but I wanted nothing more than for him to put his hand back down. Out of nowhere because, again, God is good, the waitress popped beside me, startling me and taking the wind out of Marcus' sails.

"Oh good. " I said a little too eagerly while shooting the waitress an appreciative look. I raised my glass to Marcus over the center of the table. "Salud."

"Salud." He addressed me back, looking impressed. I took at long swing from the mug and Marcus smirked at me from over his own glass.

"So where did you grow up?" Marcus settled in after we had both ordered our meals and served the first date tennis ball.

I can't breathe. I cannot breathe! My hand was on my chest and I was panting for air, absolutely hysterical. Marcus sat across the table red faced, hand over mouth, laughing in deep convulsions. He had just finished telling me a story involving him, his Italian grandmother and his ex-girlfriend who was Jamaican.

"And that is why I can never take my Abuela back to Lil Tony's Chicken and Waffles."

"You poor, *poor* man!" I was having the best first date of my life. My face hurt from laughing and smiling nonstop for the two hours that we had occupied the little room. It was absolutely refreshing and vastly unexpected how willing Marcus was to poke fun at himself and make me laugh at his expense. He was doing a hell of a job. After one last round of laughter which ended in an unexpected snort, I covered my mouth quickly with a wide eyed expression on my face.

"Whaa? What was that Ms. Piggy?" His faced held in shocked glee. I screeched through my embarrassed grin.

"I have allergies! You can't make fun of people with disabilities! Who taught you manners?" I accosted him.
He laughed and apologized insincerely. "You are right. I am awfully sorry ma'am." Then shot me a wink.
 I had been known to snort for the entirety of my life. I could usually control them, unless I was disoriented and tired from laughing too hard. In which case all bets were off. I looked at him and tried to play hurt, sticking my lower lip out ever so slightly and straightening my face. He wasn't having that.

"Uh huh. Allergies huh? Well, do me a favor and tell Kermit that I am sorry about taking out his woman. Though I may be doing him a favor, considering your and his rocky and obsessive past." I made an indignant face and stuck my tongue out at him, then giggled. I liked him teasing me. It was much like our time together at the bar but this time I was certain about one thing. He was interested in me. Marcus reached towards the center of the table for more mussels and I dipped my piece of baguette into the cast iron pot at the same time. Our skin touched freezing us both. My heart quickened as I looked slowly to his face. *Yup! Something is definitely here.* He smiled back at me and winked again at which I playfully scoffed and pulled my hand away.

After another two hours of loud talking, laughing and teasing, four and a half more beers between us, the most delicious dark chocolate and raspberry mousse I had ever tasted, which we split, and the gentle nudging of our waitress who informed us twice that the restaurant had been closed for forty five minutes, we left. As we walked out of the small dining room, me, my two roses and a beautiful Italian man, into the completely deserted main restaurant, Marcus stuck out his arm for me to take. I looked at it for a second, distastefully.

"Oh get over it." He said dramatically grabbing my hand and looped it through his. "I like you, but you have to let me treat you the way I want. As long as it's not badly, you need to just trust that it is what you deserve." His tone was soft but firm. "Just try to enjoy it, OK?" I met his eyes and made a face. I didn't object though and I hoped he took that as a small victory. We neared the stainless steel front doors and I let go of his arm and quickly stepped in front of him, grabbing the large handle, cold in my hand, and swept the door open, letting night air in, then stepped back with it to allow him passage.

"After you, sir." I smiled brightly at him, loving his reaction of slight agitation as he passed, shaking his head in disapproval. I skipped quickly to catch up with him as he waited for me, then slid my arm in his and continued walking to the car through the abandoned parking lot. "Look Marcus," I started in "I like you, but you have to let me treat you the way I want. As long as it's not badly, you need to just trust that it is what you deserve." He stopped dead in his tracks with a bemused look on his face as I finished mocking him, "Just try to enjoy it, ok?" I took a step closer to him, hoping I hadn't gone too far and offended him. I hadn't.

"You are something else." He took a step, closing the gap between us and bringing with him the perfect smell of his body. Gently he wrapped his fingers and palm around the nape of my neck and pulled me into him, placing a single brush of his lips upon mine. Then he was gone, side stepped me and walked on to the car. As silent and subtle as arsenic, that kiss had almost knocked me down. What I hoped was an inaudible noise like the coo of a dove left my lips as I tried to regain composure. I spun around to see Marcus leaning up against his blazing red car, holding my door open. I walked to him, attempting to look sexy and graceful but sure I wasn't pulling it off. I stepped into the car, purposely grazing my hand across his chest and disappeared inside.

I watched him as he settled in and started the car, turned on our seat warmers and adjusted the AC. He was very meticulous as he fixed all three mirrors even though no one had been in the car since we exited a few hours prior. We pulled away from the restaurant and exited onto the main road. I enjoyed the feeling of him shifting from first to second, to third and then back to second and I placed my hand on top of his controlling the gears. His skin was soft and warm as it powerfully switched the stick back and forth into its proper place. I could feel the muscles and tendons responding and flexing with every motion, the ignition from the engine traveling through the stick, into Marcus and then into me. I was completely exhilarated. Marcus spoke to me in soft tones, explaining the mechanics of the six speed engine as we exited onto the freeway. I knew that he wouldn't need to shift again anytime soon, but I left my hand on his because I loved the feeling it gave me. He extended his fingers, interlocking his with my own, intensifying my high. The ride went way too fast for my liking, and soon we were back at my apartment. Marcus pulled up to the curb in front of my building and turned off the engine.

He looked at me warningly. "You know what to do." I exaggerated a sigh and sat still after unbuckling my seat belt. Marcus jumped out of the car and ran around the front to open my door. I stuck my legs out again and took his hand. He pulled me up into him forcefully and slid one arm around my waist, holding me to him. Before he could make a first move I lifted my face and placed my lips on his. He inhaled quickly and then released slowly, melting further into my body. His lips were incredible, like warm pouty marshmallows. I pulled away slowly, catching sight of his breathtaking eyes only inches away. He moved his hand to the back of my neck lightly.

"You have the softest lips I have ever kissed." He said to me in a dazed whisper. I laughed out, probably killing the mood.

"I was just thinking the same thing about you." Slowly, reluctantly, I stepped away from him and closed the car door. He took my hand and began to walk with me towards the entrance of the building. I stopped quickly. "Um, you aren't coming up to my apartment Marcus." Not that I didn't want him to. I most certainly did. But I refused to build yet another relationship on the foundation of sex. Marcus flashed a playful smile at me and for an instant I changed my mind. Bending to inches before my face he whispered.

"Oh, don't worry. I won't come up until you are begging me to." He stuck out his tongue in jest and then walked on ahead of me to open the door. *That sounds like a challenge.* I walked through the entry.

"Good night. Marcus." I said as I passed and started up the stairs.

"Good night, princepessa." He called. I turned and walked quickly back down to him, grabbed his jacket and pulled him into me, kissing him.

14.

The door slammed behind me and I leaned backwards resting my head against its cool metal. Slowly a gush of air escaped my lungs and I closed my eyes. After spending several hours getting to know Marcus the connection I felt was undeniable. He had a wonderful sense of humor, was a great listener, and was very considerate. I let my mind wander back to our kiss, his hand on the base of my spine holding me supportively. Body still tingling from the beer and Marcus' touch, I skipped over into the kitchen to pour myself a glass of water. *I wonder what he's like in bed. My guess is super passionate. Powerful yet thoughtful.* A chill went through my body as I imagined him completely nude. I turned quickly to walk out of the kitchen and I caught the scent of Marcus. Digging my nose into the collar of my blouse I inhaled purposefully. He was all over me. I stood and breathed deeply for several moments, picturing his bright smile and mesmerizing eyes. In the absolute silence of my apartment a vibration came from somewhere by the door. My cell phone was buzzing from deep inside my purse. I smiled, and jogged to where I had dropped my belongings on the cream tile upon entering my home, looking for a *good night* message from Marcus.

Hey there. What's up? A text message from Cain. It was eleven thirty. I was stabbed with an emotion and recognized it immediately as disappointment. For a few short hours I had totally forgotten that Cain existed, and now he was crashing back into my consciousness, bringing with him anxiety, trepidation, and anger. I took the phone and cold water back to my bedroom and plopped down on my white down comforter. *Thirty minutes. This man waited to contact me until there was thirty minutes left in my five day deadline.* It seemed like something the arrogant Cain would do just to spite me. I took a moment to imagine what it would have been like if he hadn't contacted me and left me with a legitimate excuse to cut him out of my life forever. I had just been out on a fantastic first date with a beautiful man who wanted to treat me with all the respect I deserved and more. *Why would I want to spend my time on someone who has disregarded me and my feelings, disrespected me and showed no regret time and time again?* There was no way that I was going to respond to Cain that night. I was too afraid that he would ask me to come over.

Undressing slowly, I took note of my feelings. While I hoped I was no danger to myself, I felt the tick at the back of my head just itching to contact Cain, itching to drive down to see him, to smell him, to be held by him, to have sex with him. I lay in bed and stared at the ceiling in the dark, my fear of Cain, and myself, radiating off of me. I closed my eyes and tried to sleep, tried to think about Marcus and about the fabulous life that we would have traveling around the world, but somehow Cain's face kept creeping in where Marcus' should have been. I corrected myself several times and then finally I gave in. There Cain and I were on the Italian coast sailing sapphire waters, and then in a little town eating at a café as the sun set, and then horseback riding through an emerald vineyard. Always glowing in the sun, always smiling, always perfectly attired.

I awoke to a message from Marcus.

Thank you so much for coming to dinner with me, Myra. You are an amazing woman and I hope to spend a lot more time getting to know you in the near future. I rolled back over and smiled a thanks that I hadn't ruined my wonderful night by responding to Cain.

"Honey that thing is broken and has been broken for years. Please throw it away!" Harper sat across the table from me at our favorite Mexican restaurant. Our short red-headed waitress had just set two jumbo margaritas in front of us. The broken item that he was referring to was my "gay-dar", the ability to discern homosexual males from heterosexual ones. "I cannot believe you thought even for an instant that Marcus was gay!"
I took a sip from the salted rim in front of me and then gave him a look.

"Hello! He works at a gay club as a bartender with no shirt and a splattering of glitter on his chest. My bad, but I think it was a totally justified mistake." I dipped a golden chip into the bowl of queso in front of me, knowing that I shouldn't, being lactose intolerant and all.

"So how was the date?" Harper dismissed me with a shake of his head. The chip had almost reached my lips before I stopped and looked at Harper.

"How did you know we went out?" I hadn't gotten a chance to tell him about our date yet. It was just the night before. He looked at me and batted his long eyelashes.

"Girl please! You thought Marcus just magically wanted to go to *your favorite* restaurant?" I looked on at him in shock. *Oh, he's good!*

"You…"

"Yep! He texted me about your wallet and about how you two spent the afternoon together and I thought I'd help that brotha out! Girl he is fine, and if I can't have him… why shouldn't you?"

I smiled and laughed. "Thanks, mama! Well, has he told you how the date went yet then?"

"Oh, no. I was going to wait until you told me before I talked to him. Look at me- Mother and match maker." He twirled his wrist in the air regally. I went on to explain with painstaking detail the beginning, middle and end of our date. Harper sat across from me sipping, cheering, clapping and slapping at the table.

"I cannot believe you didn't take him upstairs with you! You would have had to pry me off of his sexy ass!"

I laughed out loud, feeling my face heat up with the thought of Marcus. I had never been with an Italian man before. *Italians are known for their passionate lovemaking skills, right? Or is that the French?*

"Yes, I am definitely attracted to him." Harper leaned towards me over the table and nodded his perfectly smooth chestnut head, "But I want to take it slow with him. We all know what happened with the last person I moved at hyper speed with." I looked down at my margarita as I finished the sentence, and then took a long sip, trying to wash down the thought of Cain.

"No girl, we really don't. What ever happened with Cain?" *Wouldn't we ALL like to know?* I explained to Harper everything from Friday, Saturday and Sunday. Then about the long silence of the week which was finally broken with a text.

"What do you mean *Hey there? What's up?* Is there something wrong with that boy? Did he really expect you to respond to that bullshit after everything? You *DIDN'T* respond, right?" Harper was appalled.

"No of course not." I said moping. It was true. I hadn't responded, but that had been a feat of sheer will, and it had been less than twenty four hours. I had to leave my cell phone in my car that day at work to stop myself from texting him. When I got back to my car after work Cain had sent me a few text messages asking me about my plans for the weekend. I put my phone in the trunk which was where it still lay. *Whatever gets the job done!* For an instant I thought that maybe Cain was asking me what my plans were for the weekend because he wanted to see me, but a quick trip through recent history convinced me that that was not the case. Cain never made plans with me for the weekends, none that he actually followed through with at least.

"That is very, very funny though. God has a sense of humor for sure." Harper chuckled to himself. "After you have a fabulous night with a good man… here comes Mr. Bad-Boy to tempt you away."

Oh yea- God is fucking hilarious.

Three days later and I still didn't see the humor. I had maintained radio silence which was fed by Cain's daily texts. I woke up every morning to the same thing.

Good morning, gorgeous. I hope you have a great day.

And at the end of every day the same,

Good night, beautiful.

When I rolled out of bed on the third day there was no text from Cain. I ran outside to my car to check my phone in its home in my glove compartment a few times that morning while at work, after a meeting and then again right before lunch. *Nothing.* The day went smoothly, and it was just as I finished my glass of Sauvignon Blanc from my couch, and looked at my phone to see no new text message that something hit me like a punch in the stomach, reverberating off the white walls of my apartment. *Why hasn't he texted me?* I sat as still as a statue. *Is this it? Is this the end of us? Is he sitting somewhere wishing that I would reach out to him? Am I making the wrong decision?*

All of the sudden I felt very alone. Out of all of the voices trumpeting in my head, I grabbed onto Lilly's telling me all of the great things I deserved. I picked my phone up off of the coffee table and started a text message.

Hey you. I hope you are having a wonderful night. I am off to bed. Let's get together soon, OK?

I selected Marcus' number from my contact list and pressed send. I felt good about my choice, and with the absence of Cain in my life, there was a space for something real and good to fill it. I climbed into bed and no sooner than I shut my eyes, I was awaken to the sound of my alarm the next morning.

My resolve lasted until about 9:00 a.m. the next day. I was completing the final review of my team's monthly invoices when a song came on over the speakers that sat in the corner of my desk. I had never heard it on the radio before although it was several years old. As the beginning notes reached my ears, I stopped reading the spreadsheet, eyes frozen on a line explaining the total service charges over the previous year of a nursing home on the far-east side. My hands, planted on top of my desk like bricks, did not respond to the command my mind gave them to change the station. I was held completely captive to the rock blues hybrid that I had listened to several times with Cain. Flashes of memories accosted me like rounds of a semi-automatic weapon. There he and I were, lying in bed, laughing and holding each other. I closed my eyes and I could feel him there with me and all the happiness and wholeness that his presence always brought. Adrenaline coursed through me, my stomach tied itself in knots, and then, as if someone was yanking at them, threatened to be ripped to shreds.

Just as I felt the sting of tears welling up, the song ended and released me. I stood quickly and walked out of the large room. In the restroom, I leaned heavily on the cold counter in front of the mirror and stared into my sad, confused eyes. I stayed there for several moments, voices booming in the silent fluorescently lit room. I didn't want to contact him, I knew that wouldn't solve the deep issues that saturated our relationship. Would he, could he ever really be present? If I contacted him, I would be committing myself to continuing in something that didn't serve my needs. Contacting him would be a clear declaration of what I thought I deserved in love, and it wasn't much. But he would be in my life, and even in the smallest capacity that seemed better than nothing at all.

Maybe if I just talk to him about it. But I had already done that. The last time I saw him I went over what I wanted from him, though perhaps not in the best setting. I had been drunk and more than a little aggressive. *If I tried again, in a more calm and rational way, maybe he would hear me.* I frowned doubtfully in the mirror. Maybe he could shed some light on what was going on with him. Something had to give and it occurred to me that no matter how much I wished the contrary I wasn't ready to let that something be me giving up.

I took a detour through the cafeteria to get a drink of water, passing the free soda fountain machine, and walked the long way back to my desk to give myself as much time as possible to think over my decision. As soon as I got back to my phone there was going to be very little stopping me from texting Cain, and I wanted to make sure that I seemed as calm as possible. *What is going to be my excuse for not responding to his texts for several days?* I knew that ignoring his communication for several days surely seemed to him as payback for him doing the same to me. That was the first morning I felt safe enough to keep my phone at my desk rather than in the trunk of my car where it had spent the work days. *I should have left it at home.* I looked at the cool black device in my hand.

Hey there. Sorry. I just got back from a business trip. Such a bold faced lie was a clear sign of my desperation, even I could see that. I had committed though, I had to sell it.

I was using a work phone. How are you?
I placed the phone on my desk and shook my head at myself, having no idea why I had just made up that story. It occurred to me that I didn't want to look like the bad guy. I shrugged off the enormous feeling of being the biggest hypocrite who ever lived and continued to work on invoices, cell phone in peripheral vision so I would notice it light up when he responded. It only took ten minutes.

Hey gorgeous. It's good to hear from you. How was your trip? You miss me?
Relief over took me like the first hit of a drug after rehab, relaxing me deeply into my chair. I realized I had been in a rigid posture since I sent the message.

It was fine. I do miss you. I am great. How are you?
I could have sprinted around the building ten times. Now all that was left was the anxiety of when I would see him again. That bug buzzed in my ear, growing increasingly louder for the next two hours, as Cain and I communicated via instant messaging on the computer, so I could at least pretend to be working as I stared at the screen. Every time he responded I expected him to extend an invitation to come and see him.

So what are you up to tonight?
Finally! I couldn't control myself quickly enough to edit my response to look less desperate.

Nothing. Want to hang out? I can bring some takeout down and we can chill.

I stared at the screen like the meaning of the universe was about to flash across it. I sat there for about twelve years, eyes locked and near watering from the strain.

Yea, sure. Ill text you. OK- Meetings for the rest of the afternoon. Talk to you later.

The email I sent to my manager wasn't a complete untruth. I tried to continue working for another hour but the anxious feeling in my stomach was making me physically ill. Every time I tried to write a sentence of a summary my mind would run away to Cain and the prospect of seeing him again. *What am I going to say?* At one point I worked myself into such a flustered state that I started writing him a letter.

I know that this may scare you, but I am so totally in love with you, and I know that we have something extraordinary here. Just let me be there for you and I will do everything I can to make you happy.

I deleted it as soon as I read it over once. *I sound like a crazy person.* The truth was that I was the one that was scared, terrified actually. After I stopped by Lilly's desk to let her know that I had a stomach ache and was going home, I jumped in my car and drove the forty minutes, daydreaming about Cain the entire way. Thank God for autopilot.

The clock on the microwave read twelve-fifteen p.m. I had at least six hours to sit and brew. My apartment was spotless, all my laundry was done and daytime television seemed like a bad idea. Right now network television was rife with talk shows featuring paternity tests and cheaters, and soap operas' stories of unrequited love. I had enough drama in my life without filling my head with other people's problems. I sat on the couch and took a deep breath, racking my brain for something to calm my nerves. My hands shook a little as I grabbed a beer from the back of my refrigerator. The carbonation stung briefly as I took long swallow, then headed to the bathroom for a hot shower. As I leaned against the cool side of the tub I let the acknowledgment that I was losing it sink in. *How much longer can I do this?* There was nothing healthy about the fact that in the same head on my shoulders I yearned to be with Cain and without him in equally desperate measures. I glanced at myself in the mirror while drying my hair, and the face I saw looked haggard, like I was in the middle of a war. The disappointment I felt in myself for the inability to keep my emotions in check was etched across my brow and swelling in the bags under my eyes.

Luckily my apartment was only five minutes away from a north side mall, and soon I found myself in a lingerie department, pulling through a rack of lacy corsets and negligees. Out of everything I was thinking, the fact that if I wanted Cain I was going to have to devote myself to getting him burned most brightly. The back and forth had to stop. I knew that I wanted us to be together. The challenge before me now was convincing him, and the black bustier I carried into the dressing room couldn't hurt. Bag in hand, feeling more calm than I had all day, after spending the entirety of my weekly grocery and gas money on my purchase, I walked past the new purses and shoes of the brightly lit store stationed with sales people milling around a few mid-day shoppers.

I came upon the transparent display cases of the jewelry department, and the back of someone's head caught my eye. The thick dark brown hair of a man was familiar and before I could fully recognize him and hide, Ralph, my most recent boyfriend turned around and locked eyes with me. A smile swept across his narrow face and mine answered his with a toothy grin accompanied with a rush of warm comfort. I began speaking from several feet away.

"I heard you would be visiting soon." Instinctively my arms rose and wrapped themselves around his small frame firmly.

"Myra. How are you?" the low growl of his voice felt amazing. I held on to him for a few seconds longer than was friendly and then stepped back, hand still resting on the bicep of my once sweetheart.

"I'm great! How are you, love?" I hadn't realized how much I had missed him. Seeing him again reminded me of how much he had loved me and how fantastic and secure that had felt. He had been devoted to me. The fact that I had underestimated the value of that swept my thoughts. His deep brown eyes shone down at me.

"I'm excellent." He motioned to his right. "Myra I want you to meet Hilary, my fiancée. She is from here. Isn't that cool?" I felt my face drop sharply. *Wait. What?* We had only been separated for six months. *You sure didn't waste any time.* I tried to pick my smile up off of the ground as I turned my head to the tall shapely blonde Barbie Doll standing next to Ralph and extended my hand.

"Oh wow! Hi! It's nice to meet you. Congratulations." I heard the lack of enthusiasm in my voice as soon as the words left my lips. I looked at the very shiny contents of the case behind them. Fiery diamond rings sparkled, mocking me intensely. Barbie accepted my hand hesitantly and gripped a few of my fingers lightly before quickly letting go, then gave me a once over. I could have kicked my own ass for wearing the pair of faded yoga pants tucked into fur lined boots and pink novelty Empire State Building long sleeved tee shirt. I looked like I just got out of bed, locs thrown up in a loose pony tail. I could hear my fashionista grandmother scolding me in a tone that said *have I taught you nothing!?* Ralph jumped in,

"Yea, we are in town to celebrate our engagement and to start making some wedding plans." I didn't care. I would have rather been having a pap smear while the entire city watched, than standing with my ex-lover and his snooty fiancée, clearly interrupting a personal and romantic moment.

"I am so incredibly happy for you Ralph, this is wonderful." *God I hope they cannot smell the insincerity rolling off of me.* "I have to get to a dentist appointment, but it was fantastic seeing you." I turned to Hilary who was disinterestedly looking at the dresses across the aisle, "And I am so glad I got to meet you, Hilary." Upon hearing her name she whipped her head back to me and gave me a half-assed smile. I reached in to give Ralph the kind of awkward hug someone gives a family member that they don't particularly like and turned to walk away.

"We are getting together at Dante's tonight with the gang who are flying in from D.C, if you would like to join us. We will be there at 8 p.m." Ralph extended an offer that we both knew I didn't want. I would have sooner died then be in a room full of Ralph's old friends, who all hated me for breaking his heart, and his new gorgeous soon to be wife, when I was alone and destined to die a spinster due to my poor life choices regarding men.

"That sounds great-I have plans with a friend-but if I have time I will certainly stop by." I looked at his soft eyes once more before I turned and walked away willing myself forcibly not to glance around. If his oh-so familiar cologne hadn't lingered in my nose all the way home I would have cast it off as a horrible hallucination.

I hadn't thought this through. Or maybe I hadn't thought about this clearly, due to the two beers and half a bottle of wine I had consumed when I got home from my shopping trip turned shell shocking blast from the past, and very public fashion faux pas.

In my room I tried on my very first lingerie purchase ever, pulled on a pair of heels from my closet and strutted around my apartment lounging on furniture and sighing like a film star. My initial plan was to wear designer jeans and a sweater over to Cain's, but as I pulled them over the undergarment of black lace and satin, it felt almost sacrilegious. I dug deep into the back of my closet and pulled out a black satin knee length dress. A deep plunging neckline led up to its thin straps which zipped in the back. I had bought it a year and a half before to attend a Christmas party with Ralph while visiting him in Washington. Since I had just seen him and he had clearly moved on to a busty beach babe, I felt it was OK.

I laid the dress on my bed and sank down next to it. *How the hell is he engaged to someone else already?* It seemed unfathomable. I wasn't even totally over him yet according to the way my stomach shivered when I saw him earlier that day. I pushed away the reality that it could have been me. A cascade of memories came streaming back into my consciousness the second that our eyes met. I knew that I didn't want him back, but there are some feelings that one never quite gets over.

I turned onto the highway, the smell of take out from the expensive steak house down the street filling my nostrils and antagonizing my stomach. I had chosen the steakhouse based on the fact that, if you can't wear jeans with lingerie, then you can't walk into a Chinese take-out place with pre-packaged soy sauce by the door wearing a thousand dollar satin and silk dress. It was all perfectly logical to me, so I charged the two hundred dollar dinner of two medium rare filets, mashed potatoes, asparagus in a butter cream sauce and one chocolate mousse with berries to share, and headed down town.

Out of the car after parking, I readjusted my knee length wool coat then grabbed the bag of food and made my way to the front door. A few young women with chipper smiles were exiting and they held the door open for me. I thanked them and passed, headed in the direction of the elevator. According to my phone it was 8:30 p.m. and I was just on time. Somewhere between my second beer and opening a bottle of Riesling, Cain had texted me and told me to be at his apartment around 8:30 p.m. I had been holding my breath that he would, in fact, contact me like he had promised but also set about making plans for if I didn't hear from him.

When I received the text from him confirming the time, I had just finished concluding that, if he did not contact me, I would send him a rather nasty text message and block his phone number. Sometime after my second glass of wine, I had decided that this was the night that I would tell Cain how I felt about him and ask that he put more effort into treating me how I deserved. I gave myself a pep talk while I walked around my apartment, stopping in the mirror to apply a full face of makeup. If Marcus, a complete stranger could treat me with grace and kindness, why couldn't Cain? He totally could, and I was going to make him, damn it.

By the time I got out of the elevator, it was filled with the rich, delicious smells seeping out of the unmarked brown paper bag I carried. All of my limbs felt weak with stress. After not speaking to Cain for over a week I was going to see him again and declare the feelings I had been wrestling with since we first met. I knocked on the door and waited a few moments. Then knocked again and turned the handle of the door- it was locked. Just as I moved my hand to call him, I heard footsteps on the hard floor from the other side of the door and then the latch of the door being lifted. The door opened slowly and Cain's angelic figure appeared, backlit in yellow light.

"Hey there, stranger." I said in the sultriest voice I could muster.

"Hi!" Cain chipped. I stepped inside, setting the bag down and stepped over to Cain, wrapping my arms around his middle. He held me and stroked my hair as I took deep breaths and let the warmth that was emerging from my heart expand across my body to the furthest reaches of my fingers and toes. I kissed his neck, and felt a sigh stretch his throat beneath my lips. He looked down at me and softly kissed me. He pulled me into him again. I pressed my entire body against him.

"I missed you." He spoke in my ear. *Why didn't you reach out to me then? I have been waiting for you.*

"I missed you too." Was all I could say. I heard Cain sniff the air once and then again.

"What is that amazing smell?"

I smiled, released him to pick up our dinner and walked it down the hallway to the kitchen counter where I began unpacking its contents, Cain following close behind.

"Are you hungry now?" I looked over at Cain sitting on a bar stool looking like an excited ten year-old on Christmas. He nodded his eyes widening over the eight ounce filets.

Another thing that I didn't quite think about was how I was going to eat all of that delicious food with my little black dress on. My underwear didn't exactly have a control top, and by the time that I had three bites of steak and a fork full of mashed potatoes I was feeling uncomfortably snug. I cursed myself and promised that I would take it home with me the next morning.

"You all done already?" Cain asked me looking up briefly before diving headfirst back into his potatoes.

"I ate a little at the work function. There were hors d'oeuvres." Soon after I had removed all of the items from the bag in preparation to eat, Cain had offered to take my coat to his room. Being swept up in the excitement of seeing him again, yet another thing I didn't think through was that he might be curious as to why I was wearing a cocktail dress and heels. After letting out a whistle and an expletive, he asked about my attire. "I had a cocktail party after work," was the first thing to pop into my mind. Lies had been flying all over the place that day. I couldn't have possibly told him the truth though: That I had based my outfit and the expensive meal that we were eating to coordinate with some overpriced underwear I had purchased for the night with him.

We continued talking about work and about the previous week while my second glass of Cain's scotch buzzed its way through my system. I had given up on having anymore of the most delicious chocolate mousse of my life after two small bites, for fear of my corset exploding and ripping my dress to pieces in the process. Instead, I stared at Cain as he explained a process at his work.

I couldn't care less. I wasn't even listening, just watching his mouth move and his full lips form into shapes. When I stood in his arms shortly after arriving, I had shortly changed my mind and decided not bring up any of my feelings that night. The first time back together after not speaking shouldn't be one of elevated emotions, but quiet, comfortable, and peaceful. *What if I scare him and he shuts down?* I would just have to hold in my feelings for yet another night. *But what if I don't see him again for another week or two?* I decided that the uncomfortable feeling of my silence was worth avoiding the devastating feeling of losing him again. The scotch, unfortunately, had a different idea about how the night should go. Finally, he put down his fork and leaned back into the couch where we had been eating and looked at me, satisfaction glowing from every pore.

"That was amazing, Myra. Thanks." He reached for the remote and pointed it at the television to power it on.

"Cain." I said abruptly. He looked over as something snapped in me. I didn't care. If I didn't tell him how I felt, how I'd been feeling over the last few months right then at the moment, then I was going to melt away into a puddle. "I really missed you over the last week." I said forcefully. "Why didn't you contact me at all? Did I do something?"
Remote frozen in midair pointed at the TV he replied.

"No." his face was soft and blank.

"Well, I reached out to you a couple of times but you didn't respond. So…" my voice trailed off.

"Oh yea. That's right, you did. I was just busy. Sorry." *Too busy to send me a five second text message?* That was unlikely. I forged ahead, fueled by alcohol and my desire.

"Look Cain." I scooted closer to him and dejectedly he sat the remote back down on the coffee table. "I know that you aren't looking for a relationship right now- which is fine. I completely get it- So I am not asking you for that. What I *am* asking is for you to put a little more effort into building something here. We can take it slow, but I need to know that there is something real here. Something worth waiting for. I just want to spend time with you and get to know you better." I paused for an instant to gauge Cain's reaction. He was biting on the corner of his lower lip.

"On Saturday night we had a great time and had a really great conversation and then you disappeared. You say that I didn't do anything wrong, but your behavior seems to state the contrary." Cain's eyes were wandering around the 20 foot tall room. "I am asking you to give just a little bit more so that at least I don't have to wonder what is going on between us. You are quickly becoming one of my favorite people in the world." That wasn't a lie. "We can spend time together in any way that you want. Grocery shopping, picking up dry cleaning, anything. I think that the more time we spend together the more comfortable we will be and the faster we can decide if this," I made a gesture indicating the two of us, "is something that we want." His eyes zipped back to mine and I sent him a small smile. As I sat and waited the ten years it took for him to respond, I took a moment out to commend myself on how well delivered my speech to Cain had just been. Apparently my skills as an orator really were improving! Just as I was feeling confident Cain opened his mouth.

"I can't. I'm sorry." Then closed it again and resumed biting his lower lip.

Uhh. What? I hadn't planned for that.

"You can't? What do you mean?" I asked, confusedly. The response he gave was silence. A swell of embarrassment came over me. I had just spilled my heart out and all he could give me was two barely complete sentences. I was shell shocked. I looked around not sure what to do next. *I guess I should leave.* My legs and arms felt dead and my heart restricted. The tar-like sadness that was beginning to envelope my body was creating physical pain and I shook my hand to remove the sharp tingling sensation gathering. I looked at Cain again who hadn't moved at all. "Are you sure?" I asked, hoping that a grin would spread across his face and, "*I am just kidding, Myra! I love you. Want to move in next weekend?*" would pop out of his mouth. Instead,

"Yes, I am sure." Cain breathed sullenly like he had had this conversation one too many times before. A loud voice interrupted the funnel cloud that was forming in my mind. *Get up! Leave now! Before any more damage to yourself is done.* From the depths of my soul, perhaps it was the last bit of dignity I had, I found the strength to stand up quickly ready to sprint out of the apartment and never look back. I turned on my heel towards my coat, purse and the door.

"Where are you going?" the words hit my back and fell on the floor, where I looked at them rather than at Cain.

"I am going home." My mouth was stiff and dry.

"Why? Why aren't you spending the night?" At this, my head whipped up to meet his. He was leaning forward towards me. I didn't say anything. *Is this fool crazy? Why would I stay?* Cain dropped his head and stood up like there was one hundred pounds on his back then pulled me into his arms again. I kept mine tightly to my sides, refusing to touch him, trying to protect myself, wanting to push him away, but unable. His strong forearms kept me in place, which was good, because I felt like my legs were going to give out at any second. Cain kissed the top of my forehead and then buried his face in my hair. *How is it that he thinks that he can take and take and take and never give anything back and that I am still going to be here?* "Myra, please stay." His voice was gentle. "Just stay here with me one more night. We don't have to do anything at all, just let me hold you. Then you never have to see me again if you don't want to. I am sorry, I really am. I just can't." With each sentence, my heart grew softer and sadder. He moved his head down and found my eyes by lifting my chin. "Please?"

I didn't say no because I couldn't. The audacity of the man before me had turned me momentarily mute. He took my hand and led me back into his bed room. I went first into the dimly lit room, the cold drafty air hitting my exposed shoulders. I felt the zipper of my dress slowly slide down and the sound of air quickly moving into Cain's mouth.

"What do we have here?" As my dress fell to the floor Cain spun me around devouring my mouth with his. I tore away after a moment as soon as my head cleared. His hands were covering my all but exposed breasts.

"I thought you said that we didn't have to do anything tonight." I was dizzy, confused, conflicting voices growing louder in my head.

Run, bitch! Run for your life! You heard him. He doesn't want anything with you. He doesn't care about you!

You were miserable without him. Just this last time. Stay with him. Show him how much you love him.

His green eyes burned into me. A mischievous, haunting smile crept over his face.

"You didn't wear that for me just to sleep, did you?" And then he swooped over me, paralyzing me for the next two hours.

When I came to, my hand moved to my lips, raw and swollen. Cain's arm was warm beneath my neck, holding my head, face stretched towards the ceiling. His words echoed in my head,

"*Just stay here with me one more night.*" I had done that, I had let him win again. I was ashamed and scared. I wanted to leave but I couldn't move, my pride was depleted. If I had had any left I would have gotten up without a word and never spoken to him again. Instead I took my last bit of strength, emotional and physical, and spoke.

"I love you, Cain."

15.

"You said *what* to him?" Ava, the usually supportive friend shouted at me from across the island counter top of Stella's granite kitchen. I dropped my head and looked to Stella for backup then checked myself realizing that I would get none there. I kept my head down and chopped at the cucumber in front of me.

"So let me get this straight," it was Stella's turn. "You asked him to be a little more open with you, to spend a little more time with you and to respect you a little bit more than the dog poo he has been treating you as," Ava made a noise of agreement at this, "And he said no. That he wasn't going to give you the satisfaction of being treated like a human being. And instead of leaving, you stayed, had sex with him, and told him you love him." *Yep! It is as pathetic as it sounds. Damn.* I didn't respond and didn't blame them for being hard on me; someone needed to be. Honestly, with all of the voices running rampant in my head around the subject of Cain, I needed opinions from the outside.

"I know guys. I just can't help myself around Cain. I don't think or see clearly." I slid the sliced cucumber off of the bamboo cutting board and on top of the salad I was making. The smell of homemade lasagna swirled through the kitchen and I took a sip of my merlot.

"Well," Ava took a softer more optimistic tone, "Do you know if he heard you? I mean, was he asleep?" I wasn't sure. He had made a grunting noise, slung his arm across me and then resumed silence. I just shrugged at both of my friends and proceeded to move the heavy glass bowl to the kitchen table.

The morning after I left Cain's apartment I received a text from him at about 11:00 a.m. which was a surprise. I hadn't expected to hear a word from him, possibly ever, again.

Thank you again for dinner. I can't get over how beautiful you are. Are you still upset with me? I sank into my chair and rocked at my desk for a moment. The truth was that I wasn't mad. I was happy as hell to see his name on my phone. Ever since I had said "I love you" to Cain, a weight had lifted. I had no idea if he heard it but I felt better regardless. And with the release came an ability to breathe just a little bit easier. With that breath came clarity of thought. *Maybe I have been too emotional, moving too fast.*

I wanted to be with Cain, sure. But the thought was solidifying that maybe I should just relax and let things happen, or not happen naturally. Especially since Cain had made it clear that nothing serious was going to happen between us anytime soon. So that was that. I made the determination to cool it, not take everything so seriously and just have fun. At least that was my plan.

Buzz…buzz…buzz. I nearly jumped out my skin as the vibrating phone jolted me alert from the sitting position on the couch that I had fallen asleep in. I scrambled for the phone on the espresso coffee table in front of me, picking it up to see that my mother was texting me. I threw it disgruntledly on the couch without reading the message, skidding it across the beige microfiber. Surging through my body for a brief moment was the thought it might be Cain texting me. I stood from my post on the couch where I had been since getting home three hours prior and walked into the kitchen. I knew that he probably wouldn't contact me today. It was Tuesday. It had been over a month since experiencing a week of no contact, and Cain and I had resumed our ritual of weekly visits. The previous Wednesday at ten-thirty p.m., just as I had lost all hope of seeing him, he contacted me, asking me to come "cuddle" with him. I had been in bed at that time, hair wrapped up, no makeup on, and quite tired from a strenuous day at the office, and still I jumped out of bed, showered *again,* dressed, slapped on some make-up and drove the distance. I was excited to see him, to talk to him and share some funny things that had happened that week before. Unlike when we first met and spent hours of the work day sending instant messages back and forth, we rarely spoke other than a *"how was your day?",* text that generally came from him late in the evening. By the time I exited the elevator onto his floor and skipped down the hall towards his door I was glowing with electricity. I knocked on the door which was partially open and entered an apartment filled with midnight blue light. Carefully maneuvering my way past the dark kitchen, up three stairs to a landing and into his bedroom, I closed the door softly behind me.

"Hello there, stranger." I said softly removing my jacket.

"Hey babe. Come get into bed." I relinquished the remainder of my clothing with the exception of my underwear and climbed onto the warm mattress, hovering just over him. In the black room I found him and held his face in my hands, letting the heat from his lips spread over every inch of my body. I rested my forehead against his.

"How was your day, sweetie?" I asked, intensely interested in the answer.

"It was OK." He answered briefly. He placed the palm of his large hand on the back of my head and directed me down to his body, my ear against the hollow of his chest like a parent urging her rambunctious child to be still. I stayed there, eyes wide open to the void of the room, waiting for him to ask me how my day was, or say anything at all. I missed his conversation, his laugh, the way he his mouth stayed slightly agape while he watched TV or read something. I listened to his breaths and the rhythm of his heart, both slowing down to resting speed.

When the first soft snore arose out of his throat, I sighed, disappointed. *If I would have known that we were just going to sleep and not actually speak to each other, I certainly would have stayed home. I could be in my own bed right now.* As soon as the thought passed through my mind I knew it was a lie. I would have gone anywhere at any time of the night or day to be in the presence of Cain, even the unconscious presence. It was annoying and agonizing that it happened so infrequently. I moved my head up slowly and softly repositioned myself as I slipped off him and onto the bed. Cain inhaled sharply just as I landed next to him, rolled to his side away from me and sleepily slurred, "Come hold me, babe." There wasn't a molecule of my person that would allow me to deny him it seemed, so I too rolled to my side and scooted up behind Cain, wrapping my slim arm around his massive frame. He hummed softly as my skin touched his and returned to deep breathing and slight snoring.

I lightly traced the smooth skin of his back the pads of my fingers. I imaged them as paintbrushes, placing beautiful strokes in every color all over the already perfect shell of him. I focused my energy on all of the love that I had, and tried to transfer it into him. I let myself marinate in the grateful feeling that soothed me by just being there. I wanted to witness him happy and I wanted him to be happy because of me. It made me sad that I wouldn't get to that night. *When will I get to, again?* I became anxious for the next time I would get to see Cain, actually interact with him, and then the satisfaction of just being there was doused with a horrible thought. *Is this the only time I'm going to see Cain this week?*

I felt nauseated. We had only been spending one night a week together, sure, but this couldn't count. *This can't count. Him sleeping while I dive into a mini panic attack? No, I'm sure I'll see him again. This is a bonus, twice in one week. Maybe it will become a trend!* Trying to force myself to believe that, I closed my eyes and did a breathing exercise to fight the mounting urge to shake Cain awake and demand that he agree to see me another night that week. What finally made me relax was imagining a scene in a cozy restaurant lit by candles. Cain and I were sitting across from each other, holding hands atop a table's wooden surface. I was telling him about my life and my dreams and he sat and listened and responded when it was appropriate, agreeing with every notion I expressed. We were seated by the front door, and right beside us a never-ending line of beautiful Victoria Secret models strode in. Cain's green-amber eyes never left my face. His gaze never faltered. He was completely enchanted by me and I knew there was no one else in the world he would rather be with.

The hard electric cords of a guitar were the next thing I remembered. Across the room, neon green lights of a high-end alarm clock blinked. Every time I spent the night at Cain's I was awakened this way, with the same song. It was becoming my favorite song in the world. It meant that the solitude of sleep was over and that I could share a few moments with Cain before the day began. Before the second bar I was wide awake, but didn't move. I could hear Cain stirring beside me. He was over at the far end of the bed and double rolled over to me. He wrapped his arms around me, kissing my ear.

"Good morning."

"Morning." I faced him. He kissed me with closed lips.

"Does my breath smell bad?" *It smells God-awful.*

"Nope." I said sweetly. The truth was that I didn't mind it at all, because it was his.

"Good." The music played on as he rolled on top of me kissing me and wiggling his way in between my legs, starting the day off in his very favorite way.

That had been five days ago. I stared into the light of the open refrigerator. I was starving but couldn't muster up the strength to make something or even order food in. A four day old box of cold pizza from a work party laid on the bottom shelf. Everyone had decided that I should be the one to take it home because I was the poor single girl without even a pet to keep me company. *I hate pity food.* I made a contemplative face and bent down to pick it up, when the slender green glass bottle of my favorite chardonnay caught my eye. I looked at it with uncertainty. It had come to my attention that since Cain and I had starting seeing each other once a week again, all six of the other days I was prone to boredom, loneliness and general listlessness. My only other prospect, Marcus, was away on a trip to Europe with his med-school team.

Luckily for me, I had formed what I thought to be an effective coping method. I would come home, pop open a bottle of wine, turn on the TV and watch about three hours' worth of crap reality shows, while effectively getting anywhere from slightly tipsy to rip-roaring drunk. Then I would turn on any of a number of 80's pop albums, Whitney Houston was my go-to, and wildly sing and dance around my apartment. When I felt satisfied with my cardio workout, I would run a hot bath adding too many bubbles which frothed up over the edge of the tub. Once inside, I daydreamed about Cain while holding conversations with him, speaking aloud as if he were sitting across from me. This generally continued for about an hour until the mixture of the heat, alcohol and exhaustion was too much and I began to get anxious that I was going to pass out in the tub and drown. Upon which, I would climb out, minimally dried myself off and pass out naked in my bed at around 9:30 p.m. This had been going on since sometime after declaring my love for Cain with no response. I never brought it back up. *How could I?* There was a chance that he hadn't heard me.

Clearly on the verge of alcoholism I had tried to limit this behavior to days when I was feeling exceptionally alone and missing Cain. My eyes averted back to the bottle.

Buzz... buzz... buzz. Damn mom! Calm down. To be fair, she hadn't heard my voice in over a week and I rarely responded to her texts. I shut the refrigerator and walked over to couch to pick up my phone, annoyed at the persistence of my mom's texts. I just wanted some space from her. I knew that if I let her too close she would know something was wrong with me and I didn't want her worry on top of everything else.

Cain's name peered at me from the screen.

"Oh my God!" I yelled, heart racing. I opened the text message.

Hey. I just got home from a work dinner. You want to come over? I checked the clock. It was 8:05 p.m., on a Tuesday! My heart sang. *It is so early! We are going to have all night together!* I shot him a quick text message that I would be leaving my apartment in about five minutes and would text him when I got downtown. Running to the bathroom, I fixed my eyeliner and mascara and pulled the ponytail holder out of my hair, letting my fast growing locs fall around my shoulders. I spread toothpaste on my toothbrush, shoved it into my mouth and ran into the closet across the hall. Pulling out medium wash skinny jeans, a navy blue tight fitting long sleeved tee shirt that Cain had mentioned was sexy, and a gray, teal and blue scarf as I continued to brush my teeth. In about three minutes flat I was ready, grabbed my purse off of the kitchen counter and headed for the door, glancing back once to ensure that all of the lights were turned off.

I pulled my car out of the complex parking lot, poking at the radio buttons until coming across some Alicia Keys. My heart was practically banging out of my chest. *Imagine, just a few minutes ago I was sad, lonely and depressed and now I am completely ecstatic!* I shook away the small voice from the back of my head that suggested sudden and extreme shifts in mood and demeanor were not healthy behavior. The exit to the freeway towards downtown was just one intersection away. I applied the gas feeling downright giddy and sped through the light as it changed from yellow to red.

More thoughts emerged from the dark corners of my mind as I jumped onto the highway. *Isn't this a little pathetic? Running, literally running, to see him every time he sends a text message? What about my own plans? Don't I seem a little too eager?* I tried to think about something else. My mind wandered to the first time Cain had visited my apartment after taking me home in the morning after a night out. I had been left downtown without a car and after an awkward string of events he had brought me home and come inside, stayed for a few hours and then disappeared for a week.

To my great delight, thirty minute's time passed in a flash and I was approaching the downtown exit that would lead me to Cain's. I pulled out my phone to text him that I was about three minutes away as I flew through another intersection under another yellow light. By the time I got parked and out of the car Cain had not yet responded to my text message, but I walked to the entrance and rang his number. Pulling my coat around me tightly and clicking the heels of my brown cowboy boots together, I waited. *There's no place like home.* I thought. *Home,* in this case, being Cain's arms. That notion satisfied me and made sense due to how I was constantly home sick for him when I was away. A few minutes passed and I rang the door again, looking up and down the empty city sidewalk illuminated gray from the bright full moon. *Maybe he is in the restroom.* I waited another minute and a half and then took out my phone. It rang several times and Cain's voice picked up in a bright and cheerful tone. "This is the voice mailbox of Cain Jones…" I hung up the phone and buzzed the door again. *This fool fell asleep didn't he?* The realization sank in and hit my heart hard. *But it is only 8:45 p.m.!* I knew from previous experience that once Cain fell asleep, there was absolutely no waking him up. I looked around for anyone on the street who might be heading in. *Still vacant.* I pulled on the door handle which didn't budge an inch. *Fuck!* The thought of driving thirty minutes back to my apartment without seeing Cain was not an option.

Hi! I am down here but you are not answering! I am going to the coffee shop on the corner and will wait thirty minutes. Call me as soon as you get this!

I put my phone away after sending the text message and walked a block north to the Starbucks. Ambling up to the counter where a scruffy looking middle-aged barista greeted me, I stared into the glass case and he rang me up for a piece of lemon pound cake and a tall medium blend coffee. I slouched into a barstool that faced the large front window and let the defeat roll over me. Not only was he inconsiderate about me taking the time and energy to come over, he was apathetic about seeing me in general. As soon as I read his invitation to come over, I felt like I had just taken a hit of cocaine (or at least I imagined that's what it felt like, having never actually done it myself). He, himself, couldn't even stay awake. Tired of taking my phone out of my pocket to check it ever few seconds, I laid it on the countertop in front of me. *Furthermore…* My mind galloped on. *Whenever I do come over late at night, is he waiting for me with open arms at the door? No! He is in bed! And it's up to me to climb over the crap in his apartment in the dark and stumble into his room like a member of a harem summoned by some sultan!* The voices in my head, that weren't nearly as impressed with Cain as my conscious voice was, were apparently having some kind of rally. *And so here I am! Stood up, for all intents and purposes. AGAIN! He is so not worth this! This isn't good enough!* The last bite of the citrus cake deliciously disappeared into my mouth, leaving traces of frosting on my lips. I finished the rest of my coffee and looked down at my phone again, turning on the screen. It had been twenty-five minutes. Feeling the sting of the first tears coming, I quickly gathered my belongings, shooting a quick glance around the room. The shop was splattered with a few students on laptops, a man reading the newspaper and a young couple speaking in quiet tones positioned closely to each other in the corner. I tossed my trash and opened the door leaving the warm smell of coffee and my illusions of seeing Cain behind.

Back in the car I turned on the engine, glanced once more at my phone, which still stared blankly back at me, and dug through my glove box for some CD's. I found a good one that I had made mid- breakup with Ralph and shoved it into the player. As angry songs of the 90's rang out I let the hate-mongering voices explode about Cain. *Who the hell does that fool think he is? I have acted like a complete idiot letting that little boy run all over me, use me and not appreciate me like this. I have given him more than his fair share of chances and he acts a jerk and shows his ass every single time!* The rage continued to build. *I will never speak to him again!* None of the voices in my head believed that one. *Well, I will never speak to him again AFTER I tell him all about himself. He is a selfish asshole who doesn't deserve a nice woman like me. The only way I would ever see him again is if he comes crawling back and begs me to give him one last chance and then straightens up completely. And starts treating me like a queen. Dinners out, movies, parties with his friends, all of that!* It was painfully true that I hadn't met any of his friends other than his roommate, but as I was having a hard enough time securing a regular spot on his calendar, that seemed to be of lesser concern.

I entered my parking space, opening the door before I was completely stopped, pulled my keys from the ignition, slammed the door and stomped all the way up to my third floor apartment. Banging my way in the door and all the way back to my bedroom before turning on a light, I tossed my purse into a chair and plowed to the bathroom to wash away the feelings of disappointment, shame and heartache. After putting on my pajamas, I grabbed my purse and carried it into my room. A sigh escaped me as I calmed down. I racked my brain looking for any trace of self-respect that I could cling to. In the car on the way home I had a chance to zoom out and look at the big picture. The truth was that I was playing the part of a desperate, naive little girl, and he the part of an average guy who was just taking what I was clearly willing to give out to him. Rubbing my eyes in emotional exhaustion, I turned back the blanket and sheets to my bed and began to climb inside when my purse hummed from across the room. It was 10:05 p.m. and that could only be one person. I stalked over to the bag, ripped out the phone and stared at the screen. It was Cain, and he was calling me. *Calling* me. *Wow! He never calls me. He must know his ass is grass.* A sense of smug satisfaction came over me and, just as I was moving my thumb to ignore the call, a flash in the form of a strong desire to answer burst forward. *No!* I tossed the phone across the room frantically and it landed softly in my dirty clothes hamper. *Absolutely not. I am not answering that!* I criticized myself for being so weak and slumped onto the bed. After a few more seconds passed, an alarm sounded which signaled a voicemail. I walked over to the hamper and checked the message.

"Hey Myra, it's Cain," *I know who it is fool!* "I'm sorry! I passed out. Please call me back as soon as you get this." In all of my anger, a part of my heart melted at the sound of his voice but I straightened up quickly, afraid of being scolded again by myself. With my phone, I climbed into bed and turned off the light, pulling the soft comforter and sheets around me snugly. I was sad; more than sad, I was disappointed. More in myself than anyone. How had I let this get so out of control? I had asked Cain to treat me better and he had flat out denied me. How could I be angry with him when he had clearly told me what he could give me and I had been too weak to walk away from the lack? The phone buzzed again. It was a text from Cain.

Are you awake beautiful? I am so sorry, please text me to let me know you are OK. A sigh escaped my lips. I didn't want him to think that something bad happened to me. It was late, he was tired and he might worry.

Yea. I'm fine. Good night. Thirty more seconds went by.

I'm sorry. You are pissed huh? I threw my phone down on the bed. I couldn't believe the balls of steel this kid had. Of course I was pissed. I stuffed the phone under my pillow as if that would keep him from texting me again and keep me from reading said text. Predictably, after a minute and a half my phone started vibrating. Again he was calling me.

"Hello!" I shouted angrily into the phone.

"Oh, um. Hello. How are you?" I let silence answer his obviously rhetorical question. "Myra, I'm really sorry. I didn't mean to fall asleep." I stayed quiet, pinched my eyes closed and tried to fortify my stony, cold resistance to his apology. "I got home from dinner after having a few drinks and I was really tired."

"Then why did you invite me over? I drove all the way down there and you couldn't even stay awake to let me in? You are a fucking asshole" was what I wanted to say. Instead I just mumbled, "Yea, whatever." Tears were forming behind my eyes.

"I know. I'm an idiot." *Damn right, you are.* "I just really missed you,"
You what, now? "And I really wanted to see you." *Oh, snap.* "I guess I was
just over excited and not thinking about the fact that I was too tired." *Overly
excited?* Something began to glow. First it was a tiny ember and before I
knew it, my whole being was aflame. My mouth was spread tightly in a
smile. *He missed me! He was excited about seeing me!* I remained silent.
"Do you want to come back down?" *What the hell did you just ask me?* His
last comment went a little too far and the anger flared back up, but only as a
ghost of what it had been before.

"Are you crazy? Hell no! I am not going to come back downtown!
Seriously, Cain!"

"Oh, I'm sorry, you're right. You're right." He tried to back track. "May
I please see you tomorrow?" His voice pleaded and although I wanted to
shout yes, the less convinced voices in my head wanted to make him pay a
little.

"And what, may I ask, will we be doing?" I wanted to make sure this
wasn't going to be one of our standard eating an instant meal on the couch
while watching TV and then going into his room to have sex and going to
sleep dates.

"Let's go to dinner. We haven't done that in a while. And have some
drinks." I liked the sound of that. A small smile crept back on my face.
"Where would you like to go?" His voice was sweet.

"Cain, I don't know. You figure it out. All I know is that my ass isn't
driving back downtown, so you can come here and pick me up and drive to
our destination."

"OK. I can do that. That sounds perfect." There was a real earnestness
to his voice and my heart softened further.

"Good." I said with finality. "I am going to bed. I will wait for your call
or text tomorrow, good night."

"Goo.." and with that I hung up the phone. Placed it theatrically beside
me, pulled the covers over my head and let out a loud, earsplitting shriek of
victory. I fell asleep with a huge smile on my face and closed my eyes not
able to fight the hope that things might be different from here on out.

16.

My nasal passaged pounded into the bridge of my glasses. I stood, barefoot on the dirty kitchen floor and I had not a care in the world of all of the bacteria and organisms my feet were sinking in as I opened drawer after drawer looking for coffee filters. Cain was convinced that sex was the best cure for a hangover, all of the endorphins rushing to the nervous system was better than any pain reliever you could take. Sex couldn't last forever though, so a couple of hours after waking there I was, suffering the consequences of the overindulgent previous night with Cain. For whatever reason, one of our new favorite things to do was to go out together, just he and I and drink and laugh and talk until we were thoroughly lubricated and then come home and drink some more. It was heaven to me, and I smiled at the new town I found myself living in called Reciprocity. Cain seemed very willing to spend at least one weekend night with me a week, and we were spending two weekday nights together. A wave of nausea came over me just as I remembered the deep and touching conversation he and I had explored the night before about his grandmother. I held onto the side of the laminate topped counter for stability.

"Cain! Where the hell are your filters?" I screamed harshly. I closed my eyes and dropped my head forward to give myself a break while I waited for him to answer. I heard the bathroom door open and Cain come into the kitchen.

"That bad huh?" he asked supportively and guided me, my eyes still shut, to the bar stool at the end of the counter. I sank into it and held my head in my hands. Cain milled around the kitchen, turned on water faucets and opened cabinets. A few moments later I heard a glass make contact with the counter top and I opened my eyes. Water and three ibuprofen lay in front of me. "Here, babe. Drink the whole thing."

"Thank you, baby." I said in a pouty voice. I looked up to him, hair still damp, body wrapped in a towel, turning on the coffee maker. I downed the glass and then rested my head on the cool counter top, inches away from some indistinguishable crumbs. I was sure my head was in them. I decided to close my eyes instead of move. I didn't open them again until Cain was back in the kitchen completely dressed.

"The shower is ready for you *My*. Go ahead and get in there. It will make you feel better." I hopped down from the stool and walked into the bathroom without a word. After stripping down in front of the fog covered mirror, I stepped into the hot shower and sat immediately down on the floor. The water hit me in the head like drumsticks so I leaned further back, letting the water rain on my chest and stomach.

As each moment passed I felt my head clear. *Cain called me My just now. Who is My? Is that my nickname? Did he really give me a nickname?* I contemplated all of the things that could mean. None of which were negative. I stayed there, legs stretched along the smooth white surface of the tub for a few more minutes, then stood, grabbed the body wash that hung on the shower head and went about washing up. I felt about ten times better than I had before I entered the shower but still twelve times worse than I wanted to. I wrapped up with the brown oversized towel Cain had set aside for me. The same towel that fit him perfectly swallowed me whole. Walking towards the door through the steam, I stepped on my overnight bag. Apparently he had thought of everything.

After I dressed, I found Cain on the couch and collapsed next to him, pulling my feet up and snuggling into his side. Sports news was on his sixty inch flat screen and he didn't look over at me when he asked, "You feel any better babe?" and reached his arm around my shoulders to hold me closer to him.

"Yea, I do. Thank you. Hey Cain?" He stood up quickly and called back over his shoulder to me in acknowledgment. I continued. "Did you call me *My* earlier?" I heard the cupboard and refrigerator both open and close. He popped his head around the corner, visible again.

"Do you want some cereal? It's high in protein so it will help you feel better. And yes. I did. Why? Do you not like it or something?"
The name that I went by, Myra, is actually already a nickname, short for my full name, Almyra.

"Yes, I would love some cereal and no I don't mind the name. No one else calls me that." I smiled to myself as he ducked back around the corner to fix my breakfast.

After I ate I felt even closer to normal, which was still considerably abnormal, but the progress was much appreciated. I rinsed my bowl in the sink and walked back over to the couch.

"Thank you for breakfast. Would you like me to leave now?" Cain didn't look over at me from the TV until I was done talking.

"No. Do you want to leave?" He stared up at me with a blank expression.

"No." I said quietly, feeling a little vulnerable and embarrassed. There was nothing worse to a man than a woman who overstayed her welcome. Or at least I figured there was nothing worse. Cain reached out his hand to me and I sat back on the couch and squirmed back into him.

"If I want you to leave, I will tell you." Cain remarked bluntly before kissing the top of my head. *Oh. I have no doubt about that.*

After spending two hours on the couch crawling all over each other trying to get comfortable and failing miserably to do so we decided what we needed was crisp fresh air and sunshine. Cain had a few errands to run, so I found my shoes while he poured us two travel cups of coffee and we piled into his blue sedan. Despite my still very intense headache, as I let the late February sun warm my face, I felt the kind of happiness that was indicative of being around Cain. I smiled and giggled and joked and chatted merrily with him while sipping my coffee in the passenger's seat.

"Now how do you feel, Gorgeous?" Cain grabbed my hand and intertwined his fingers in mine.

"So much better!" And it was true, the coffee really seemed to help.

"Yea, the best thing for a severe hangover is an Irish Coffee. Are you almost done?" *Irish Coffee? Wait, but that's whiskey and Irish cream with the coffee.* My mouth dropped open. I felt guilty for putting my body through so much. My alcohol intake wasn't at an all-time high, but it was pretty close, and I wasn't twenty-one anymore.

"I thought it was spending time with you that was making me feel better. I didn't know that you were liquoring me up again." I spoke accusatorily. Cain laughed.

"Why can't it be both?" I thought for a moment. I guessed it could be. Cain and I had never been closer. It was the little things that we both enjoyed: being close to each other and spending time talking about family and friends, watching sports and eating.

"Ok." I said resignedly, "It's both."

The single most exhilarating shopping trip of my life was realized in that south side super center pushing a ridiculously squeaky cart up and down the overcrowded aisles. I followed behind Cain as he picked things off the shelf, pretended to look at them for a second and then tossed them into the cart from wherever he was standing, an obnoxious, and yet totally endearing behavior that made me smile. While in the paper goods section my phone vibrated, a text from my mother, and I looked down to respond to her. With the quickness of an air strike Cain threw two rolls of paper towels and a package of toilet paper at my head.

"Cain! What is wrong with you?" My phone had flown out of my hand and I had been startled half to death. Cain looked like an eleven year old who had just been caught tantalizing his sister, eyes wide and mouth fixed in a rounded position. I couldn't even pretend to be mad. I didn't care about my phone, or even about being hit in the head with a paper towel roll; I was experiencing what it would be like to really be with Cain. This was a snapshot into a life with a man that I desperately wanted. I marched over to Cain and he straightened up, perhaps expecting to be reprimanded. I grabbed the front of his shirt and pulled him into me, threw my arms around his neck and held him, my nose pressed against his neck. I loved him. I loved the way the he talked and walked and dressed. I loved the way he touched me, talked to me, played with me. I loved how he made me feel, be, desire, know. I told him that I loved him every night we spent together. The first time I uttered the words aloud to him, I didn't know that he was asleep and therefore didn't hear me, but every time since I had made sure he was. It was cowardly of me but I validated it by telling myself that somewhere in his subconscious mind he was getting the message. I kissed him softly, grabbed his arm roughly spinning him to the side and slapped his butt then marched back to the cart.

17.

"So if I had some information about you, you would want me to share it right?" Lilly reached over the linoleum table top and stole a French fry.

"Well, yea. I guess. Is it about work?" I moved the double cheeseburger around in my mouth so that I could speak more clearly then took a sip of strawberry shake to try to wash it down. The thick half-liquid didn't help my situation and just mixed the sweet fruity taste with salty beef, making me grimace.

"Well, you are going to be called into your director's office later on today…" Lilly stopped and took a bite of her chicken sandwich and then flipped the page of her tabloid magazine. I stared at her.

"And?!" *What the hell for?* I had just had a meeting with him, what could he possibly want?

"I don't know the specifics," she pushed out her bottom lip hinting at the fact that it wasn't good. "I wasn't even supposed to know. So don't say anything."

Fucking fantastic. It was Friday. Everyone in that place knew that Fridays were the days that people got sacked. It was like the ultimate- *Have a good weekend! An extended weekend, please don't come back.* There was a period of time a few months back when people wouldn't show up for work on Fridays just because they didn't want to give management a chance to give them the boot. They suddenly had a medical procedure or came down with bronchitis. I threw the burger I was holding down into the paper wrapper from whence it came and swore under my breath.

"Well it was nice working with you." I looked at Lilly then started thinking about all of the implications of being laid-off. *Will I get severance? How will I pay my credit card bills?* I couldn't even lean on them because they were all almost maxed out anyway. My father had always stressed living within my means, and had I listened to him? No. I had not. I had just charged bananas and milk the week before, I could not survive being unemployed. "If I get evicted, I expect you to let me live with you." Lilly smiled back at me. *Shit. I can't live with her. She has cats and I am allergic.* "What are you smiling about?" I rose my voice at her.

"Just kidding!" Lilly grinned widely at me. "I got your ass. You look terrified." *You bitch.*

"You bitch!" I threw a french fry at her. Lilly and I lived for the prank. Every couple of months we would try to trick each other, each time worse than the last. The October before I had moved her car while we were at work and convinced her that someone had stolen it. Remembering this I laughed. "Ok. Ok. You got me."

"You do have a meeting with your director today though. I saw it on his calendar earlier." She took a sip of her diet soda.

"I had no idea." Worry flew back into my mind and my mouth turned downwards.

"Myra! You lead a department which has increased claim payment by two-hundred percent last quarter. You are probably getting a raise or something." This was true. My department had been kicking ass since I had taken over. To be fair, the man I had replaced had been inept as a manager. It hadn't taken much for me to look like a super star.

Sure enough, when I returned to my desk there was an email from my director asking me to report to his office at three that afternoon. Truth be told, I thought my director was a jerk. He seemed like that kid in school who got made fun of a lot and let the adversity turn him into a spiteful asshole instead of a compassionate, empathetic person like God had intended. I sat down in the chair outside of his office door, which was perpetually closed, at 2:50 p.m. I had a notepad and my favorite orange pen in hand. I had concluded that Lilly was right. I probably wasn't going to be canned, but that still left a lot of other possibilities, not all of them even remotely good. At 3:15 p.m. Ben opened the door to his office and summoned me inside. I sat in the stiff plastic chair across from him.

"Good afternoon, Ben."

"Myra." That was all that I got. He seemed visibly disturbed as he shuffled through a stack of papers. *I'm fucked.* I took a deep breath and started praying for my financial livelihood. After about a minute he turned to his computer exasperated and pulled up an email. *Is he going to read me a pink slip?* My mind zoomed to my apartment and all of the things I could sell to make money. I put my hand to my forehead as I thought of the designer purse I had just purchased. *Can I return that shit? I've only worn it a handful of times.*

"Are you OK?" Ben had apparently noticed my distress. A sound came from the printer next to him and he grabbed a sheet off of the tray. I nodded weakly. "OK. Good. Look Myra. How attached are you to this building and your family and friends here in the city?" That was an odd question. *Is he threatening me?* I didn't answer but made a face urging him to continue. "The corporate office in Chicago wants you. Well, Cody, the "Big Dog", wants you in Chicago." My mouth dropped open. I remained silent. "You would leave in two months to be the team lead of the contract team that oversees the east and south east regions. *Oh my God. Is this for real?* I stared at him for a few moments with a confused look on my face. "Myra! Do you have anything to say?"

"Thank you?" My frozen mind asked the question. "Thank you!" I rearranged my tone into a statement.

"So, yes, then? You would be interested if this were to get approval?" Ben was starting to look annoyed.

"Yes." I shook my head to get a grip. "I'm sorry Ben, this is just a big shock. Of course. What an amazing opportunity! I would be more than happy to represent this great billing center at corporate." *There we go. Talk like you have an ounce of professionalism in you.* I smiled broadly at him. He sighed back at me.

"Well, I am happy for you. I will let Cody know that it's a go." He swiveled his chair away from me and towards his computer. I took that as my cue to leave. I stood and walked to the door.

"Thank you, Ben. I know you had to approve this too, and I appreciate you for it." Ben nodded his head at me and gave me a brief, forced smile.

"Close the door behind you." I stepped out of his office and pulled the handle of the door until it clicked then leaned briefly against its wood.

Lilly responded to my cryptic email "Meet me in the parking lot directly after work." And was standing by my car when I exited the building. The sun was directly behind her and I shaded my eyes to find her face and then shoot her an excited face as I sprinted the remainder of the way to the driver's side, yelling at her to get in the car.

"What the hell is going on, Myra? What happened?" She slammed the car door behind her. Her face was screwed up in concern. Initially, I was going to tell her that I had, in fact, gotten fired, but I was too excited to

waste time. Instead I went on to tell her what had occurred in Ben's office.
She pulled me into a tight hug. Then screamed in glee. "Oh my God! This
is amazing! I am coming apartment hunting with you!" She shrieked again
and clapped her hands together.

"Of course!" As her words sunk in I realized that I would have to move
away leaving my family, friends, and… Cain. She kissed me on the cheek
and exited the car, wishing me a great weekend. She was going home to her
longtime boyfriend, and I started the drive home to my extensive wine and
beer collection.

18.

Bright blue light crept past my eyelids and I slowly woke up to the sound of men's voices penetrating the wall of the bedroom where I lay. I rolled over onto my back, my naked skin sinking into the cool mattress. I looked up at Cain's ceiling and smiled. He had sent me a text message at midnight inviting me to come over. I was downtown with a couple of friends from work and had immediately left them, taking a five dollar cab to his apartment. The night before I had stumbled into his apartment giggling, mind lubricated with cocktails. He had shushed and kissed me while unbuttoning my pants in the entry hall. His friends from college in town for the weekend were sleeping in his living room. I had never met any of his friends.

Looking around the sunlit room I started to contemplate how I was going to slip out unnoticed to avoid humiliation, when I heard the door to Cain's room begin to open slowly. I whipped the white sheet up to my chin. *Shit! No, please don't come in here.* I spotted my pink and lavender bra and panty set laying on the floor in front of the door. *Oh, God. No. Please...* The door sprang open and in strode a man, Cain's age, with short brown hair and a sun kissed face. He was looking over his shoulder having a conversation with his fellows in the other room. His eyes went to the floor, apparently looking for something, when he caught sight of my lingerie, then slowly looked from them to me in the bed.

"Hi." I said weakly. He gasped and started.

"Oh, shit! Sorry! I didn't know you were in here! Sorry." He grabbed a duffle bag from the floor, spun, and left the room, softly closing the door behind him. *Seriously?* I looked up and imagined God laughing at me and then sat up in bed, wrapping the sheets around me in case someone else should enter. I could hear whispers from the other room and a soft chuckle.

Now that they knew of my presence, my prerogative was to escape as quickly as possible. Cain had gone to work that morning at five and had insisted that I stay after he left. It was the first time he had ever left me at his house and, at the time, I relished in the trust he had shown. But now, as I crawled out of the bed and gathered my belongings from the bed side table, all I felt was embarrassed and abandoned to be tried by a jury of my peers alone. I picked up my jeans and blouse from the director's chair that Cain had placed them on after he removed them from my body.

Fully clothed again, I stared at the door, frozen in place by fear of what could happen when I ventured to the other side. *Just open the door and walk out!* I could hear that the group of people on the other side of the door had congregated in the kitchen. I would have to walk right past them as I left. I pressed my ear to the cold wood and placed my hand on the knob. *Maybe I can just stay in here until Cain comes back.* Resolving that staying for the next five hours would make me look like a crazy person and that there was no other option, I wiped below my eyes, hoping to erase any eye makeup that had gone askew and slowly opened the door. *Maybe they won't even acknowledge me. If they have any decency at all they will just pretend not to see me. Please God, make them pretend not to see me. Just keep walking, Myra. Hell- RUN if you have to, out the door.* I made a mental note that my gold Carlos Santana pumps were sitting beside the front door. I could still hear the guys talking, there were two conversations going on. *How many of them are there? Geez! I didn't realize Cain was hosting a frat boy convention.* I stepped from behind the door, out into the hallway that connected to the kitchen, eyes to the coal blue carpet. All voices stopped immediately and I looked up at six grown men staring at me. *Dear Lord. please strike me dead.* A weak smile crept over my face.

"Hey guys." There was a moment of silence.

"Hey there!" A very tall and thin brunette wearing an apron walked from behind the island counter with his hand extended. "I'm Chuck. I'm Cain's roommate." I took his hand.

"Hi, I'm Myra." I smiled, still hoping that God would end this agony by any means.

"Yea, it's great to meet you. I've heard a lot about you." Chuck smiled sincerely down at me. *Really? Like what?* My mind wandered to all of the embarrassing things that Cain had surely shared with him about our sex life and I winced. I turned and faced the rest of the men and one by one they introduced themselves.

"These guys all came to town to watch the college basketball games tonight." Chuck spoke to me, still smiling. "Are you going to watch them?"

"Oh, I hadn't made any plans to yet actually." Basketball was not my sport. Just then the oven timer went off. I hadn't noticed until then the sweet and spicy smell in the air. Chuck punched a few buttons and opened the oven after placing mitts on his hands. When he turned back around he had two trays covered with at least twenty huge cinnamon rolls extended towards the island.

"Alright boys, eat up." He smiled. "Myra, why don't you stay for a while and have breakfast? We have coffee." He added with a smirk. I looked around. The guys seemed nice enough. If Cain wasn't going to integrate me into his life in a timely fashion, I would. Or at least I wouldn't pass up an opportunity to do so when it was presented. Besides that, I was starving, hung over and in desperate need of caffeine.

"So when she didn't answer his phone calls he, being the drunk ass that he so often is, decided to go over to her apartment." Brighton, one of Cain's friends sputtered out the words between laughs. The other five men were red from the hilarity of the story they had surely heard several times before. Apparently it hadn't gotten old yet. I took a long sip of coffee and then a big bite of gooey cinnamon roll, licking frosting off of my top lip. "When he got there he started throwing rocks from the garden at her window to get her attention," I dropped my head, smile wide, horrified of what was to come. "I don't know exactly what happened next. Cain says he doesn't remember much, but all I know is what the report says from the police picking him up, passed out in the bushes, completely naked, clothes laying all around him." As he finished he threw back his head and roared a deep laugh. I looked back up at Brighton and then around at the rest of the group, an amused look of mortification on my face.

"Yup. That's our good buddy Cain. Always good for entertainment." Another friend Dave stood up and walked to the kitchen for another cinnamon roll.

"That is great." I shook my head. "He certainly is one of a kind." That was the third tremendously embarrassing story about Cain I had heard in the course of an hour. I was thoroughly enjoying my time there. It was amazing to learn a side of the man I spent the majority of my time thinking about. All of the men in the room knew Cain in a completely different way than I did. The experience made me feel I was missing out on so much. I

missed him then, even though I had just seen him. I felt like I missed a part
of him I hadn't even been introduced to yet.

Afraid of overstaying my welcome I looked at the clock and decided it
was time to get home even though I truly didn't want to go. I felt
completely comfortable in the company of these strangers, each so
interesting and fun in his own way. It was amazing to have something so
deep in common with a group of strangers. There was a bond shared in the
room. Everyone present loved Cain dearly. I stood up and carried my plate
to the kitchen.

"Do you need help cleaning up, Chuck? I think I am going to head home
now." I called to the roommate.

"Oh, no that's OK. I am about to start making chili for later. You should
definitely come back for the games. More people will get here around four.
Some of these guys invited their girlfriends." There was a collective groan at
the mention of females coming to ruin their "bro time". I laughed.

"Thanks Chuck, that is really sweet. I will talk to Cain. I would love
too." I grabbed my clutch from the kitchen counter, slipped on my shoes
and called into the living room a farewell. All of the guys said good bye and
I walked out of the apartment and down onto the street to hail a cab to return
me to my car a few blocks away.

I walked in to my apartment and the smell of alcohol greeted me. "Ugh!"
I covered my nose with my hand. It smelled like a bar. I walked over to the
table on which sat an open bottle of tequila and a half full shot glass. *How
much did I drink last night before I went downtown?* I shook my head at my
alcohol consumption as I replaced the cap on the Jose Quervo and carried it
and the shot into the kitchen and placed them next to several empty bottles
of beer. *I was definitely the only person here last night, so why does it look
like I had a party of heavy drinkers?* Sometimes I drank on a weekend
morning to curb a hangover from the night before, a little trick I had learned
at school with Ava. As I cleaned and tried to remember the last Saturday
morning I hadn't been hung over, I got a slight headache. Chuck had fixed
me some coffee which helped tremendously, but I was still a little light
headed. I looked towards a bottle of Sauvignon Blanc on my counter. *Nah,
I will just take some Advil. I want to be fresh for when I go back over to
Cain's later.* After I swallowed the pain reliever with some much needed
water, I climbed onto the couch, phone in hand and started a text message.

"Hey there! I woke up to your friends in the apartment and we had cinnamon rolls! It was really fun. I think they like me! Your roommate invited me to come over when you get off to watch the game with you guys! How awesome is that? Would you like me to?" I flipped on the TV to a reality series and before the first commercial break I was asleep.

I jolted awake to my phone ringing, scrambled, and tossed the blanket I had wrapped up in around to find the cell in the folds. It was my mother calling. *I'll call her back later.* After the screen cleared I saw that I had two new text messages from Cain. I grinned and opened the alerts.

"Hey. How long were you at my apartment? You hung out with my friends?"

My face grimaced at his less than enthusiastic response. I braced myself for the next message, rightfully so.

"I think that it is just going to be us guys tonight. Sorry."

"What is the problem?" I tossed my head back in agitation. I thought that my meeting his friends would make him at least happy to have it over with. I could feel the anger start to rise from my stomach. It was unfair for him to be upset with me. He had invited me over and left me knowing that there was a possibility that I would meet them. *What did he expect me to do? Sneak out of there like some whore?* I scowled at the indignity of it and then remembered. *Well, I tried that but it didn't work!*

I only stayed for an hour. Brighton walked in on me in your bed. After that, all bets were off. Chuck said that some of the guys are having their girlfriends over to watch, so I won't be the only girl there.

I took a breath and went out on a limb.

I would love to be included.

Another snake of anger wound itself in my stomach. I was basically begging. I felt like a child asking her father for a play date. I dropped the phone on the coffee table and walked to the restroom to start a shower. I had a suspicion that whatever Cain was going to respond with was not going to be one conducive to me seeing him tonight. As I stripped off my clothes from the night before, I looked at the clock. It was 2:30 p.m. and I was just now bathing and changing clothes. I knew that I smelled rank and I looked even worse as I glanced at my reflection in the mirror.

I let the water and smell of lavender honey embrace my body and mind, trying to prepare myself for the message from Cain. Although I didn't think it was going to be positive news I couldn't stop myself from imagining what it would be like to socialize with Cain and his closest friends. We had never hung out with other people before, and I was so anxious to be a part of his social life it hurt. I closed my eyes as I washed my hair and pictured myself in the amazing Dior dress and Jimmy Choo shoes I had just seen in a Saks Fifth Avenue catalog. In my daydream, Cain and I were captivating everyone at his basketball pitch-in, which my imagination had turned into a black tie cocktail party. All of the women there were much older and far less beautiful than I, and all of the men were shorter than and not nearly as attractive as Cain, who was dressed in a suit that would put 007 to shame. All of the men wanted me and all of the women wanted him, but we only had eyes for each other. As the fairy tale continued, somewhere after Cain and I waltzed in the center of the room while the guests, (hundreds of them at this point), clapped and watched on in admiration, Cain declaring his undying love for me to the crowd, I felt the hot water begin to run out. I opened my eyes to much less fabulous reality of the situation and quickly finished bathing.

I felt a world better as I dried off and wrapped my robe around me. I sank back on the couch in the living room and picked up my phone from the table. *New Text Message (1).* I opened it, took a deep breath and read.

Maybe some other time OK? Have a good night.

I wasn't shocked, but I was still hurt. My elaborate daydream hadn't helped. *Damn my optimistic imagination.* I had hoped that maybe he wouldn't be the predictably aloof and inconsiderate man that I had grown to know. I couldn't understand why he refused to let me be a part of his circle. I laid my head back on the soft cushion of the couch. I was falling more and more in love with Cain every day. That was obvious. What was also quite apparent was that I was getting more and more used to his rejection even though I always hoped to be spared. I was less offended then I should have been because I was expecting it. The real shock would have come if he would have actually agreed to include me.

"Oh, yea, that is not exactly a good sign. He wasn't ready to formally introduce you to his friends, but it was fine for them to see you crawling out of his bed at nine in the morning. What a gentleman." Stella was not and had never been impressed with Cain. Whenever I had questions about a relationship, I always consulted Ava and Stella. We had all written the manual that we generally abided by for dating. But the more time passed I realized that I was not following any of the rules we had established with Cain. Expectations and boundaries were demolished by him.

"Have you thought about the fact that," Stella's tone was harsh. She modified it, bringing it into a sweeter register, and then continued, "That this guy may not actually like you? At least in the same way that you like him. I mean, you are at his disposal, there whenever he calls, however he calls, and are more than willing to run back for more, no matter how he treats you."

"Yes," I interjected roughly to stop her from continuing, "I guess so. We have a lot of fun together and he seems really comfortable around me. You don't see what it's like when it's just us. Maybe I have been hoping to change his mind." My friends looked back at me doubtfully. Stella was the first to speak.

"Yea, well that isn't working." She took a big bite of her chicken taco. Ava looked at her in disbelief and shook her head.

"Myra, the real issue is that you don't have to convince anyone to like you or want to be with you. You are amazing." I nodded my head in agreement as I sipped my long island iced tea. I had heard it all before at this point. Lilly, Mama, Lucas and now them, but somehow it wasn't hitting home. "Have you thought about cutting him loose and dating other people? What ever happened to that Marcus guy from the bar? He seemed like he was really interested." After I spent an afternoon with Marcus at the bar while he worked, we went out for dinner few days later and had an amazing time. He was sweet, intelligent and gorgeous. He also liked to poke fun at himself which I appreciated. He had an uncommon amount of humility for someone as stunningly attractive as he was, not to mention the fact that he was going to be a doctor. The problem was that I only wanted Cain. It made me feel uncomfortable, even dirty, to think about dating someone else.

"Marcus is out of town for the next two weeks." Both Ava and Stella looked disappointed at that.

"Well damn. In that case, what are we doing tonight?" Ava posed the question to both Stella and me. I wasn't in the mood to go out. I just wanted to be at home, or better yet, at Cain's home with him and his friends.

"Oh no." Stella was resolute, "I am not going out. I paid my dues a few weeks ago." Ava moved on quickly from her, sensing a lost cause.

"Myra, love? What are we doing tonight?" *Might as well be a good wing-man. Plus, maybe Cain will be out tonight.* I smiled halfheartedly and put two thumbs in the air.

"Oh, my god!" The walls of my bedroom were spinning in the morning light. I sat up quickly and felt my stomach lurch. I jumped up and ran, stumbling into the wall, and just made it into the bathroom before I got sick. After a few minutes, feeling better but still only inches from death, I slowly made my way to the sink to splash water on my sweaty face. My eyes were red and puffy like I had been crying. *What the hell happened last night?* I had no recollection of what had transpired after Ava and I had left my apartment via taxi to a bar close by. I walked out of the bathroom and sat on the end of my bed, head in hands. Three days straight of drinking had finally gotten the best of me. I heard a laugh from the living room.

"Ava? Is that you?" Painstakingly I made my way through my bedroom and down the hall to the voices. Ava was laying on the couch next to a man I had never seen before.

"Hey girl." Ava said, slurring.

"Hi Ava, and gentleman I don't know." I smiled and walked into the kitchen, every inch of my body in agony. I shook my head at Ava as I poured myself a shot of Vodka. *Hair of the dog that bit you is the best cure. Bottoms up.* I lifted the glass to my lips and held back a second wave of nausea. Ava and her friend giggled from the couch.

"Stop it!" She squealed at him in a teasing voice. I replaced the cap onto the bottle of alcohol, wiped my mouth on the sleeve of the dress I was still wearing from the night before and shook my head. *Come on Ava, what are we, in college again?* I was referring to her one night stand and not seeing the hypocrisy in my own drunken stupor. I shuffled back into my room, closed the door and dove under the covers until 8:00 p.m.

19.

Hey there, Myra! Do you still remember me?

That depends on how many presents you brought me back (wink face).

The morning sun shone through the window a week later and warmed the couch where I lay sprawled out watching MTV. A bowl of cereal on my stomach, I placed my cell phone next to me on the cushion and continued to watch a reality TV show. The night before I had begun to look at available apartments in Chicago, close to the corporate office. The thought of moving to the largest city in the mid-west was surreal and made me anxious. The opportunity was amazing and I would have been a fool to pass it up, but moving away from all of my family and friends wasn't something that I had ever contemplated before. At least not so soon after finishing school and while still single. I decided to hold off on the house hunting until my move there was approved. My phone vibrated again within moments. I wasn't used to Marcus' style of rapid response texting. Cain would generally let hours settle before he replied to me, if he replied at all, a fact that I loathed.

I have many, many presents for you of immeasurable value and all I ask in return is that you let me take you out tonight, or as soon as you are free. If I had to guess, I would venture that you have some pretty amazing plans for tonight though.

I really didn't. I had been spending most of my weekends in my apartment drinking alone and avoiding my friends who were out in the real world and wanted me to join them. Several times now, Cain had contacted me in the latest hours of the night and asked me to come join him once he returned home from the bars. Somehow, I always found an excuse to be at home and close to my phone just in case. It vibrated again.

Whenever works for you. I am just excited to see you again. I've thought about you a lot.

After an amazing first date, Marcus had left the country for Kosovo to do a research program with a professor of his med school team. He had been chosen out of two hundred students from three universities as the gynecological representative in the study.

"He's up and coming in the vag business." Ava had teased. "That is good news for you, my friend!" Ava knew very well that Marcus had seen neither hide nor hair of my "vag". We had only shared a few rather passionate kisses before he left for Europe. I thought about it glancing over at the clock. It was only 9:30 a.m. Honestly, the thought of sitting at home alone all day and evening on this gorgeous early spring day did seem a bit droll. Agreeing to the date would also give me an excuse to get up, go to the mall, buy a new outfit and get dolled up. I looked down at the old and wrinkled over-sized shirt and sweat pants I was donning and turned to look back at the TV. A glimpse of red caught my eye. A bright red stain on the side of my shirt looked to be spreading. Oh my God! Am I bleeding? I tossed my bowl of cereal on the table next to me and jumped up, frantically grabbing at my side. The red liquid was dried and on second glance a little too orange in color to be blood. I sniffed it cautiously and images of my late night McDonald's trip flashed in my head. In the midst of a fried food craving, I hadn't even bothered to change out of my pajamas before hopping in my car and pointing it towards the nearest drive thru line. The red on my shirt was ketchup from the french fries I had eaten. *Yea... I need to get out.* I picked up my phone.

"You are in luck my friend. I am free this evening."

I carried the phone with me into the bathroom and turned on the hot water of the shower. The shelf next to the mirror was lined with makeup and beauty products that had been neglected for the past few months. The only time I bothered with them was when I was going to see Cain, or the couple of times I had met up with Marcus. Since those times were few and far between, the majority of the world had gotten Plain-Jane Myra. I grabbed a towel from the closet and just as I lifted my leg to step into the tub, my phone vibrated again.

"Great. I will pick you up at around 7:30 p.m. You in the mood for an adventure?"

I smiled at his enthusiasm.

"Oh. I am ALWAYS in the mood for an adventure."

I entered the stream of water wondering what the night had in store, and happy that I had someone to fill the time with.

The mall was a zoo. Saturday morning soccer moms with their hordes of uniform wearing children filled every isle. I didn't dare venture out of the Macy's where I had parked and wandered around until I got to the shoe department. I loved shoes. I really loved heels. My love of heels was directly related to my preference to date men of at least six-feet in height. As a tall woman of five feet seven inches on flat feet, I found that anything shorter than six-feet wouldn't allow me to wear my collection of shoes and still be shorter than my date. Which, for whatever reason, was very important to me. The weather was getting warmer and platforms and wedges in bright spring colors promised new and flirty fun. I picked up a pair of cream leather Mary Jane platform pumps. Before I could turn around a masculine voice was in my ear.

"May I get those for you?" I looked to find a tall young man in his early twenties, his deep brown eyes lined with full gorgeous lashes.

"Yes. Yes, you may. Size nine, please." After I bought the BCBG shoes, I headed over to my favorite department for date-apparel. It took me an hour and a half to divide, conquer and purchase a sea-foam green sheer top and a cream camisole to go under it. I decided that Marcus' "adventure" might call for skinny jeans rather than a dress or a skirt. I would toss a pair of flats in my bag just in case a lot of walking was involved. I almost made it out of the store without anything else, but was stopped cold by a pair of earrings and a bracelet that matched my shirt with perfection. A few hundred dollars lighter, and more confident, I walked out into the mid-fifty degree air. I looked at my phone once I was settled in the driver's seat. One of the things that I hated most about my relationship with Cain was that I always felt so scared. Scared to contact him and risk smothering him, scared of speaking up about what I wanted and risk upsetting him. It was a beautiful Saturday and I wanted to share it with him. There I was preparing myself for a date with another man, a great man, and all I wanted was for it to be Cain I was planning to see. I took my phone out of my purse as the car began to warm up from the sun.

"Hey there, bud. What are you up to today?"

I placed the phone back in my purse and started the ignition.

My day rejoining society was a delightful success. I got a mani-pedi and then took myself to my favorite Chinese restaurant for soup and an order of crab rangoon, sitting at the table thoroughly enjoying people, watching and letting my imagination run wild. The restaurant was extremely crowded and even more waited to be seated but I took my sweet time and even asked for an extra fortune cookie as I left. Past the store fronts back to my car, I walked by the first of spring's flowers for sale and wished I had somewhere to grow them. My balcony was too windy for them to do well up there. The clock on my dashboard said 5:02p.m. I was right on schedule to get home, take a shower and begin getting ready. After I sent Cain the text earlier inquiring about his day, I had checked my phone every few minutes for a response. After about an hour, I got the hint and hadn't checked since. I had never gone out and sat at a restaurant alone before. It hadn't been nearly as terrible as I had imagined, but one thing had become very clear to me. I missed having someone to share my life with- the everyday, non- events as well as the important stuff. I wanted someone to sit across the table from me and share the bowl of fried crunchies that I dipped in my soup. I wanted that person to be Cain. The notion of that desire as a reality was, like the afternoon, slowing fading into dark.

I stepped out of the hot shower for the second time that day to my phone ringing.

"Hello Marcus. How are you?"

"Myra! I am very well. How are you?"

"I am well too! What's up?"

"Well, I guess I am not that great. My uncle just called me, his bartender for the night was in a car accident and is at the hospital, and no one else can cover. I have to head over there in about an hour and work the night shift." Shit. I had really been looking forward to seeing him. I walked into my room and stared down at my perfect outfit lying on the bed and remained silent. "Will you be able to find something else to do? If not I will tell my uncle I can't help him out." This guy was over the top chivalrous. I felt a little bit of anger rise up, some residual bruised ego from being stood up by Cain one too many times, but as soon as he offered to see me despite the situation, which was in no way his fault, my heart melted.

"This is not your fault, Marcus. Of course I will be just fine. I think you are a great guy for stepping up."

"Thanks, Myra." I started to tell Marcus to have a good night when he spoke again in an enlightened tone. "You know. If you would like, you can come down and hang out with me. Maybe even bring a friend or have Harper and Lucas meet you. It shouldn't be very busy tonight and I can guarantee that you will get free drinks all night." I smiled broadly.

"Yea. That sounds great Marcus. I will definitely be there and I will bring a few friends as well. Thank you for inviting me!"

Marcus was dead wrong about one thing. Solomon's was absolutely packed. I had never seen so many people lined up outside waiting to get in. Is the doorman holding a list? I fell in line behind a group of middle-aged men and addressed one, shouting over the music that could be heard pumping through the brick wall of the dance floor. His hair was colored stark black with intentional sections of greyish white. It actually looked really good. He looked like a male Cruella Deville.

"What is going on? Why are there so many people?" The salt and pepper turned and faced me.

"The LGBT film festival was cancelled due to a water main break. Fucking conservative-ass city. How fucking convenient."

"That's awful. Do we know how long the wait is?" I genuinely felt bad about the festival. I had heard that people would be coming from all over the country to attend the weekend long event.

"People that are in there aren't going to come out. It is only 8:00 p.m. and this place doesn't usually get going until midnight. This is bullshit." Mr. C. Deville had a point. No one was going to come out, and soon they would start turning people away all together.

"I wonder what Venture is like." Venture was another gay club just up the road. It was bigger, louder and more electric, with elevations to stand and dance on and a stage to vogue walk across if you had the nerve. It also hosted the best drag show in the city.

"My friend just called me from there," the gentleman spoke to me over his shoulder, "they stopped letting people in an hour ago and the line is at least a block long. Thank God for the open container law." I silently agreed with the man. There in the city it was perfectly legal to drink alcohol out on the street. I was sure people were getting quite colorful while waiting in line. Fifteen minutes later and we hadn't moved an inch. I had taken a few steps back, in fact. I was beginning to seriously doubt that I was going to see Marcus that night. I noticed a man walk to the front of the line to the bouncer and motion towards the list. Quickly the bouncer shook his head and pointed to the end of the line. Maybe Marcus put my name on the list? I was sure there were tons of A-listers on the piece of paper. I looked around for Harper and Lucas, who I had invited to meet me. Unable to see them, I gathered up some courage, asked the man in front of me to hold my spot and walked towards the bouncer, my new shoes clicking poignantly the whole way.

"Good luck, honey!" One of my new friend's buddies called.

I caught the bouncer's eye about twelve feet from him and he didn't move them away from me.

"Hi." I started. I looked to the left and glimpsed a couple next to me giving me an encouraging smile.

"Name." The bouncer barked. I looked around, trying to count how many people I was about to get embarrassed in front of and spoke softly.

"Myra Knight." The bouncer leaned in.

"Who?"

"Myra Knight!" I yelled over a raucous group of passers-by. The bouncer looked at the list, then back up at me and smiled.

"Well finally. Our guest of honor has arrived." He turned the "list" over to face me and I read the only thing scribbled on it. Allow Ms. Myra Knight and any/all of her friends in upon their arrival. She may add to this list as well. Nothing could have stopped the gigantic smile that spread across my face. I laughed a little and placed my hand over my heart.

"Do you have anyone that you want in with you?" the bouncer asked. The group of people in the front of the line were all staring at me as if they should have known who I was, but didn't.

"Go head Miss Lady!" A man in a bright blue shorts and gray tee shirt called out. His muscles were deeply defined in his arms and chest. The rest of the group laughed and made similar comments. I turned back to the bouncer and requested that he put the names of Harper Tale and guests and Lucas Michaels and guests on the list and walked back to where I had been in line. The group of men were looking increasingly annoyed having still not moved.

"Hey guys! I am on the list and I can bring guests." They turned to me and stared.

"Seriously, hun?" Mr. Deville asked.

"Yea!" I grinned happily. "You ready?" The group of seven followed me up to the front, turning heads all the way, and went in ahead of me while I thanked the bouncer. I moved to walk into the building and heard from one of the guys at the front.

"Miss. Lady, you know you are fierce! Werk!" I whipped my hair around, gave him my best model look, and said to the bouncer.

"And this group too, please." He laughed and gave me a quick nod while I sashayed into the building. I didn't make it very far. The line to the pay for admittance was almost as long as the wait outside and in the dark inner hallway, the music was already too loud to speak over. I began to move to the music and let the excitement of being VIP and seeing Marcus sink in. Soon the group from the front of the line caught up with me.

"Hey Lady! Thank you so much." One of the friends flung his arm around me. I turned around and smiled warmly, sticking out my hand.

"I'm Myra Knight. You are very, very welcome." For the next few minutes we laughed and danced in the crowded space while it slowly progressed. Out of the vague static of voices, I heard my name.

"Myra Knight!"

I looked around and opened my mouth to answer but my new friends were too quick.

"Yes! That bad bitch is right here! Here she comes," and pushed me up to the front. I found my way to the front and face to face with a hulk of a man with a bald head and a baby face.

"Hi." I looked at him suspiciously. "I am Myra." He took my hand and shook once.

"I'm Max. Marcus asked me to bring you to the bar as soon as you got here. Sorry about the wait- Ed outside didn't call you in until just now."

"Oh that is quite alright." I couldn't believe the treatment I was getting.

"It is crazy in there, so I will escort you to make sure you can get through. The bar area is out of control." He grabbed my hand and led me into the madness. The closer to the bar we got, the more congested it became, until it was almost impossible to move. "Hey! Clear the way!" Max's voice boomed and people shoved themselves away from him, giving us an extra couple of inches to work with. I winced as I felt my beautiful new shoes being stepped on and scuffed with almost every movement. I tried not to think about their cream leather being ruined. It would have been easier if I could have climbed up onto Max's shoulders, and he definitely could have carried me, but I didn't want to push my luck by suggesting that. Finally, we made it to the bar, and he pulled up the countertop and let me inside. Everyone on the other side was staring at me, and I smiled weakly and looked for Marcus. In a flash, a figure I could only assume was him popped up from behind the bar and started moving faster than any person I had ever seen other than an Olympic track star. He was buzzing from person to person collecting orders, and then flung ten plastic cups out in front of him and began pouring different drinks. He was amazingly efficient. I wasn't quite sure what to do. I watched him as he filled a few more orders, his biceps flexing and pects creating mounds in the tight heather gray tee shirt he wore.

He wiped a fine gloss off of his forehead and caught sight of me at the same time. A violently bright smile took over his face, and it was as if the world stopped. He turned and started towards me from the other end of the bar. I, who had been leaning up against the beer cooler all but drooling over him, straightened up, shook my shoulders, and raised a hand to wave. Marcus gained speed and was in a light jog towards me like some kind of charging tiger, muscles jolting with each step. He got to three feet before me, dipped quickly, wrapped his arms around my waist and picked me up, twirling as we went. We spun for a couple of seconds to the sound of some of the bar patrons clapping and hooting and others shouting for him to hurry up and get them their drinks. He set me down very gently and kissed me briefly on the lips. That got another round of approving noises and I turned the color of a cherry.

"You look absolutely stunning." He beamed down at me panting slightly, "How was your day today? Thank you so much for coming out."

"My day was great. I am so happy to see you." I smiled up at him and then glanced around the bar. I was afraid that if we kept them waiting much longer they would start a riot. "Are you the only bartender?" Marcus looked around and wiped his face again.

"Yea, it's insane. There is no way I can do this alone." I looked down at my gorgeous shoes then looked up at his beautiful eyes and knew what I had to do.

I had absolutely no experience behind the bar, but, as far as I was concerned, I had frequented enough of them to have an idea of how to make drinks, and my limited experience in this mob was better than nothing. It didn't take very long to convince Marcus to let me tend, with or without a license. The facility was way over building capacity code and if the fire marshal showed up, I would be the least of his worries. He just looked down at me smirking,

"Alright kid," he said after giving me a two-minute review of the register and adding my name to the server list as "Myra-Love", "Good luck." He kissed me again and walked off to the other side of the bar, buzzing all over

the place again. I turned around slowly to about fifty faces at the corner of
the bar that locked eyes on me like piranhas spotting a human foot in the
water.

"OK, guys." Yes, they were all men, "I have never done this before!" I
yelled to the thirsty crowd. "So be gentle!" And we were off. I moved
from person to person taking orders, making drinks and handing out beers.
If the drink was too complicated and I didn't know how to make it, I asked
them to order something simpler. I was sweet and charming and smiled a
lot, moving as quickly as I could,, but still not quickly enough. The crowd
just kept coming. I was about an hour in and started to feel tired. I turned
around and pulled a red bull out of the refrigerator, slurping it down before
moving onto my next customer. I hadn't seen Marcus again and I hoped
that he was OK and hadn't been overrun by the throngs of men. I pulled my
hair off of the back of my neck, which was slick with sweat. The thin
material of my new blouse was starting to stick to my skin. I'll be damned
if I am going to ruin my shoes AND my blouse! As I walked to the other
side of my area I grabbed the bottom of the sheer material and pulled it up
and over my head. The crowd in front of me cheered.

"Yes honey! Put in work!" I smiled back at them and looked up to see
Marcus standing, mouth open, staring at me. Earlier that day at Macy's they
had only had large and extra small in the cream camisole that I wanted. I
normally wore a medium, a small on a very good day. So promising myself
that I would never dry it, I bought the extra small. So what if my breasts
were bursting out of the top? No one would see that under my blouse. Or
so I had thought. Marcus took a deep breath and closed his eyes to regain
composure, then grabbed the bottom of his own tee and ripped it off. From
the screams emanating from the crowd you would have thought someone
had been brutally stabbed. Everyone, including me was staring at the
glistening, rippling body of "Marcus the Roman." I wasn't completely sure
that one of those screams hadn't come from me. As if that wasn't enough,
he walked over to me turned to the bar, quickly poured two shots of tequila
and handed me one, holding his out for me to tap. We threw them back in
unison and then he grabbed my face again, kissed me, and then was off. I
walked back over to the bar front and leaned up against it looking dazed. I
found the eyes of my next customer, an elderly man who was sitting on a
stool, deep chestnut fingers covered in rings. He smiled slyly at me.

"That is a whole lot of man, honey. Good for you." He winked at me and ordered a bourbon.

Time wore on and I was actually starting to get the hang of serving. I found that the more I smiled, sparkled and called the customers "honey" the happier they seemed to be. After the first hour I had text messaged Lucas and Harper to let them know that they could come anytime and that they and whoever else they wanted were on the list. Just about every sixty minutes Marcus would come by and check on me and make me a drink and hand me a bottle of water.

"I owe you big time for this." He whispered in my ear and placed his large heavy hand on my waist, sending a pulse through my entire body. I stuck my tongue out at him and then bit my lip as he walked away. I had always been attracted to Marcus, because I was a heterosexual woman with a pulse, but being behind that bar with him drove my desire to a whole new level. I just wished someone would give us five minutes so that I could take him back to the store room and have him. I was trying my luck at making five lemon drops for a group of women celebrating a bachelorette party when I heard my name.

"Myra! Here she is! She is behind the bar!" I looked up and say the beautiful faces of Lucas, Harper, and a few of our other friends.

"Hey guys!" They shoved their way over to right in front of me.

"Girl. WHAT are you doing back there? You look fabulous by the way." Lucas shouted over the music and I explained to the group about Marcus needing some help.

"Yes, honey. Stand by your man!" Harper called out. I quickly made them all vodka cranberries, extra strong, and slid them across the bar with a wink. The crowd didn't die down until the overhead lights came on signaling the closing of the club at which point Marcus and I could finally stop serving.

The last thing on my mind at that very moment were my throbbing feet. I looked around the room glowing warmly with rich yellows and greens, and examined the original oil and acrylic paintings encompassed in reflective bronze frames, when my eyes should have been closed, enjoying my mouth being enclosed by Marcus. The all too common duel was in full swing in my mind. I was attracted to Marcus and everything about him. The way he smelled, tasted, spoke to me, and treated me. The way his home held the perfect combination of exotic colors and contemporary style and smelled like nutmeg. The way he attempted to control himself as his sweet kisses gradually intensified to long, searching strokes and then, as if pulled from a trance, he abruptly resumed his soft restrained grazes. We sat on his copper brown leather sectional, my legs in front of me, crossed and tense with the pressure I exerted to keep them closed, and he sat next to me, whole body oriented towards me slightly crouching his massive frame to my level.

After everyone left the bar, and I had finished my fourth vodka tonic, Marcus suggested that I come home with him rather than drive, under the pretense that he "would remain a perfect gentleman."

"You can take me anywhere you want and do anything you want with me as long as I don't have to walk in those shoes." I glanced towards the ruined platforms sitting on the chair next to me and then stared at him feeling warm. I wasn't afraid of what Marcus might do to me. I was afraid of what I might do to Marcus.

I had hopped on his back and he carried me to his red German sports car parked just outside the entrance of the bar and then carried me again into his home a few miles away when we arrived. His lamp-lined street was tucked into a small historic neighborhood just outside of downtown. The large Victorian homes lining the streets slept silently in the early morning dark, and the sound of Marcus' car door slamming echoed off the wood and brick facades all around us, making us both wince. I looked up at the three story, Gothic Revival, deep gray structure with soaring pitches of varying heights and a full wrap around porch, and breathed a soft oooh. Inside Marcus gently let me off his back and set about turning on lights. I followed closely behind Marcus as he moved through the house, illuminating rooms as he went. The home had been completely remodeled with all of the most modern and luxurious amenities, and popped and sparked in rich textiles and woods. After examining a beautiful silver chandelier hanging in the library amongst floor to ceiling bookshelves and plush suede couches for some time, I realized that I had lost Marcus. I tiptoed towards the end of the hallway, trying my best not to make noise and wake the other inhabitants of the home who were, no doubt, sleeping. I entered the open kitchen of mesquite colored wood cabinets that touched the ceiling and a tan, black and cream stone backsplash and found where Marcus had been. Fresh tomatoes, onions and spinach lay on the polished concrete counter top in front of me. I walked around it slowly, letting the cold, smooth surface run under my fingertips and looked around at the room. It was perfect- everything in it flowed seamlessly together and in and of itself was filling to the appetite. I could live in this room for the rest of my life. Again, my mind was taken back to my own undecorated, scarcely furnished apartment and I grimaced, thankful that Marcus had not visited it yet.

I was pulled from my ambient induced haze by my name being called from some faraway place in the house. I turned from the kitchen and quickly moved down the hall from where I had come, trying to locate Marcus.

I found him at the top of the gracefully curving spiral staircase.

"Hey Myra! Come up here." He spoke loudly at which I winced and shushed him then began to climb the hardwood stairs.

"Marcus, you are going to wake everyone up." I whispered, then stopped to listen for any note of disturbance. There was nothing but a soft humming sound coming from down the hall. I reached Marcus and he looked down at me.

"That is really considerate, but I live here alone. So, unless you are afraid of waking the ghosts that are in the attic," he grinned in jest, "you can be as loud as you want." I smiled back at him as another hundred questions popped into my head. How in the world does he have this house? Does he rent it? Is he house sitting? "I have something ready for you," He placed his hand against my cheek, "follow me." Marcus led me down to the end of the hallway through a breathtaking bedroom, which I hoped was the Master Suite and not a guest room, and into a glistening bathroom. On a ledge next to an ivory clawfoot tub lay a towel and set of Marcus' basketball shorts and a tee shirt. Across the room was a glass shower that could hold at least five people, its numerous chrome shower heads spraying water in all directions. "I thought you might want to relax while I fix us some shamefully late dinner." I looked up at him, mouth slightly open and brows furrowed. It was like a dream. My hand moved to his chest and I wrapped my arms around him, tempted to ask him to join me. I wanted to lift his smelly shirt over his head, free him of his jeans and lead him into the shower with me. Instead I reached up and kissed him delicately on the cheek then turned away from him to undress. He moved quickly and was out of the bathroom in an instant, clicking the heavy door behind him. And then I opened the glass door and stepped into a misty heaven.

Twenty five minutes went by in what felt like five. I was shocked when I exited the steaming tiled shower and looked at my cell phone. Afraid of seeming rude, I dressed in his baggy clothes as quickly as possible and rushed down the stairs, hair high on top of my head in a bun. I walked through the kitchen, which smelled like an Italian restaurant, towards Marcus who was stretched out sleepily on the sectional watching a recording of the day's news.

"Hi, there." I spoke as I got closer to him, "I am so sorry, I took so long. I think I got lost in there!"

Marcus perked up quickly and smiled at me.

"I was afraid I was going to have to come in after you." As he spoke he stood and stretched his large biceps towards the ceiling. I watched him with interest. *I wish you would have.* He walked powerfully towards me, stopping briefly to lead me over to the large kitchen table. I moved quickly in front of him to pull out and then scoot in my own chair before he got a chance to do it for me. I heard him scoff playfully behind me, and I looked back giving him a goading smile.

Marcus brought me a glass of wine and then set a plate of lasagna and salad on my plate. It looked amazing. I could smell the ricotta cheese and tomato sauce with the faintest trace of fennel seed.

"Did you make this?" I couldn't believe it. I looked at him interrogatively.

He stopped shaking out his napkin and left it hanging in midair- responding to my skepticism.

"What?" he feigned defense, "Well, not just now- But last night I did. Why?" His face fell a little. "Do you hate left-overs?"

Ha! I just ate a piece of nine day old meatloaf a few days ago. Of course I don't hate leftovers.

"Oh no! I love them. Really! I eat them and everyone else's all the time." I responded to his look of disbelief. "I am just amazed that you made this." Not that I blamed him. I looked past into the gourmet kitchen with sparkling appliances and the question crept back into my head. Whose house is this? I decided that it would be rude to ask. I resumed eating the delicious pasta and my eyes continued to scan. There was so much to take in. Antique plates and dishes lined shelves, small paintings and vases sat on the countertops. The largest wine refrigerator I had ever seen, which was as big as a full sized freezer, sat next to a bar area. Above that was a large iron clock that read... *four forty-five? In the morning?*

"Oh my God!" I covered my mouth. Marcus whipped to attention as I
pointed at the large clock.

"Oh. Yea." He shrugged his shoulders. "I hope you didn't have anything
to do today. Generally after I work the bar I come home and relax for a
while, then sleep for eight hours and get up around noon and start my day."
He stood up and picked up his empty plate and then moved around to mine
and picked it up as well. "It didn't even occur to me to warn you about that."

I should have been exhausted, but I wasn't. I felt like it was only about
10:00 p.m.

I stood up to follow Marcus into the kitchen and then stood next to him at
the sink as he rinsed.

"What are you doing, sweetheart?" He asked without taking his eyes
away from the sponge and plate in his hand. I knew where this was going
but didn't give up.

"I would like to help clean up please." I faced him and waiting for him
to acknowledge me with his eyes. He glanced my way, a small smile on his
face.

"OK. You want to help? Please grab the bottle of wine and put more in
both of our glasses, then meet me on the couch." I knew there was no point
in arguing, he wasn't going to let me help, but I was not about to let him get
off scot-free. I leaned in very slowly then rose on my toes next to the
stubble of his cheek, lingered for a moment then placed my lips ever so
slightly on the seam of his neck. I felt his broad shoulders brush my chest as
he relaxed them, exhaling a sigh. As silently as I had come, I moved away
from him to the table, where I refilled our glasses and took my place on the
couch next to the wood burning fireplace.

So there on the couch we were engaged in a slow kiss. I moved my legs
under my bottom and turned towards Marcus' body, mirroring his posture.
His pillowy lips took control of mine and we tasted the wine on each other.
Firm hands supported and gripped my back through his baggy tee shirt, and
held me firmly against him as I ran my hand along the back of his neck and
through his thick course hair. A moan escaped him. He pulled away from
me, eyes burning and apprehensive at the same time. I returned his fiery
gaze and dove back into our embrace lifting up into a kneeling position. I
kissed him roughly as I began to let the restraints that had been confining
me slip away. I moved my hands down to the small of his back and rested
them on the curve of his back side. Gracefully, almost imperceptibly,

Marcus wrapped his arms around my back and upper legs and lifted me slightly, sliding me forward and then laid me down on the cool of the leather couch and positioned himself above me. We played, tasting and teasing each other's lips and tongues; my hand found its way to the opening at the bottom of Marcus' shirt and I slid my hand under to feel the hardness of his stomach and chest. I placed my palm over his heart and caressed softly with the pads of my fingers. Another moan escaped him and he gently guided his way between my legs, pressing against my core through the thinness of the basketball shorts that covered me. Heat began to swirl there and I wrapped my legs around his solid frame and pulled him closer. I was in a fog of excitement, happiness, and exhaustion.

The exhaustion was the culprit for the slip of the mental curtain that I had so carefully hung to block out certain people from my consciousness. As Marcus' hand moved from my soft stomach past my ribcage and settled on my breast, cautiously at first and then assuredly, I relaxed just enough to let unwelcome images in. I wanted Marcus. I moved my hips against him and kissed and nibbled at his neck and jaw, feeling him tremble above me, making me absolutely certain that he wanted me as well. And just as I had resolved to take him all, out of the shadows came Cain's face crashing through my lust and stopping it dead. Marcus found my lips again and I attempted to push Cain out of my mind but I couldn't. Suddenly Marcus' lips, chest, and waist were Cain's and a wave of guilt washed over me. Myra, snap out of it. I mentally shook myself.

Marcus rose from me and pulled his shirt up over his head which help bring my attention back to the present. His olive complexion was slightly rosy from the heat, chest covered lightly with dark hair. My eyes took all of him in then locked onto his fantastic eyes which seemed to pull my body up to him. As I sat up, I gently pulled the oversized shirt above my head dropped it on the floor next to me. In a flash Marcus had spread over me again, this time with twice the passion and power. His wet lips found my breasts burying kisses in them. I gently guided him up again to rest against the back of the couch and swung my leg over each side of his large thighs, straddling him. His chest was heaving, face flushed, mouth swollen from kissing. He was absolutely stunning. I leaned down to him and kissed him. His hands moved to my chest again and his mouth followed, placing long kisses around the lace of my black and violet bra. My eyes closed and head fell back as he liberated the straps of the garment from my shoulders, and the cool air of the room met my exposed skin and then was quickly over taken by Marcus' hot mouth, licking and sucking at my sensitive flesh.

It was in that moment of bliss that Cain's face came to me again, shocking me, stealing away the joy that I was experiencing and this time he didn't leave. Marcus found my mouth again, his strong arm supporting my back and slowly began to rock back and forth then in one incredibly fluid movement stood up and placed me back down on the couch. I laid there topless while he knelt next to me on the floor and covered my stomach with kisses then moved north to my chest and neck. He placed his large hand on the inside of my thigh beneath the hiked up shorts and massaged closer and closer to my core. The closer he got to the center of me, the clearer Cain came to my conscious. I shouldn't be doing this. I felt like I was cheating on Cain even though we weren't technically in a relationship and all of a sudden it felt terribly uncomfortable to be in the arms of someone else. I wanted to stop, I wanted to leave. I wanted to be with Cain. I took deep breaths and kissed Marcus as he gently kissed my bottom lip and then hovered inches from my face.

"Are you OK, Myra? What's wrong?" He moved back a few more inches so he could take in my face. Apparently the conflict within had spilled out. I couldn't hide what I was feeling or the pained expression that covered my face. "Too fast?" Marcus dropped his head obviously disappointed with himself, "I am sorry, Myra." He raised from me back into a sitting position.

Childishly, I covered my breasts with my hands as if he hadn't seen and become quite familiar with them over the past half hour.

"Please don't apologize." I looked away from his eyes. "I thought that I was ready, but I think we should stop for tonight." I paused then looking back to him. "Is that OK?" I hoped he wouldn't shut down on me, or maybe I wished that he would so that I could gather my things and get the hell out of there. Marcus moved his hand to my face. "Of course." He smiled at me and then reached down to the floor and picked up my bra and shirt and handed them to me sheepishly.

"Thanks." I took them and laughed, shaking my head. After I was fully clothed once more Marcus stood and reached out his hand. I took it and he led my back up the stairs and into the large room connected to the bathroom I had showered in.

"I have a couple of guest rooms, but this is the most comfortable mattress. Would you like to sleep here?" I nodded sleepily. The madness at the bar, the alcohol, the heavy dinner and the intense endorphin rush from the passion with Marcus had all wiped me of energy. I followed Marcus to the king sized bed and was past him and into it before he had gotten a chance to turn down the sheets. I grabbed a huge pillow and pushed my legs under the covers. Looking at him through half closed eyes and smiled.

"Good night, Myra. He walked over to where I laid and kissed me softly on the forehead then turned to leave the room.

I shot up like a spring board, "Where are you going?" I asked in a concerned voice. The thought of him not being next to me was unsettling. Marcus looked around and shrugged. I reached my hand out to him. "Please sleep in here with me." He smiled and walked back to the bed then climbed inside. I scooted over to him, brushed my lips against his, and laid my head on his chest.

20.

"So what is the problem?" Stella sat on the couch next to me and looked at me like I was blind, deaf and dumb. I definitely wasn't. I had just explain to her my reasoning for not sleeping with Marcus the week before. I had wanted to. God, had I wanted to. Ever since he dropped me off at my car the next day I had been thinking about him, and not just the outrageous chemistry we shared, but how thoroughly I enjoyed his company. He was, for lack of a better term, my dream guy. Everything I could possibly want except one big thing that he would never, and could never be. Cain.

"Well, as you know I have been seeing Cain for a while now..."

"Oh please! Do you honestly believe that he is only sleeping with you? Seriously, Myra. Be honest with yourself." She sneered at me while shaking her head. Her hostility caught me off guard. *Where is this attitude coming from?* I stared at the TV in front of us and tried to think about something else before my stinging nose progressed to full on tears. After a few moments of silence I spoke again.

"Cain and I talked about it and we both agreed that even though we are not ready to be in an exclusive relationship we would let the other know if we became physical with anyone else." Cain and I had laid in bed one night and discussed our feelings for what felt like the twentieth time. I had quickly poo-pooed my inner voice telling me to hide my true feelings for him. After all, I wanted him more than anything in the world and he should know it. What would happen if he grew to wanting me in the same way? I might miss my opportunity. After he didn't reciprocate my desire for monogamy, he made his kind of a deal.

"Alright babe, how about this? If I have sex with anyone else, I will tell you immediately, and before you and I have sex again?" *Isn't that a given?* I blocked out the reasoning that since he was just now making that deal, he could have been having sex with other women and not telling me up to that point. I chose to believe he wasn't. A decision that Stella was now disemboweling alive.

"Wait. You both made the decision? Or did he tell you that he didn't want to be exclusive and you just went along with it?" Stella looked at me severely. *Damn, do you have me wire tapped or something?*

"We both decided!" I answered defensively. We knew that was a lie. Stella was making me feel like an imbecile, however, I refused to give her more fuel willingly.

"And you think that he would tell you? After all of the proof that he has displayed that he is a scumbag?" She laughed coldly and changed the channel.

"He doesn't care about you, Myra. And he probably never will. Marcus is a nice guy, practically perfect, and you are going to throw him away and regret it for a long, long time." Stella stood up from the couch and walked out of her family room towards the direction of the bathroom. I sat trying to will myself to gather up my things and go home, just thankful that I had made it through her reign of degradation alive. Suddenly Stella came back around the corner,

"So we have established that Cain doesn't care about you," Oh my God! Is she going in for another round? TKO! TKO! I looked up at her with a warning stare. The kind that signaled she should back off. I had had enough and not nearly adequate time to swallow anything she had said. It just sat cold and slimy in my throat in the form of a lump. Stella knelt in front of me and placed her hand on my leg, "When are you going to start caring about you? I care about you and so does Ava, Marcus wants to care about you if you let him." She sighed deeply. "The person who is really hurting you isn't Cain, it's you. And the sooner you realize that you are letting all of this happen to you, the sooner you can stop it." She stood up again and walked back towards the bathroom. This time I was able to gather up the shredded pieces of my ego, along with my belongings, and exit the house.

I left Stella's house feeling awful. I didn't know what her problem was but everything that seemed to come out of her mouth was hurtful. Everything that came out of her mouth was also true. I didn't want to believe it. Stella was ruthlessly protective of me and wasn't afraid to tell me or Ava when we were messing up big time. But this was a matter of the heart and I didn't feel like she had the right to judge me. It later came to me that she did have to right to judge me because of the fact that I had shared every intimate detail with her. She knew everything that I said, did and felt when it came to Cain. Our relationship was painful and frustrating to me, but I hadn't taken into account what it had done to the people who loved me, who were watching, and waiting for me to snap out of it.

21.

"Are you wearing two pairs of socks?" Marcus' shadow fell over me as I bent to tie the tattered and brown shoelaces of the neon green rental shoes.

"Yes, absolutely." I looked up in alarm, "Why? Aren't you?" Marcus' face was made dark by the florescent light shining directly above him. I squinted then continued, "Do you have any idea how many people's potentially fungus infested feet have been in these things?" I finished the second knot and leaned up from my crouching position, grabbing my large brown leather messenger bag and digging through it. "Here!" I reached up, handing a pair of socks to Marcus. He took them hesitantly but then extended them back to me

"Oh, no that's…"

"It's not a problem really," I interjected, standing up and dusting my hands off quickly. "I have a whole package of new socks in my trunk." I smiled brightly at him, then walked over to the scoring computer, then twirled around, realizing how I must have sounded. "I am not a germaphobe or anything."

"Hey, no judgment!" Marcus put his hands up in defense, a large smile taking his face captive.

"I'm not!" I giggled. Then gave him a serious look, "But seriously, put that second pair on. Better safe than sorry." He rolled his eyes and plopped down in the plastic bench, removing his shoes to pacify me.

We collected beer and hot dogs from the concession stand and then made our way back to our lane. Retro Wednesday at the north side bowling alley was in full effect. Strobe lights and disco balls shot lights and colors through the dusty air, while music from the 70's and 80's played over the sound of plastic balls colliding with wooden pins. After choosing nicknames for my opponent "Marcus the Roman" and for myself "Myra the Pin Destroyer", Marcus and I played a round of Paper-Rock-Scissors to see who would be the first to roll because I was not accepting his Ladies First rationality. Halfway into my fifth consecutive gutter ball set, I stood standing at the red line of the lane, looking around, hoping to steal technique from my neighbors. To my left, a little girl, I guessed she was seven, with a pink dress on and pigtails, walked up to the line holding a sparkly purple ball. She looked up at me expectantly.

"Go ahead, honey." I called to her and smiled. She smiled back, revealing two rows of tiny sharp looking white teeth and then bowled. The lilac ball sped down the alley and smashed into the pins leaving none but two surviving.

"Ah, shucks!" She called out then looked at me. Waved sweetly and skipped back to the ball return, pigtails bouncing the whole way. All right, Myra. If that little child can knock some pins over, you can roll the ball and keep it from going in the gutter. I took a deep breath, looked back over my shoulder to Marcus who gave me a thumbs up, then started my roll. The ball arched into the air upon my late release and then landed with a loud thud onto the wooden floor, rolling slowly into the gutter less than half way down the lane. Embarrassed by being showed up by a first grader, I spun around quickly, head down, refusing to look at Marcus, and shuffled back to the ball return. By the time I turned around, the ball had just reached the end of the lane and had fallen weakly into the trap at the end. Crap. I gave a quick look around to see if anyone had witnessed my disgrace and, sure enough, the little pigtailed girl was looking at me with concern. I grabbed another ball from the return and walked back to the line where the little girl was waiting. She smiled at me and walked over with the confidence of a thirty-two year old vice president.

"I asked my mommy if I could help you and she said I could." She said brightly. Isn't it just my lucky fucking day. I looked up at her mother who smiled weakly at me, looking a little embarrassed, and probably hoping that I was civilized and not going to cuss out her baby.

"Well thank you! I would really appreciate that! You are very good." Is what I said. *"Look little kid. I'm gonna need you to take your blonde butt back over with your parents and stop meddling in grown folks business!"* -is what I wanted to say. She took about five minutes to go over the fundamentals of bringing the ball straight back and releasing right as it passed my side. After being summoned by her mother, she gave me an encouraging thumbs up and ran away shouting,

"You can do it! Girl power!" over her shoulder. *Seriously? Did that toddler just school me?*

I did my best to keep a smile on my face as I lifted the ball to my shoulder, took it straight back and released just past my hip. The ball rolled down the alley, if slowly, in a diagonal line just straight enough to knock over two pins.

"Yeees!" I screamed and jumped up and down clapping. I looked over to the little girl who was doing the exact same thing, looking like a proud mentor. "Thank you for all of your help!" I called over to her and strode proudly back over to Marcus, landing in the seat next to him. His arm was stretched across the back of the bench, ankle resting on the knee of his leg, wearing a smirk. "See if you can beat that." I said smugly.

"You are the most adorable woman I have ever seen." He leaned over to kiss me on the forehead and stood to take his turn. Adorable is good, right? I watched him pick up a ball from the rack, it was at least six pounds heavier than mine, and walk to the line. In one fluid motion he rocketed it down the center of the lane. I flinched with the resulting explosion, which rendered all of the pins defeated.

"Mommy! Did you see how fast that ball went?" the little girl next door gushed. Marcus walked to the end of the platform and bowed at me. Show off.

By the end of the game Marcus' score was over five times more than mine but I didn't care. I printed out the score sheet at the counter and drew a smiley face and a heart on the top. "Here you go." I handed it to Marcus who smiled down at it. "Our first competition."

Marcus put his car in fourth gear as we jumped onto the highway. Exhausted from a long day at work, the vibration from the tires on the road and the engine were gently rocking me to sleep. Marcus broke the silence, "That little girl was really funny." I opened my eyes and turned my head, which was heavily resting on the seat, to him.

"Yea. She was cute for sure, but I don't appreciate it when parents let their children interrupt adults like that." I yawned loudly and continued, "I understand that parents have to think their children are adorable, but they should realize that not everyone feels the same or wants to be bothered. You know?" I closed my eyes again. After a few moments I realized that Marcus had not responded. I opened one eye to see him staring out of the window, jaw slightly clinched. "You OK buddy? Are you tired?"

"No I am fine." He stopped, then started again, "So what? You don't like children?" I paused. I hadn't yet asked Marcus if he had any children. That would definitely be a different, although not shocking twist.

"Oh no, it's not that! I like children that I know or have a connection with." I decided to be completely honest even when I didn't have to be, "But as for just anyone's child? I don't feel a fondness towards them. No."

"Oh, Ok." Marcus responded quietly. The car was silent again for another few minutes while we weaved in and out of evening traffic. "I guess I understand that." He looked over at me and smiled then placed his hand on my leg. I lightly set my hand on top of his. "You want to have kids one day, right?" I froze. Whoa! We have only known each other for a few months! We haven't even had sex yet. It wasn't that I didn't want to have sex with him. I definitely did and if I hadn't been sleeping with Cain I would have already traveled that no doubt glorious road. The very personal question seemed very premature. It wasn't that I didn't want kids, it's just that I didn't know that I did, either. I bit my lip and tried to dig up something to say. "It's just that I know that I want to have kids." Marcus started in slowly. "I'm Italian, remember?!" he joked. "So that is kind of a deal breaker." I remained silently at a loss. I am only twenty-three years old. I have no idea if I want to have a family one day. Is that something I should know already? I made a mental note to ask my older siblings whether there was a time limit on someone knowing whether they wanted to be a parent in their lifetime or not. "Anyway, not trying to freak you out." I could hear in his voice that he was regretful that he had taken the conversation to that place. I closed my eyes again and squeezed his hand under mine.

Marcus pulled to the front of my apartment and jumped out of the car to get my door. I stepped out of the red coupe and took his hand as he walked me to the entrance. I turned into him and watched as he raised the back of my hand to his lips then placed my palm against his cheek. His bright eyes bore into mine, looking encouraging and sincere. I gently put my lips to his and then pulled away.

"Thank you so much for taking me bowling." I leaned in for a hug, wrapping my arms over his broad shoulders. I buried my nose into his neck and took a deep breath.

"You are very welcome." He pulled back and kissed my nose. I lowered myself back to flat feet and walked through the doors and up the stairs to my apartment.

"Do you want kids?" I asked over the loud crowd around us. I sat, elbows on the counter, and took a large bite of my BBQ burger and followed it swiftly with a swig of my favorite micro brewed beverage.

"Shit no!" he barked almost choking on his own hamburger. Visibly disturbed, he took a long sip of water and then, like something had just occurred to him, whipped around to me. "Are you pregnant? Jesus fucking Christ!" People next to us began to stare. All color had drained from his face. I rolled my eyes.

"No, Cain. For God's sake! I was just trying to have a conversation with you." Cain's body relaxed.

"Oh," he exhaled loudly, "well next time please preface that before you start talking about children." We were downtown, just a few blocks away from Cain's apartment, at the bar to watch a basketball game. One of his friends from work, Collin, was meeting us. For the first time I was going to meet someone from Cain's work. I was excited and intent upon making a fabulous impression. "You know, the mother of Collin's son was a one night stand? One night!" I looked over at Cain, unimpressed as he rambled on about how it would feel to have life as you know it end over one slip up. Sometimes it baffled me just how insensitive he was. More than likely, Collin thought that his son was the best thing that ever happened to him. Most parents did. I wanted to tell Cain that there was more to life than philandering frat boy-hood, but of course I didn't.

"So you never want kids? What about Dyson?" Cain's brother had made him an uncle four years ago and Dyson was the love of Cain's life as far as I could tell. "I thought you said that Dyson made you realize that you might want kids." I took another bite of my burger and grease oozed out, down my chin and landed with a plop on my plate. I watched Cain intently as I dabbed at my face with a napkin, making a mental note to reapply my lip gloss later.

"Nah. He's great. I love that little guy, but I don't want any of my own." His eyes remained glued on the fifty inch screen above our heads. "I would definitely want to be married before I had any kids," I perked right up "and every guy I know who is married hates his life. So that will probably never happen either." *Cain you are really fucked up.* I kept that to myself also and looked around the room disgustedly. Sometimes Cain said things that made me really reevaluate my connection with him. If he never wanted to get married then why was I there? I wanted to get married. I pushed those things aside and saw a man in his mid-thirties with light brown hair walk through the door and glance around. He looked down at his gold watch, caught my eyes and then, seeing Cain next to me, smiled and waved. Cain was completely oblivious as Collin made his way over to us and I rose from my bar stool to meet him.

"Hi Collin!" I said loudly, snapping Cain from his sports hypnosis and reaching my hand to him.

"Hello, Myra! I have heard a lot about you. It's great to finally meet you." It always felt good to know that the guy you liked talked about you to his friends, but it always made me embarrassed to think about what exactly Cain said about me. He wasn't exactly a gentleman. Cain and Collin greeted each other and Collin took the stool next to Cain.

"So Collin how was your day?" I asked him. Upon meeting I always tried to talk to people like it wasn't our first introduction by asking them everyday questions. Not the: *Where did you go to school? What did you major in? Where did you grow up?* - but the real questions. The kind of questions, that clue you in on who a person really was.

"It was good!" *He was enthusiastic*; "I worked my tail off with Cain here." *He was hard working and a team player, not afraid to share credit or acknowledge the contributions of others.* "Then snuck out early to play a pick-up game of basketball to blow off some steam." *Understands the importance of physical activity as an effective stress management tool. So far so good!*

"That sounds awesome! Where do you play?"

"I play at a park near my house on the North side of town. In Kensington." Kensington was a very moneyed address. The information just kept rolling in. I was able to gather that he and the mother of his son lived approximately five minutes apart so that they could split custody. He had a part time nanny to help keep the house up and on the evenings when he couldn't get home before the bus came. He was thinking about getting his son a puppy but didn't want to have to keep it kenneled when he went out of town on business, so Eric's, his son's, mother would have to be willing to let the dog stay with her every once and a while. His relationship with his son's mom seemed pretty polite.

Collin and I continued to chat over Cain while he watched the pre-game highlight show and interjected during the commercial breaks. I liked Collin. He was quick, funny and adorably endearing. Moments before the game began, Cain excused himself and found his way through the now packed bar to the restroom. I ordered Collin and me another round and he promised to share an order of breadsticks with me.

"You know," Collin said as he lifted his glass to his mouth and drained the remainder of his first beer. "Cain really likes you. He was pretty bummed when you guys weren't talking a while back." I looked at him in shock.

"It was only for like a week! He couldn't have been."

"I'm telling you," Collin interrupted, "He was. He even came over and made me talk to him about it, give him ideas of what to do," He winked at me and I turned to the bartender who had delivered our fresh round of drinks. And the best you clowns could come up with was a *"Hey there. What's up." text?* I couldn't deny the feeling of contentment rising up from my stomach. Cain came back in a few minutes and grabbed my hand as he sat, then held it on his knee. I looked over at him and noticed for the first time how relaxed he seemed. Like he was just hanging with his buddy and girlfriend. He caught me staring at him and winked at me. I giggled and squeezed his hand, then settled in for the basketball game.

"I like Collin, a lot." I spoke loudly from inside Cain's walk in closet. I stood in my underwear and looked in dismay at the disorganized ball of cotton t-shirts as I tried to pull a ragged white one out to sleep in.

"Oh, yea? I think he likes you too. I'm glad you finally got to meet. He is a nice guy." Cain's voice got nearer and nearer until I felt his arms wrap around my middle and pull me into him. "Why are you looking for a shirt when you know I am just going to take it off of you in a second? That seems like poor time management." I spun around to face him, still in his hold.

"I will need it for after you are done with me then," I said teasingly.

"I don't think you will," he leaned in close and then quickly kissed me, taking my breath away. I wrapped my arms around his neck and pulled my legs up to encompass his waist never once losing connection with him.

My head lay on his chest. The lights were on and I could see the few blonde hairs that were scattered across the two distinct hills of his pectorals. Every fifth hair I found, I kissed. I was only up to twelve and I was pretty sure I had counted a couple of them twice. Cain's hand was on my head, every so often he would flex his palm and his fingers would grip my scalp. I soon gave up on counting and closed my eyes breathing him in. Things had gotten so much better. We were seeing each other several times a week and getting out of his room and into the real world. We were getting closer and closer, and although I was satisfied, I couldn't help but wonder when we would make our relationship more official. I breathed again, this time with my nostrils against his skin, like I was trying to snort him up.

"Has it ever been like this for you before?" Cain's voice pierced the room. *Like what before? How I want to be with you every second. Or how I think about you all the time, how I feel you every second of every day. Or maybe how every decision I make I compare and contrast what you might want, think or feel? How I have absolutely no self-control when it comes to you and that scares me because I don't even care?*

"Like what before, Cain?" I decided that was the best answer.

"Our sex. It's amazing, the passion. It feels so good," I raised my eyes to him. *Of course you had to take the most superficial route possible.* Cain continued to speak in fragments, "So amazing. So intense! Like nothing I have ever experienced." I smiled. I agreed, it was intense and very pleasurable, but it didn't hold a candle to the deep desire I had for every inch of Cain's mind, body, and soul. I wanted his physique less than any other part of him. "Any way, you are amazing." I lifted my head off of him and extended my neck towards him, lips puckered. He kissed me, reached over to turn off the light and then pulled me up next to him where he held me until I fell asleep, the shirt I had picked out, still abandoned on the floor.

22.

"I'll be out in a second!" Cain shouted over the sound of rushing water through the cracked door of the steam filled room. I poked my head around the corner towards the yellow light of the bathroom, having half a mind to join him in the soup-scented shower. It had taken me quite a while to put on my makeup in preparation for the evening and I didn't have any of my supplies for reapplication so I decided against it. Cain had planned a lovely Saturday evening for us, which was how I knew that our relationship was progressing in his mind, if even subconsciously. Saturday was prime real estate. Dinner and the new action movie he had read a few reviews on. The lead actor was a ridiculously well chiseled Englishman with dazzling green eyes and deltoids to die for. I had no issue with the prospect of watching him run shirtless through crowded European streets and underground military laboratories for two hours. No issue at all.

I plopped my bag and jacket down on the floor in Cain's bedroom, helped myself to a piece of spearmint gum lying on Cain's desk then sat on the side of the bed next to the night stand. There, splayed across the dusty wood surface, were his wallet, his keys, his cell phone and work ID and a pile of change next to a plastic cup. Shaking my head I picked up the quarters, nickels and few pennies and dropped them one by one in the cup with the rest of Cain's coins. How hard was it to place them in the container rather than next to it? I had come to accept the fact that Cain was not the neatest or cleanest person I knew. Not by far. I wasn't sure if he just couldn't see the disorganization, dirt and general distressed state of his apartment or if he just didn't care. Whichever the culprit, I had developed a habit of cleaning up Cain's space whenever I had the time. It wasn't just esthetic for me. I had suffered for all of my life with allergies and after one particularly bad asthma attack from sleeping underneath Cain's dust ridden ceiling fan, I decided that I may have to take matters into my own hands. Cain was a pretty terrible cook as well, so when we ate in at his place, I was chef. I couldn't be expected to prepare a three-course meal in a dirty kitchen, so sometimes I cleaned that as well. Despite all the excuses, deep

193

down, I knew that Cain brought out the domestic in me. I just wanted to take care of him, for him to not have to worry about trivialities and focus on being a rock-star. Which he clearly was. It was the exact model that I learned from my parents. The one I swore I would never duplicate.

After I wiped my hands on my light pink mini dress, and then checked where I had just touched for smudges, I collapsed back on the bed behind me, grabbing a steel blue pillow from the headboard and stuffing it under my head. I was going to tell Cain that I loved him that night. I was going to tell him while he was awake and conscious and while it was light outside, rather than in the dark while he was asleep and I was sure he couldn't hear me. I was sure it was obvious at that point, anyway. Today marked the fifth month since the day that we met. I turned to the side and nestled into the cool pillow, smiling sweetly to myself while taking deep breaths of Cain's scent into me, glad that I had washed his sheets the last time I had visited.

My right eye opened slightly, allowing it to focus on the tiny fibers on the cotton cloth supporting my head. Suddenly, sunlight broke through the high window of Cain's bed and something inches away from my face caught the light and shimmered. I lifted my head slightly and before I consciously directed my fingers to do so, they were holding a long blonde hair. My mouth dropped open. *What the hell is this?* Accusations flew wildly through my mind. My heart's rhythm picked up. *That bastard!* I felt my fist tighten into a ball. *Myra! Calm down.* I worked over time to defuse the situation. That hair probably got picked up in the laundry or something. I had never seen Cain's roommate there with a blonde woman before. In fact, out of the six or seven girls that Chuck had brought home, they had all been brunette. Doubt and anger rose back up, there was no logical place this hair had come from other than a woman in Cain's bed. *Myra! There is no way that you can take responsibility for witnessing every single girl that Chuck sleeps with!* I thought that over and had to agree. I took a deep breath as I tried to convince myself that the hair was from the dryer. I left the bed and grabbed my purse to find my lip gloss, listening for sounds from the bathroom down the hall. The shower was still running.

After I pulled the slender body of the gloss from the bottom of my unkempt bag, I walked over to a mirror that hung on the inside of the closet door. I felt much better. *One hair does not a cheater make.* I smiled, relaxed and took note of how upset I had just gotten over the idea of Cain sleeping with another woman. It was all the more reason to tell him that I loved him and move our relationship to the next level. *Should I tell him at dinner?* I screwed the applicator wand back into the nude pink bottle. *What if he responds badly at dinner?* We would have to skip the movie. I repeated some positive affirmations to myself and ran my finger underneath my lower lashes to neaten my eyeliner. *I don't know that I will be able to last through an entire movie without telling him.* My brown hand reached up to my hair to fluff out my locs. I ran my hand through them once, then again and then I felt something catch on my index finger. *What the hell is on my finger?* I swiftly brought my hand to my face where not one, but two long blonde hairs had wrapped themselves around my index and middle fingers after being emancipated from my locs. They had obviously hitched a ride with me while I was lying on Cain's bed.

With stray hair follicles in my hand I sat down on the bed silently. I could feel the corners of my mouth lower in pain. *Myra he's not.* I tried to console myself but couldn't finish the thought. *Myra he's not...* I didn't want it to be true. I tried to keep an open minded. There could be a perfectly good explanation. *Myra he's not...*

"Hey babe! How are y…" Cain burst into the room in the midst of my last plea to the universe that he was not sleeping with anyone else. As soon as I looked at his face I knew in my gut that he was, in fact, fucking other women. The only thing left to do was to get a confession. Cain, not being an idiot, knew from the look on my face and my sunken posture that something was not right. "Are you O..." I didn't wait.

"How many women are you having sex with, Cain?" I looked up at him from the floor, two pieces of hard evidence still clutched in my hand. I had a slight urge to jump up in his face and start flailing around like an idiot. I had only ever seen this kind of confrontation happen on trashy talk shows and was completely at a loss for how much dramatics was acceptable. "Don't lie to me, please. Just tell me the truth." I reserved myself to that from the bed. Cain's eyebrows raised, then he looked quickly around the room and walked in the direction of his nightstand, picked up his phone and looked at it as if he expected to see evidence of my tampering with it. *Guilty.* Cain looked at me, anxiety in his eyes, then sat on the bed a few feet from me.

"Not very many Myra." I whipped my body around to square him. *Is this fool serious? Not very many?* "And I am not spending time with any of them like I do with you." Like that was supposed to make it better.

"Cain, you promised. You *promised* me that if you ever had sex with anyone else that you would tell me *immediately* after." Ironically, Cain and I had been sitting in this exact spot. We had also talked about protection. I had made the decision that since I was on birth control and neither of us were sleeping with anyone else at the time that it would be fine if Cain didn't wear a condom. The agreement was that if he did sleep with someone other than me then he would protect himself and also tell me what had happened before we were intimate again. As I heard the words come out of my mouth they fell like dominoes of truth, each one setting off another one to come. I looked at the ceiling. *Jesus.* "You have been sleeping with other women the entire time we have dated haven't you?" I looked at him like I was asking about the weather. Initially, I had been afraid that I was going to fly off the handle, strike at him or strangle him. The reality was that I was quiet, calm. There was no more emotion to be had. He looked at me pitifully, ran his perfectly massive hand across his forehead, sighed and then nodded three times, each one more committed than the last.

"You have to be fucking kidding me." I dropped my head, shaking it. Here I was about to profess my love to this creature. A smiled spread across my face. I had a weird quirk that made me laugh at things that were terribly sad, or unfortunate- especially when they were at my own expense. The irony of this situation was palpable. I had just started to get comfortable, feeling it was safe to let my guard down and trust this man with my heart. The night before as I laid in my bed, I scripted the whole conversation to be had. We would be sitting across from each other, perhaps at a café after our movie, sipping coffee, watching people passing outside in the mild air. I would wait until there was a lag in conversation, a long pause, and then I would say it. *Cain, I love you. You mean so much to me and I love you.* In my now preposterous fantasy, he would grab my hand and tell me something similar. We would go home and make passionate love after which Cain would demand that we begin a monogamous relationship, and that he couldn't fathom being with anyone else and certainly didn't want me to be. I had slept sweetly under that dream, warm with expectation. There would certainly be no profession now. Unrequited love was the worst, and since he was sleeping with "not that many" other women, which meant about ten, I was pretty sure he didn't share my feelings.

"This is…" my voice was strong and powerful until I felt a sharp pain to my heart. My voice became soft, weak, almost a whimper. "You are unbelievable, Cain." My stomach churned with red hot lava causing nausea. He was gazing at the floor with a cold, sad look on his face.

"Myra, look." He scooted closer to me. "It's not like we are exclusively dating right? I told you I didn't want a serious relationship." I refused to look him in the eyes.

"You lied to me, Cain." My voice was soft. "You've known all along that I thought that I was the only one… in that way." I looked from the floor to his face. "You are a liar."
That stung him and his face winced.

"Myra, I care about you. I just didn't want to hurt you. But I didn't want a serious relationship."

"No. You manipulated me into getting exactly what you wanted from me. You didn't want to just be with me, but you didn't want to be without me, so you broke your word to satisfy your own desires. You are a child." Cain dropped his head back down and my heart ached for him, the bastard. Even though I hated him, I didn't want him to hurt.

My stomach lurched again as I realized how badly I wanted to go back fifteen minutes. Before I found what some other woman had left behind while she was kissing, touching, holding and ultimately having sex with the man that I loved. *How many other women have sat right here?* Images emerged of white women, Asian women, Latino women. *Was he also dating other African American women?* Had he used protection with all of them? Any of them? Another wave of nausea rolled over me as I thought about the repercussions of being intimate with a sexually frivolous man. It was dangerous. Was I ready to deal with those consequences? That thought rocketed me out of my seat startling Cain.

"What are you doing?" he was monotone. I was looking around for my purse and shoes and then walked around the room to the other surfaces to make sure I hadn't left an earring or bracelet. I prayed I didn't find some other woman's personal effects instead, because they might send me over the edge into a murderous rage. I had been betrayed, but more uncomfortable than that, I felt like the world's biggest fool. I needed some relief.

"I am going home." I looked at him and our eyes met. There was nothing in him. No desire for me to stay, in fact, he seemed relieved that I was going. I looked around a final time, walked towards the door and turned towards him. "Goodbye, Cain." I whispered. I wasn't sure if he responded or not due to the intense ringing that enveloped my entire head.

I made it out of the apartment, sprinted to the elevator, jabbed at the button and slipped through the partially open doors, pinning myself to the sidewall of the car just before a loud sob escaped my mouth. I took deep breaths and hid my face, as a passenger entered the car on the next floor. I felt like I was being jabbed by a hundred knives. Cain hadn't stopped me from leaving, didn't reach out to comfort me didn't even apologize. *He said he did it to keep me in his life.* A small voice tried to stand up for Cain. I stomped the weak bitch out.

By the time I had reached the main floor I was livid. All sadness had been replaced with rancid rage that needed to be neutralized. The most aggravating thing was that he had tried to justify his actions. *He didn't want to hurt me.* I had no doubt that he was hesitant about hurting me but that came tertiary to his ridiculous ego and his stunted emotional capacity. He had manipulated me like I could have never imagined possible. I laughed loudly as I opened my car door, catching the attention of a few men walking a dog, who glanced my way. I peered at them quickly in embarrassment and then jumped into my car. As I drove away, my mind raced back to a fight that Stella and I had had over Cain. She had insisted that Cain was a creep and had predicted the very situation I found myself in. I remembered the conversation and thought about how she had championed Marcus. Marcus, my protector. He had asked me earlier in the week if I wanted to have dinner with him tonight. Of course I had to decline because of my plans with Cain, but now I wanted nothing more than to be with someone who made me feel good. I needed him to make me feel all the way better.

The seven minutes it took me to get Marcus' street and park in front of his house was not enough time for me to adequately cool down. I should have just gone home but instead I climbed out of the car and walked the sidewalk up to the front steps and rang the doorbell. Marcus had been thrilled when I called him and told him about a "change in plans." He had insisted that I come over and let him fix us dinner. I was determined to drive any thought of Cain out of my mind. I sat on a stool at the large counter and watched Marcus, donned in a white "Grill Master" apron, cut up vegetables and a chicken. I had never seen a man cut a whole chicken up into individual parts before. He was hacking away, missing joints and breaking bones until he was left with eleven pieces of meat. I was pretty sure there was only supposed to be eight, but I kept that to myself. As he continued to maul the poultry, he asked me about my day. I described my morning, one of cleaning my apartment and doing laundry.

"Naturally." He commented, looking quizzically at a single chicken piece made up of half a leg and a thigh combined. Marcus often teased me about my insatiable desire to clean my apartment. I had never really thought about it but cleaning calmed me and I did spend a considerable amount of time doing it.

Usually, I would have smiled and laughed. Maybe even mocked him back, but today his teasing seemed rude and uncalled for. My already bloodied feelings, through no fault of Marcus', began to throb again. I stopped talking immediately and looked away, feeling attacked. I knew that I was being dramatic, but I couldn't pull myself out of the bad place I was in. It occurred to me that Marcus wasn't going to be able to either. After a moment of silence Marcus looked up at me,

"And? What else."

I gave him a blank look and shrugged my shoulders, hopping down off the stool as he watched and walked into the powder room off the kitchen. After shutting the door behind me, I stared in the mirror and grabbed a tissue from the dispenser on the counter, then wiped under my eyes. This was not going well. I felt distant from Marcus. *He didn't even kiss me when I came in. Only a hug. And if he doesn't stop massacring that chicken I am going to scream.* I turned off the light and walked out into the hallway and into the entry of the kitchen.

"Is everything OK?" Marcus looked concerned.

I inhaled deeply.

"Yes." I answered sharply, "Why wouldn't it be?" I sounded like an ornery eight year-old. Marcus raised his eyebrows at me and then turned around to open the oven before placing the seasoned chicken and vegetables in then turned back around.

"I don't know babe, you seem upset about something. Why don't you tell me what's going on so I can help fix the problem?"

Damn it, Marcus! Do you have to say just the right thing in every situation? I felt like an asshole.

"Well..." I started, "You didn't kiss me when I came in." It was completely absurd, but it felt good to complain about something, especially to someone who I knew was listening, so I continued. "Is something going on? Would you rather just be friends?"

I heard a voice in my head, this time it was my dad's. *Neurotic Nancy Needs a Nap.* It was something that he often said when people were being ridiculous. I knew he was right. I was trying too hard to be OK after the "great reveal" with Cain and the pressure was causing me to unhinge. By the time I had determined to snap out of it and act normal, Marcus had crossed his HGTV kitchen and put his arms around me, slowly tracing my back.

"Absolutely not, I don't want to be just friends." He kissed my head. "In all honesty, I ate some barbeque bacon chips before you came over. *That* is why I didn't kiss you." He pulled away and smiled brightly at me.

"Oh." I answered, mortified by my temper tantrum.

As he held me I tried to summon up any of the passion I felt for Cain when he did the same. There was a glimmer, but it was so slight that I questioned whether or not I made it up. Marcus stood, still holding me, not pulling away, not rushing me, just content in being the support that I needed. I buried my nose in his shirt and took a deep breath. He smelled amazing, like pine and cinnamon. I relaxed, putting more of weight against him broad chest. Marcus moved swiftly, putting his arms under my legs and around my back and picked me up. I buried my face in his neck and kissed him once softly as he carried me over the couch and sat with me still on top of him.

"What's wrong, babe?" Marcus spoke sweetly.

I shook my head then stared into his eyes. *Marcus is what I need.* I kissed him. I kissed him slowly and sensually, filling his mouth with my tongue. He was right. He did taste like barbeque and bacon. I kissed deeper, holding his face in my hands. He pulled away to look me in the eyes again, but I buried my face into his neck and kissed the spot right behind his ear. He moaned softly and held me tightly. I found my way back to his mouth and sucked at his bottom lip, feeling his breath quivering. I needed to know once and for all what was here and what wasn't. Gently I moved off of him and stood before him. I didn't take my eyes away from his as I unbuttoned my jeans and slid them off of my body, exposing bright pink lace panties. His eyes flashed down quickly and then back up to my mine. Next, I pulled my tee shirt up over my head and laid it on the ottoman next to me. Marcus again broke eye contact only for a second and then resumed gazing into my eyes though his breath had quickened. My hands went to my panties, and, after taking a deep breath of courage, those fell to the floor too. I wondered what Marcus was thinking or if he was waiting for an invitation to join me.

My arms moved to my back and in one motion I unhooked my bra and let it slowly fall off my breasts. I stood there for a second and watched as Marcus took all of me in, motionless. Just about the time I worried that I was not being well received, he shot up from the couch and was all over me. He kissed me passionately, hands roving over my breasts, hips and butt. I moved into him, taking hold of his belt buckle and fumbling with until it was unlatched, and then undid his jeans, pushing them down towards the Earth as he leaned over to kiss my neck and cheek. He stood tall to discard his shirt. He stumbled a little and freed his ankles from the pants, then stood upright again, standing in front of me. I took a step back and washed my eyes over every inch of him. His strong legs, bulging with muscle, powerfully led to his bright blue briefs and the essence of his manliness, which jutted out at a ninety degree angle to his body. I was startled to see how much of him was there, hidden in his underwear. I walked the two steps to him and placed a hand on each side of his waist, sliding my fingers inside the band of his underwear, and moved them down carefully, revealing the most perfect penis I had ever seen. Marcus stepped out of the blue briefs on the floor and pulled me into him, pressing against my stomach. He kissed me and walked back to the couch sitting down slowly. I followed, still moving my mouth with his, and placed my hand on the hard length of him. He moaned deeply into my mouth and the rest of his body became rigid as well.

"Myra." He moaned. Then kissed me again. I pulled away, intrigued by what laid hotly in my hand. I placed my mouth on his neck, then his chest and then his stomach, creating a trail down his body until I was face to face with his desire for me. I kissed it once. Marcus hand shot out and gripped the pillow next to him. I kissed it again and watch Marcus' bite his bottom lip, seemingly helpless. I looked him in the eye one final time before I took all of him into my mouth, tasting his smooth and salty flesh, letting my tongue move over every ridge. Marcus' strong legs shot out in front of him and then collapsed to the ground and I continued my work, carefully fitting my mouth around him and pulling at his sweetness. More than anything I was enjoying the symphony of sounds escaping Marcus above me. To know just how much pleasure he was experiencing made me want to continue. So

I did, intensifying my efforts little by little, causing Marcus' music to crescendo and crescendo until, much sooner than I anticipated, he erupted a final bar, in long, loud notes. I popped up to find him sprawled across the couch, eyes closed and panting. I moved back up to his body and laid my head on his chest, sitting next to him.

"Wait, I'm not done." He sputtered, wearily placing his hand on my head. "Just give me a minute." I smiled to myself and kissed his shoulder, then laid my head back down. I closed my eyes and listened to his breath regulate, becoming slow and deep. He hadn't even touched me intimately but I was fine with that. My mind wandered off to what had just happened. It didn't feel wrong. I hadn't thought about Cain once, but the question of if I had done this to get back at him reared its ugly head. *No. I wanted to see how things would feel with Marcus.* They felt amazing. They felt real. A part of me felt relieved that I could feel passion outside of Cain. A few minutes later the timer for the oven went off. Marcus, who had fallen asleep jolted awake and I jumped up to turn off the oven and remove the chicken and vegetables. I set them on the glass stove top and walked back over into the living room and stooped to gather our clothes, handing his shirt to Marcus who had been watching my naked body move around the house, grinning.

"What do I need that for?" he asked smirking.
I laughed and tossed it at him.

"Aren't you hungry? The chicken just needs to cool for a moment and then it will be ready." Marcus leaned forward and grabbed my hand, pulling me to him, my face very close to his.

"I told you. I'm not done yet."
Two hours later Marcus came through the bedroom door still naked and holding a tray filled with a large plate of chicken and veggies and two large glasses of water. He placed it on the king sized bed amuck with tousled sheets and pillows. I clapped and cheered for him as he climbed back in bed and handed me one of the glasses.

"And now, for dinner." He took the plate from the tray and scooted back next to me against the tufted headboard. "I had to nuke it." He said apologetically. I kissed him on the cheek and took a bite of chicken. It was delicious. I was sweaty and sticky after the two hours of sex with one whose prowess had proven to be unmatched by anyone I had ever heard of. Where Cain used pure strength and brute force in the bedroom, Marcus used finesse, was agile and intentional in every move. The salt from the chicken stung my raw lips and I licked at them feverishly. After we finished eating, Marcus pulled back the sheet and I climbed under it. He followed and spread his arm. "So what is the deal with the tattoo, Marcus? Really. I want the whole story." I smiled warmly up at him then stretched the lower half of my body which was stiff from activity and dehydration.

"You know I could watch you do that all day, right?" Marcus sighed blissfully, then snatched the sheet off of my body exposing me. I shrieked playfully and snatched back at it and in an instant he was back on top of me, kissing my neck and chest. I pushed at him trying, but not really trying, to wiggle away until he stopped and looked at me with displeasure.

"Well?" I encouraged him. "What about the tattoo?" He smiled and rolled off of me, I followed him and perched on his chest looking up at him.

"I was eighteen and in Italy,"

"You were only eighteen when you got that?" I interrupted.

"Shh!" Marcus started over, "I was eighteen and in Italy. I had just graduated and it's a custom in my family to spend the summer between high school and college in the Amalfi Coast, in Salerno." He continued to speak like I had any idea where that was. I didn't. "That is where my paternal grandparents are from." He stopped and looked at me as if I was going to ask a question and then continued when I did not. "So I was there for four months, and I met this young lady in the village. Her name was Giana. She was the most beautiful girl I had ever seen and I fell in love with her, head over heels." As I intently listened to the story, I tried to imagine an eighteen year old version of him, then felt perverted, as I was attracted to the younger version of him as well. "Well we spent the summer together and towards the end we became," Marcus paused, "intimate." Marcus looked away, apparently slightly embarrassed, and then back at me. His cheeks and nose were a little rosy and he wore a smirk. "Well, somehow Giana convinced me to have this tattoo done in her image, telling me, '*you should never forget your first.*" My mouth dropped. *Really?*

"Wow. You were really honest about that." I stammered.

"Yep. I was young."

"The tattoo certainly doesn't *look* to be of an eighteen year old." I sat up and turned around to get a closer view of the design. I traced my finger along the ink running over a large blue vein that cut off the mistress' torso. Marcus' bicep was hard and flexed.

"That is because she was thirty-five." He finished his story.
I whipped my head to him, eyes wide in horror and then fell backwards in hysteria, slapping at the bed next to me in glee. Marcus scoffed and jumped on top of me holding my hands above my head and pinned to the bed

"What the hell is so funny?" He asked me over my laughter, trying to look stern, but failing to hide a smile.

"Young lady, my ass!" I did my best to calm down and leaned up towards his face. He kissed me softly and then rolled over off of me and pulled me to my side. I laid my head back on his bicep after kissing his first lover, and sunk against his large frame.

"I am falling for you pretty hard, kid." He whispered into my ear from behind me. I turned around briefly and kissed him, then laid back down, not sure if I felt the same.

23.

"Final-Fucking-Ly!" Lilly screamed out into the afternoon air and proceeded to jump around the parking lot like a child. She ran a lap around, laughing, then stopped in front of me. "Finally, bitch! Finally!" I shook my head at her, smiling wide.

"Are you done yet?" I asked her, impatiently.

"Yes!" She took a puff of her cigarette, "Now tell me everything."

It was Monday, after spending both Saturday and Sunday night with Marcus. He studied, while I read and watched TV and used his computer to log in to the server for work and replied to emails. We had sex more times than I was willing to admit, even to myself. Every hour that I spent with him ticked away the doubts about him and me more and more. That morning when I had gotten into my car to go home I looked at my phone for the first time in a day. *No New Text Messages.* Cain hadn't tried to reach out to me at all. I wasn't sad about it in the slightest.

Back in the office a few hours later, Ben stopped by my desk and asked me to meet with him in one of the small conference rooms. I followed him down the hall and sat next to him in the cold room, uncertain what was going on. He pulled the speaker phone that rested in the center of the glass table closer to us and then dialed a number, tones echoing off of the sterile gray walls. A deep voice picked up after several rings.

"This is Cody." It was the Big-Dog. "Hello Cody, this is Ben and Almyra Knight."

"Hello there, Almyra!" Recognition permeated his voice. I looked to Ben who nodded in approval.

"Hello, Cody. How are you?" I answered, understanding dawning. This was it. I had been waiting for months after having a conversation with Ben about a potential position at our ambulance company's corporate office. My guess was that the approval had finally gone through.

"I am well! Listen," he cut to the chase. "Ben tells me that you are willing to come and work up here at corporate as the regional manager for contracts. Is this true?" My heart was racing. A lot had changed since that initial talk with Ben, but a lot was still the same. I took a deep breath and took the plunge.

"That is correct. I would be honored." I smiled at Ben and he looked relieved. It would have been smart of him to follow up with me in private, a thought that seemed to occur to him too late.

"Fantastic!" Cody boomed. "It looks like you will be starting here in three months. Does that sound OK to you?"

It sounded as good as any other time to me. I wondered how I would go about telling me family and friends. How I would tell Marcus. It struck me that I may not have to tell Cain. I wouldn't be surprised if I never heard from him again.

"That sounds great. I am ready as soon as you need me."

"Perfect. I will be back in touch with you and you should be hearing from HR regarding your salary increase and moving bonus." *Salary increase and moving bonus?* I smiled widely. "I am off to a meeting but I will talk to you again soon. Thank you Ben." And then he was gone.

I sat perfectly still until I was addressed by Ben. He stuck his rough hand out to me. I took it and shook firmly.

"I will need you to help me find your replacement here," was the only thing he said as he stood and left the room. I watched the door close behind him and laughed.

As I pulled up to my apartment building, I contemplated who I would tell first about my relocation. *My parents, surely.* It still felt like a dream. I was having a hard time visualizing living in another city after spending my entire life there. In a daze, which was why I wasn't more observant, I walked across the parking lot and opened the first door into the building with my keys ready to unlock the second. I saw a figure move quickly and stand in the corner of my eye. I screamed and jumped away from it, then looked to find Cain.

"Cain!" I tried to catch my breath. "What that fuck are you doing here?" I yelled. He put his hands up innocently. "It's just me. Sorry. I didn't mean to scare you." He said apologetically.

"Yea, well. Don't lurk in corners and jump out at people then! Jesus." I bent to pick up the keys that had flown out of my hand and snatched them from the ground. I looked up at him again. "What are you doing here?" I demanded. He looked down and then up at the ceiling. *Oh Lord. Just come out with it.* I had no idea why he had darkened my doorstep, but I was finding myself a lot less curious than I should have been.

"I need to talk to you." He said softly.

I scoffed at him and rolled my eyes, then moved to unlock the door. My feet were starting to get sore in my heels and I wanted to sit down.

"Fine." I opened the door and looked back at him as I walked through the entrance, signaling him to follow me. We walked up the stairs and down the hall in silence. I didn't have anything to say. I could have asked him how his day had been, but I really didn't care. I just wanted him to say his piece and be gone. I had much more important things to deal with. I opened the door to my apartment, removed my shoes and set my belongings on the table. "I'm going to get changed." I glanced at him. "You can have a seat." I walked to my bedroom and closed the door behind me, then leaned against it for a second, before heading towards my closet. I felt completely numb. I didn't want to talk to him but slowly the intrigue was setting in. This was behavior unlike anything I had seen from Cain. *Showing up unannounced and uninvited to my apartment?* I still loved him and that fact was slowly bubbling to the surface as I pulled on a tee shirt and jeans then checked my reflection in the mirror. A sense of worry for his well-being struck me. *I hope everything is OK.*

I entered the family room where Cain was seated at the edge of the sofa, leaning forward, hands clasped. I sat in the chair opposite him.

"OK." I looked at him sternly. "What do you want?" The harshness in my voice even caught me off guard. Cain winced.

"My," he looked at me with sad eyes. "I'm sorry." I stayed silent. Unwilling to give him anything he didn't deserve. I had done too much of that already.

"I know that I am an asshole and that what I did to you was inexcusable." My eyes darted away from his to the floor where I stared at the shadow of a vase as the sunlight streaked into the room. "You are right. I broke a promise and I lied to you." *You are coming clean a little too late.* "I didn't want to lose you but I didn't know how to give you what you deserve. I was selfish." My eyes moved back to him. His eyes were red and glossy looking but I couldn't risk believing that he was being sincere. "I want you," he paused, "No. I need you in my life. I am closer to you than anyone else in the world." I scoffed and rolled my eyes, but he continued anyway. "You are the best person I know." I could feel my lips tightening. "Please forgive me." He dropped his head and slid his hand across his face.

We sat in silence for a few minutes. There were so many things I wanted to say, but all of them were knotted so tightly in my throat that nothing escaped. I felt fear in every inch of my body. I wanted to move next to him. To take him in my arms and kiss him. This was what I had been waiting for. *This is not enough.* A sad voice stood out among the rest. Slowly, and with strength I didn't realize I had, I stood from my seat and looked down at him.

"Are you finished?" I was cold. As cold, if not colder, than I had always accused him of being. Never taking his eyes off me, Cain stood and took a single step closer to me. Then something occurred to me to ask, although I was pretty sure I already knew the answer. "Why did your ex-girlfriend, Myra, stop having sex with you, Cain?" The question brought a look of shock to his face. He opened his mouth once to speak, but nothing came out. The wetness in eyes increased and his face turned red before he spoke.

"Because I cheated on her. I slept with other women and at first she tried to forgive me." His voice got weaker with each word, until it trembled. "But I didn't stop until it was too late."
I nodded silently, firmly and then turned to walk towards the door to let him out. That confession was all I needed.

"I love you too, Myra." He spoke gently. I froze where I stood.

"What?" I mumbled, my back still to him, shaking my head in confusion.

"I love you. So much."
I felt my legs begin to shake beneath me. My heart felt like it was being wrenched from my chest. He continued.

"I heard you. The first time you told me," His voice was getting closer. "Do you remember?" I didn't answer. I couldn't answer. "And the next time as well." He was right behind me, I could feel the warmth coming off of him pulling at me like a magnet. "And every time after. I wait for you to say it every night that we are together. Sometimes I think that you aren't going to but you always do. You always love me." I felt his hand lightly touch my arm. It startled me and I gasped. Turning around slowly I found his eyes. "Please don't stop, My." He raised his hand and cupped my cheek. "Please. I love you."
And just like that everything crumbled. I fell into his arms and held him, rubbing his back and listening to him sniff his tears away as he kissed my head then moved to my forehead, cheeks and then lips. He kissed my lips

and a bolt of electricity surged through me. His lips were hungry and remorseful and loving. The longer he kissed me the more deeply I fell, harder and farther than I had ever before. Love enclosed my heart for this man once more and sealed itself in. He pulled me close and lifted me to his eye level, causing my feet to dangle over the floor. I pulled away, breaking the kiss, and spoke, still in the air.

"It can't be how it was, Cain. Almost everything has to change." He returned my stare.

"Everything except love?" He asked in a whisper. I nodded and touched my forehead to his.

"Everything except love."